THE DARK STREETS

JOHN SHANNON

THE DARK STREETS

A Jack Liffey Mystery

PEGASUS BOOKS
NEW YORK

THE DARK STREETS

Pegasus Books LLC
45 Wall Street, Suite 1021
New York, NY 10005

First Pegasus Books edition 2006

Library of Congress Cataloging-in-Publication Data
is available.

ISBN: 1-933648-20-1

Printed in the United States of America
Distributed by Consortium

For David MacDougall

Author's Note

The names have been changed, but the testimony of the "comfort women" is based on actual testimonies given to the Korean Council for The Women Drafted for Military Sexual Slavery by Japan, testaments given in an effort to wrench some form of justice from a country that has never formally apologized to these women.

In the middle of the journey of our lives
I found myself upon a dark path.

—Dante

THE DARK STREETS

One

The Post-Ironic Age

He'd already been fixed up with a lot of edifying advice about "dealing with Koreans." Everybody had a hot tip on these hot-blooded people from the Land of the Morning Calm, even Maeve. But he forgot all the index-card opinions about as fast as he filed them away. Despite Tolstoy, Jack Liffey thought, it wasn't really true that families were all alike, happy or otherwise. Especially in this big L.A. melting pot where nobody melted any longer—with the marginal day-labor Latinos fifteen to a house, professional white couples peering out from behind their armored gates, African Americans escaping in dribs and drabs out to Riverside and Palmdale on the periphery to cling to the ragged edge of the dream. Not to mention the many thousands of angry grandchildren of the dust-bowl refugees, who'd earned their tract homes and then tacked on sweat-equity family rooms only to be laid off for good from aerospace and steel and auto.

Still, in his experience, you could say that every family that had just lost an 18-year-old girl was pretty much alike. Caught up in the first throes of that stomach-wrenching, unfathomable event, they were going to *present*, as doctors said, a bit frantic, as dazed as a jacklighted deer, desperate for any word of hope, and touch-ingly grateful to anyone who offered to help.

So went his thoughts on the day's expectations, and he figured he'd probably get that wrong, too. He drove west from Gloria's place in East L.A., where he was living now, across the dense out-post of Central America that crowded into the triangle of Pico-Union just south of Downtown L.A., offering a terrain of tiny pupusa stalls and sidewalk flea markets, and rolling on into the gaudy streets of K-town, to the address off 8th and Normandie he'd been given. Long ago, he'd got into the habit of worrying things to death in advance, and it was a hard one to break. Natu-rally, though, things never really worked out the way he antici-pated, which left him relying on one of the little anxiety pills his doc had been pushing on him.

He parked the old pickup truck, a recent acquisition, in the one free spot in the cramped minimall lot, spotting the Han-Kook Do-Nut shop at one end, address 4240-G. A cardboard sign in the window said: YUPPIES WELCOME, suggesting there might be some question. The L-shaped strip mall also contained a dry cleaners, a nail salon, a travel agency that seemed to special-ize in trips to Asia, two empty shops, and a minimart at the far end.

He struggled a little with the door handle—he'd have to fix that—and finally got out. His VW bug had burned up in a big Malibu fire six months back, and this was the discard of an old friend from his tech-writing days who had moved up to a Lexus. The pickup had so much low-end torque that it got lousy mileage, but it seemed reliable.

An old Korean woman struggled out of an SUV and into the cleaners with an armload of clothing. Amazing that he hadn't had a Korean case before now, he thought. There were a couple of hundred thousand Korean immigrants in L.A., outnumbered only by the Latinos and blacks. He guessed that one reason he hadn't had any Korean runaways yet was because they simply didn't have that many. Or they never turned to outsiders for help.

He walked around the long building, just to get his bearings. An old black woman had homesteaded the alley behind the mini-mart, building a warm-looking windbreak out of big rolls of rags tied with string. Jack Liffey took careful note of the technique, never certain that some day he might not need to know stuff like this.

A maddening *screech* went off inside his head as he entered the doughnut shop and tripped some signal, but it soon cut off. After a moment a young man with bright red hair came out of the back holding a small video camera up in front of himself on one palm like Eve offering the apple. Inexplicably, it was aimed back at himself.

"Yes, sir. Can I help you?"

Now he turned the camera around to pick up Jack Liffey's reply.

"I'm looking for Mr. Kim. Tae-jin Kim." He knew he was saying the name backwards, the reverse of the Korean order which gave the family name first, but this was the way he had been told it.

The young man held the camera away to the side, deftly ma-nipulating the zoom with his thumb to widen out and presum-ably take in both of them. "That's my father. You must be here about Soon-Lin." The young man looked about nineteen, but it was hard to tell. He had a wisp of beard under his lower lip— what musicians called a jazzdab—and he wore faded jeans. There was an abstractedness about him, as if he were listening for sig-nals that would be coming in from time to time from some other world.

"Yes. My name is Jack Liffey."

"Would you mind buying something, Mr. Liffey? You're the first customer today. It's one of our superstitions that the morning's first customer sets a pattern, and mother would appreciate seeing the early time-stamp."

Jack Liffey looked over the trays of doughnuts, but could not escape the unpleasant awareness of belly overhang, a consequence of the immobility he'd been forced to endure after having a collapsed lung. His condition was okay now, but at his age, weight stayed with you until you took extraordinary measures. "I'll have a double espresso. No milk. Are you related to Soon-Lin?"

He nodded. "I'm her *oppa*, her older brother. Peter. Many of us use an American name. It adds a certain piquancy of ambiguity about who I really am."

He hoped brewing the drink would force the young man to shed the camera, which it did, but not quite as Jack Liffey anticipated. Instead, he set it gently on top of a juice machine and left it recording the room.

"Are you a film student?" Jack Liffey asked.

"In a manner of speaking. I'm trying to record the rather second-rate life I'm currently inhabiting, and then, in some way, redeem it in the edit."

"How on earth do you do that?"

Peter began to fiddle with the coffee apparatus. "At least I can edit out some of my wiseguy inclinations. Wouldn't you say we've entered a post-ironic age, especially after 9/11? We all have a certain responsibility to lead an earnest life."

"I think after 9/11 things changed forever for about six months."

The young man smiled. "Ah—but the secret of all theory is that there is no absolute truth. There are only relations of power." He seemed to prefer off-center answers, steering the conversation off onto some strange tangent of his own.

"Two plus two equals four," Jack Liffey tried.

"Two-plus-two might equal four, in certain circumstances, but only if it's *signed*—to establish its authority."

Jack Liffey decided he wasn't going to get very far along this irritating tack. "Is your father here?"

"He's on his way. You want china or a paper cup?"

The big Italian machine began to steam and rumble.

"Let's try china. And that's not a political statement, just a *cup*."

Peter gave him a grin as he rotated home a little brewing infuser.

"Did you grow up here?" Jack Liffey asked.

"I'm not sure I've grown up. I was born here. My father came in the late seventies as part of a *kye*. Do you know what that is?" The espresso stopped dripping and the young man decanted it into a tiny thick-walled cup, handing it over the counter with two hands.

"Thank you. No, I don't." Anything to get him talking about the real world.

"A *kye* is a kind of pooling of capital. A half-dozen pals and relatives in the old country put their resources into one sock and then draw straws for it. The winner takes all the ready cash and emigrates here to start a business. He works his butt off until he can sponsor the next one in the *kye*. And so on."

The espresso was strong, with something off about the taste, though he went on sipping politely. Peter waved his hand around the shop without much enthusiasm.

"What you see here is the typical *kye* business. Low initial investment, eighteen-hour days, the whole family has to work. A generation of pink sprinkles and crullers, and we've brought over mother, grandfather, and three uncles. I'm in college and I'm expected to become something substantial."

"Doctor or lawyer," Jack Liffey suggested.

"Computer whiz would do. As long as it's on track for the bucks." He made a face.

Jack Liffey took a guess. "Your parents don't look kindly on a struggling filmmaker."

"I hint. They change the subject. We are all very robust in our positions but indirect."

"Materialism doesn't interest you?"

"It repulses me. But here comes Father." Through the plate glass, Jack Liffey saw a full-size Ford pickup with lifts and big knobby tires pull up in front and a big-shouldered man get out. The car even had rally lights and a gun rack, everything but a Confederate flag—about the last vehicle he would have expected.

Jack Liffey looked dubiously at the man as he came toward the door.

"If you expect us to be the shy type, you've read the wrong books," said Peter.

"I see." But he didn't.

"I think I'll remove my camera now." Peter brought his face close to the lens and said, "April sixth. Seven forty-five A.M. Cut."

It wasn't 7:45 A.M., Jack Liffey thought. It was after nine, but who was he to object when there was no truth?

CLOSE, young Korean woman's face, in repose. All at once she looks straight up at us, noticing the camera.

YOUNG WOMAN
I wish you'd turn that off.

MALE VOICE, off shot
History is a slaughter-bench, according to
Hegel. I'm obliged to find out why.

YOUNG WOMAN

Oh, for chrissake. Peter, I'm tired.

MALE VOICE, off

But you're the one with the courage to take
action. I admire you. I worship you. I envy
your principles.

YOUNG WOMAN

I thought we'd passed out of the age of irony.
Into the age of some tiresome French rhetoric.

MALE VOICE, off

Ninety-nine percent of the French philosophers give the rest a bad name. I want to
know about Asians United.

YOUNG WOMAN

You know about it. I told you we're opposing
the developers' plans for turning the old Y
where all the old people live into a luxury
hotel.

MALE VOICE, off

But how, little sister? Tell me how you plan
to defeat a great zaibatsu that makes computers and turbines and road graders and
nuclear reactors.

YOUNG WOMAN

You know how, and it's very personal. As
personal as this.

> She raises a middle finger without emotion to
> the camera.

Kim Tae-Jin had given some instructions in Korean to his son and then invited Liffey Jack aboard his vehicle. He had driven him to a double-deck golf driving range just off Olympic. It was an immense screened space, like an aviary, with the whole lower tier hard at it, Korean men in colorful golf pants flailing away with irons and woods at target numbers that hung from the screening in the distance. A weird little mowerlike vehicle with a protective cage over the cab was tootling around the course raking in the white mushrooms that sprouted all over the lawn.

The man took Jack Liffey to the near empty upper deck, where they sat as a surly waitress delivered two tonic waters.

"Was that really a gun rack?" Jack Liffey asked. "Did it come with the truck?" He wouldn't have been asking about something so off the point, but the man hadn't expressed any worry about his daughter or shown much interest in talking about her.

"Yes. I haven't been duck hunting in a long time, but I still go fishing every year. Do you, Mr. Liffey?"

"For years I've been trying to train rainbow trout to use automatic weapons so they'll have a fighting chance."

"If you eat them, it's fair, isn't it? Doughnuts don't have a fighting chance either."

"Can you support a family with one doughnut shop?"

"No," he admitted. "The shop does not do so well. Had I not branched out, I'd never have been able to bring others over. I have several minimarkets and a furniture store. The dress shop inside the mall is my big earner. Back in Korea, I owned a newspaper."

"Why give that up?"

"Too many papers. Most of them connected to political parties. And the print business we had on the side was being killed by offset machines, same as here. And there was no democracy when I left in 1978. America offers a good life."

Jack Liffey liked the man for some reason. Another immigrant with all the self-starting skills. But it was time to get down to business.

"I think you'd better tell me about your daughter. Was she in college like her brother?"

"Sure, okay. Both my kids are crazy about movies. Strong kids. You think our girls cover their mouth with two hands and giggle, you'd be wrong. The girl is full of power. The boy wants to be some kind of Nam June Paik. You know him?"

"Video art, I think?"

"That's him. Really strange stuff. Peter makes installations on little TV sets that talk back to you and annoy you. My daughter wants to be more normal. She makes documentaries—The Struggle of Yellow People in America, like that."

"Are they in film school?"

"Soon-Lin went to USC and studied visual anthropology. She graduated. My son is still at UCLA. I am crazy for allowing this. Somebody's got to run my businesses."

"In my experience, Mr. Kim, kids do what they want. At least in this country."

He grinned unexpectedly. "I think I am having too much fun in life to fight my children, Mr. Liffey. They will either grow out of it or have fun, too."

"Didn't you contact me because she's disappeared?"

"I think she is probably in Las Vegas with a boyfriend, or maybe a girlfriend. She's over eighteen. It's my wife who's worried, she insists. Would you come this evening to the house and talk to her mother? That would be most helpful, I think." He gave Jack Liffey a card, with an address in Hancock Park. The area had once been wall-to-wall old money, filled with Tudoresque and Spanish mansions, and it still looked the same today. But it was swallowed up by the sprawl of K-town, and Koreans had bought up quite a bit of it.

"In fact," Kim said and offered his surprise grin again. "Hankook means 'Korean' in Korean. "Lucky we didn't all move somewhere that means 'asshole' in Korean."

When Gloria got home from work, Jack's seventeen-year-old daughter Maeve was lying down in the small guest room upstairs that they saved for her, surrounded by bags of CDs and books and her new Gore-Tex suitcase. It looked like she planned on staying for a while. Even Loco, the somewhat unpredictable half-coyote Liffey dog, had come up to lay his head sadly on the bed beside her.

"Hey. What's up, sweetie?" Maeve was petting Loco absently.

"Hi, Glor. Brad seems to be gone for good and Mom's hormones are raging. She brings home these guys who aren't even very nice, she's dying her hair bright red, and she's got these really embarrassing new black undie outfits. Not even Victoria's Secret stuff—much grosser. It's like *Desperate Housewives* or something. I thought I'd give her some space so she can work on her new dating tricks without an audience. It's okay, isn't it?"

Gloria sat on the edge of the bed and rested her hand on Maeve's leg. "Of course it is, hon, you know that. Where's your dad?"

"There's a note on the fridge. He's meeting a client. He won't make it for dinner."

Gloria winked. "*Good*, that'll give us a chance to have some food just for us."

"Like what?"

"I don't know, something that doesn't have a big chunk of meat floating on it."

Maeve smiled, but her heart was too heavy to get behind it.

Gloria cocked her head. "You're not hoping Jack and your mom get back together, are you?"

"I know better. Anyway, I'm crazy about you. Remember, it was me who pushed Dad and you together in the first place." She sat up and hugged Gloria, being careful not to touch the pistol on the woman's waistband. Sergeant Gloria Ramirez was an LAPD detective, assigned for now to the Harbor Division.

"Sorry, I'll get the hardware off, and then we can make some plans. There's not much in the house. Maybe we can shop." She stood up and unclipped her waist holster with its shorty Glock, then bounced it in her hand for a moment as if weighing it, too tired to move right away.

"Can I ask you something?" Maeve said.

"That sounds serious. Let me get some *horchatas*. If you want a soft drink, it's that or your dad's Vernor's."

"Horchata's fine." Maeve had grown to like the sweet rice and almond drink. Instead of buying the bottled kind, Gloria kept a batch of homemade going in a pitcher in the fridge.

While Gloria was changing, Maeve decided to get off the bed and stop moping. She gave Loco a hug and then peered out the side window that looked over the Montalvos' yard next door. The big son, the gangbanger she'd never met, was out in the back yard with his shirt off, doing speed-presses with his homemade barbells—two cans of concrete cast onto a length of water pipe. He was pretty buff and had strange bluish tattoos all over him, words and names in old fashioned script and a few pictures, too— a Virgin of Guadalupe with the full-body aura, a spider web, and a flaming heart. She could pretty much understand the allure of colorful tattoos of animals and designs, but she wondered why anyone would think such poorly executed ones attractive.

Gloria came back and caught her peeking. "His name's Beto, and he's a hard case. He's an O.G. in the Greenwoods."

"O.G.?"

"Old Gangster. It just means a guy who's been through a generation of that crap and lived to talk about it."

"A police officer and an O.G. next door. Strange."

"I talk to him now and then. I don't really know him well." She handed Maeve a glass of the milky horchata. "What did you want to ask?"

Maeve let the window curtain fall, and they went down to the living room to be more comfortable. Gloria had already swapped the jacket of her business suit and silk blouse for a pullover peasant top, embroidered, with a gather at the neck.

"I don't mean it to be such a big thing. I just wonder how you and Dad are doing. I haven't seen you in a while."

"And it's not a time that you're exactly ready to embrace more change," Gloria suggested.

"Yeah, I suppose. But please don't just tell me everything's fine, if it's not."

Gloria raised her bushy eyebrows. "I'm a handful, Maeve. You've got to know that. I still haven't figured out the full extent of what it did to me inside—being half-blood Paiute and raised by Indian-hating fosters. I don't know if I should even be here or with my people up north. Jack's a wonderful guy, I love him—I love you, too—but he's been through a lot, and he's more fragile than he makes out. You and me tiptoed around it last year, but that was as near as anyone needs to get to a nervous breakdown."

"Wow. Maybe you saw that, but I didn't. I guess he never lets me know how bad it is."

"So that's the picture. We're a pretty strange combination, but then again who isn't?"

Maeve smiled, not wanting to dwell on her father's vulnerabilities. "At least I hope the sex is good."

Gloria wagged a finger. "That is definitely not within a daughter's need to know." She winked. "But it's pretty damn good. Not to change the subject, but how's your scar doing?"

They compared notes from time to time. Gloria had lost her right breast to cancer and then had it rebuilt, and Maeve had been shot in a drive-by and had had a stoma and colostomy bag for about six months. They'd reattached her intestine now and it was healing up pretty well.

They both raised their blouses. Gloria unhooked her bra. The hang of her large rebuilt breast looked almost like the real one, except for a perfect ring in lighter color as if it were detachable. They'd even saved her big brown nipple. In fact Maeve's scar looked worse, a fresher starburst on her right side that had no natural anatomy to explain it.

"It'll get less and less noticeable," Gloria reassured her.

"I don't really mind. I'll never be a bikini model."

They lowered their clothes, and Maeve gave Gloria a warm hug. "If you and Dad ever break up, can we stay friends?"

"Don't worry about it so much, hon. We're looking out for each other, and that includes you."

Two

El Yonque

"Wait, please! I get you the pictures!" Emotion erupted again through the crust of her voice, and the woman hurried away, her bright silk dress billowing like a giant bird.

It was a full-bore Tudor-style house—with half-timbering, diamond-paned windows, a big twisty brick chimney, and a steep-pitched roof made of real slate that would go on waiting a very long time for the snow it was designed for.

Mrs. Kim came back carrying a shoebox full of photographs. "These all Soon-Lin."

She started by yanking out and unrolling one of those panoramic class photos everyone has in a box somewhere. This one showed twenty or so little girls in two lines. Most of them were Korean and he wasn't sure which seven-year-old was Soon-Lin. They were all in school uniform and all had the same jet black bangs and ponytails. Next he saw a graduation pose in the usual mortarboard, a prom shot in a pink gown, and some vacation shots. He tried to steer Mrs. Kim gently to the newspaper clippings that she had promised.

She couldn't resist showing off one more photo. "That Soon-Lin today. You take it."

It looked like a passport photo, the woman's pretty daughter caught in an unpretty pose, her face wearing an uncomfortable wince.

"She's a very attractive girl," Jack Liffey said, wondering about the sour expression. He took the photo from her. Among the various predigested tips he'd been given, he'd been warned not to pocket anything offered—a business card, a note—without studying it appreciatively first.

"She always say 'young woman,' Mr. Liffey. She very strong about that."

"She's a feminist."

"Oh, yes, and many other ist, too. She was leader of Stand Up Angry in L.A. High School. She went to Seattle for World Trade demonstration. Now she with Asian United."

"She's been busy."

"Soon-Lin a busybody." She shook her head, then sighed. dramatically. "I never had no sign *Question Everything* on my books when I was in school."

Mrs. Kim was a beautiful woman, with hair dyed a deep henna-tinged brown, and he would never have guessed she had a grown daughter.

"Kids today, they want to fix things," she told him. She sighed again.

"Bless them. My daughter, too, though she's not as active as yours."

"How old?"

"Seventeen, going on thirty."

Mrs. Kim laughed. "Soon-Lin twenty-two, going on five hundred. But she got good heart, wonderful heart." She pointed to her chest, as if to make sure he knew where the heart was, and shook her head. "But she won't believe the—what?—the danger out there. Bad people out there, Mr. Liffey, even wearing expensive suits."

"Especially wearing expensive suits," Jack Liffey said. "Can I see the clippings you mentioned?"

She handed him the shoebox. As he reached in under the photographs—once again spading up someone else's life—he had the weirdest sensation that he had no specific density of his own. He was an inquisitive ghost in a world of more solid people. Maybe it was time to get out of this business, he thought.

The first clipping announced that Soon-Lin Kim was working on a documentary video about comfort women of World War II. Much of the film, it said, would be based on an interview with Korean-born women living in Los Angeles now who had been forced into prostitution by the Japanese during the 1930s and 1940s.

He knew a little about the "comfort women"—tens of thousands of Koreans and Filipinas and Indonesians and even a few Dutch women who'd been rounded up and forced into brothels for the Japanese army—"servicing" as many as seventy men a night. That horrible number had stuck in his head, as it seemed to work out to about ten minutes each. Why not just have the troops masturbate? he'd thought. It couldn't be any less satisfying.

The second article was about International House, a one-time YWCA on Loma off Third, just on the Downtown edge of Koreatown.

ACTIVISTS ARRESTED AT
INTERNATIONAL HOUSE PROTEST

Police yesterday removed three women who had chained themselves together across the driveway of International

House at 306 Loma Drive. Soon-Lin Kim, 22, Carol Park, 21, and a 16-year-old minor claimed to be protesting the eviction of longtime elderly tenants who are being displaced by redevelopment of the site.

The adults were charged with misdemeanor trespass and taken to Parker Center, and the minor was released to her parents.

Formerly the Mary Andrews Clark Residence, the chateau-style building, constructed in 1913 by the Young Women's Christian Association, for 80 years offered housing for working and single women.

In 1988, according to the YWCA of Greater Los Angeles spokesperson Lisa Taylor, the changing demographics of the neighborhood led to its closing.

In 1994 it reopened as International House, with its tenants city-subsidized senior citizens.

Now, a decade later, once again owing to changing demographics, the site has been put up by the city for redevelopment, and the elderly tenants forced to seek homes elsewhere.

Soon-Lin Kim, one of the arrested women, speaking on behalf of a group she identified as Asians United, blamed the Seoul-based Korean conglomerate Daeshin for what she called the "vile treatment of poor elderly men and women whom our culture would have us honor."

Preliminary plans for the redevelopment of International House as a luxury hotel are being proposed by Westlake Hotel Partners, a subsidiary of Daeshin.

The redevelopment plans are the subject of further controversy because of other, historically based allegations made against Daeshin. "They are war criminals," says Ms. Kim.

"The company has a policy of not commenting on irresponsible allegations," replied Frank Fowler of Milford-Kubek, the public relations firm representing Westlake Partners.

However, Roz Sanchez, the Los Angeles city council member whose district includes Koreatown, has made her own response to the controversy a procedural one: she has put the question of planning permission for the historic building back on the council agenda.

Mrs. Kum Hak-Soo, 82, designated to speak for the remaining six residents of International House, claims that they have nowhere else to go. "This is our home," she said angrily, "and we are too old to live on the streets."

According to Mr. Fowler, Westlake has found alternative accommodation for all of the residents. Their moving costs are to be paid and ongoing rent subsidies have been offered. But, to date, Mrs. Kum and the other residents have stated their intention to remain in residence at International House.

"Whatever they are saying, we don't trust them," says Mrs. Kum. "They say they are showing us respect, but they are just pretending until they get us out of here."

"Do you know what newspaper this is from?" Jack Liffey asked. The byline, Jennie No, didn't mean anything to him.

"No."

The back of the article was a slice of a large display ad that didn't help. He guessed it was from one of the weeklies or even a bilingual Koreatown paper.

"Could I see Soon-Lin's room now?"

She had to think about it for a moment. "She had everything she need, every toy and doll."

The room was upstairs, along a hall, and after leading him there, Mrs. Kim left him alone. He shut the door softly. Much of the furniture looked as if it hadn't been chosen by Soon-Lin. There was a canopied bed, a big mahogany wardrobe in lieu of a closet, and a desk too fragile to sustain much real work. However, there was a Mac on the desk—one of those models that looked like a big shaving mirror—but no papers or books. He didn't think she did much work here.

One long shelf high over the desk held a row of dolls in Asian costume that didn't look like they'd been touched in years. Hanging in the wardrobe were some frilly pastel dresses, but stacked below them were much more serviceable pedal pushers, jeans, and T-shirts. There was nothing in any of the pockets. He found no evidence of her interest in video except a single tiny unlabelled tape on the floor of the wardrobe that he recognized as a digital videocassette. He slipped it into his pocket, though he had no immediate way to view it in his own low-tech world.

He sat in the rickety chair in front of the computer and tried to put himself in the girl's shoes. Despite being American-born, she would have been intensely aware of being Korean—of being *other*—all her life. He closed his eyes, smelling a faint aroma of spice from a sachet somewhere. A wind-buffeted tree branch scraped and tapped on the second-floor window, like something from a horror film. The harder he worked at imagining her, the more his mind's eye kept picturing Maeve in the chair, her face morphing into Korean features, her innocence palpable. But why innocence? he thought. The room was a little too sanitized to tell him much, in fact too sanitized to believe. Either the parents had tidied it or else she hadn't spent much time there in recent years.

He opened his eyes and focused on a small plastic robot standing guard beside the computer. When he touched it, it burst into an antic little dance, stamping its feet alternately in high dudgeon and buzzing angrily. He shut it off quickly and held it tight for a moment. Slowly calming down, he realized it was only a gimmick alarm clock. He could see it was to go off at 19:45. Why would she set an alarm for then? A TV show at eight? A date? Was it just for the evening of her disappearance, or every night?

He slid open a thin drawer on one side of the desk. A small digital photo, printed on plain paper, lay in the otherwise empty space. He held it close enough to tell that it showed a political demonstration. But his near vision had begun to go, and so he slid out of his wallet a card-thin plastic fresnel lens that he used to peer at the photo like some updated Sherlock Holmes. Soon-Lin could have been any of several young women, but, try as he might, he could not make out the words on any of the picket signs they were carrying. Several sawhorses and yellow police tape held them back on a sidewalk, with a gingerbready Victorian house down the street.

Putting the photo back, he noticed there was also a name tag, just one of those self-adhesive stickers you wore at mixers, with a blue border and leftover cloth fuzz stuck to the adhesive side. It was hand lettered with a felt-tip pen: SOON-LIN, ASIANS UNITED. He closed the drawer slowly, then opened it again and felt the underside for anything taped there. Just old habits of suspicion, but there was nothing.

He closed his eyes again and forced himself to breathe slowly and deeply for a while, trying to slow his heart rate. It was a phony sort of meditation that he still practiced from time to time, the last vestige of a hateful regimen he had been forced into by a not-quite-quack psychologist who had been thrust upon him. Dickie Auslander had harried him regularly with an assortment of his goofiest jargon—*functional nervous affection, transient episode, personality disintegration.*

Jack Liffey had gone through a bad patch, true enough, and

he'd been helplessly anxious, given to unexpected crying jags and
some tremors of the hand that he still had trouble controlling
from time to time. But he'd also had a collapsed lung back then
and figured it had to have been at least half physical. Not counting being dumped by a girlfriend he'd come to count on, plus his
finances dwindling way too close to the bone. All in all, he figured he'd done pretty well to come out the other end strong
enough to take care of Gloria Ramirez, who had her own problems.

He was interrupted by a knock, and Mrs. Kim looked in.

"Can I get you something to drink, Mr. Liffey?"

He figured she was mainly curious about what he was doing.

"Thank you, no. I have to leave soon. Could you please make
me a list of the names and phone numbers of Soon-Lin's closest
friends?"

"I can think of only few. You know the young today." She
looked at him for understanding.

"Whatever names you've got, that'll be fine," he said.

She hurried away. Her husband had already promised him a
reasonable retainer, and it was just the sort of case he liked, really.
He'd be a bit lost mucking around Koreatown, of course, but the
odds were good that nothing serious was wrong. No dead bodies,
no ransoms, no threatening gangsters. Some poking around and
it would sort itself out. Already he could feel his thumping heart
slowing.

CLOSE, the weathered hands of an old woman, ROH EUN-SU,
kneading nervously.

ROH EUN-SU'S VOICE, over
The Emperor ordered unmarried Korean girls
to come work in a Japanese military factory

for three years. They said you can make a lot
of money and that my family had a debt of
200 won. My adopted mother was grateful,
and she said she would marry me to a good
family when I come back.

CAMERA PULLS BACK to show the head and shoulders of a
very old woman, her face even more weathered than her
hands, speaking with a sad and resigned expression.

ROH EUN-SU

I think each country in the Empire had a
quota, but Korea's was the biggest. This was
the third lunar month of 1941 and I was seventeen. I went to the train with a big cloth
sack that contained underwear, soap, warm
clothes, toothbrush, and menstrual pads. They
put all of us from the village on a military
railcar that had black oilcloth shades on all
the windows. All the girls were crying to be
leaving home. I bent low to look out through
a gap and saw the man who brought me getting a big roll of money from a military policeman. I never forgot what I witnessed—
and I curse him today—but I had to sit back
up fast. Soldiers in our car were watching us
closely.

The woman glances up at the camera quizzically, as if be-
seeching someone, then looks back down at her hands.

Two times a day in the train they gave us

rice balls and water. We rode many days, and
I learned later we were taken to somewhere
in China, I don't know the Chinese name. We
stopped at a troop compound and they took
us to a barracks, a koya, which is a big arch
of metal. I thought we were going to work for
the Japanese soldiers, doing washing, but the
women already there would not tell us. Next
day a soldier came and took us one by one. I
was taken to an officer who, as soon as the
door closed, tried to embrace me. I shouted
and said no. He slapped me hard and said he
can have me killed. I say, kill me. Then he
tore my skirt off and took out his sword to
cut my underwear off. It hurt when he cut
me. I had a thick braid then and he grabbed
my braid and made me do what he wanted.
Then a soldier took me back to the women's
koya. I was crying and a woman there said,
See, we didn't want to tell you. We won't get
out of here alive.

Maeve retreated to her bedroom upstairs. She set up her laptop,
plugged in the phone line and downloaded her algebra home-
work from Mr. Bridges—one pipe filling a swimming pool at a
certain rate, another emptying it, and so many liters present at
the start. She knew there had to be an X and a Y there somewhere, but the logic of it all resisted her. Usually, it didn't take
this long for her to "get" things, but algebra was putting up the
shutters and throwing the bolts. It didn't help that, in general,
she was feeling a little lost and confused in her life.

There was a scritch at the door, and when she got up to let

Loco in, she heard a faint rattle of many voices from the back yard next door. The concentration she had been trying to summon up for gushing pipes waned rapidly. She put out the light in the room and knelt at the window, wrapping the curtains tight around both sides of her face. With no light behind her, she should be invisible. She felt Loco lie down next to her leg.

A floodlight over the back door of the house next door revealed an accumulation of discarded junk in the back corner of the yard—an old washing machine, a fan, a Hoover, car tires, two tricycles, a sheet of iron, a section of metal fence, and a whole tangle of unrecognizable stuff, even a park bench swiped from somewhere. It was a *yonque*—*norteño* Spanish for an unofficial junk-pile. A girl named Xaviera in her class at Redondo High, who insisted scornfully that she was pure Spanish, told her disdainfully that all Mexicans had *yonques* in their back yards. "Where else would they get the spare parts for their Chevies?"

A half dozen teens had pushed this *yonque* around to make a kind of hanging-out place. The guy that Gloria had said was named Beto sat on the park bench holding one of those oversize beer bottles in a paper bag. A group of other boys, younger and smaller but with the same sort of tattoos showing on their arms, bumped shoulders atop the ruins. They all had moustaches and two had baseball caps on backward, plus white socks and big unlaced Nikes. One had his boxer shorts hiked up so high that more of the cloth showed than was covered by his low-riding baggy jeans.

There were two girls who sat on an old car seat, primping, and trying not to seem like they were posing for the boys. They wore those orange raw leather work shoes and skimpy tops with about half of their bras showing. Their dark red lipstick looked almost black. Everything and everyone faced a little toward Beto, who raised his beer and said something to the boys. Everybody readjusted a little in response. Maeve eyed the girls closely. They wore a lot of glittery rings and bracelets and big hoop earrings. One was a bottle blonde, which looked a little weird with her olive skin and black eyebrows, but not unpleasant.

"That stupid hooker look," Xaviera had told her one lunch. "They're just peasants from some village in Sonora. They even dress up six-year-old girls like that. It's disgusting." Eventually Maeve had discovered that Xaviera's parents had come north from a tiny village in Sonora.

Spying on the girls now, Maeve had to admire their stubborn insistence on keeping to their own standards of dress and beauty while living in a world of MTV and HBO that would never compare them favorably to Sarah Jessica Parker or Calista Flockhart.

One boy in the middle of a broken divan said something, causing two of his friends to beat on his shoulders with their fists. The blows looked pretty hard for fun-and-games, but he didn't object.

The girls ignored the roughhouse and passed a hand mirror back and forth. They both wore tight jeans and had long painted nails. There was no question that they were looking at themselves through the eyes of the boys. Every scowl and primp and tug of the hair was a mating cry.

Maeve was surprised at herself. She actually felt herself envying them. Paint up your lips, show off your bra, smile a little, and one of the stronger predators might notice you and carry you back to his lair . . . and ravish you. The idea excited her a little.

One of the younger boys said something to the girls, and the blonde picked up an old oil can and threw it at him. The can missed and buried itself in the *yonque*, which all but the girl and boy found hilarious.

"Have you gone to sleep?"

The room light came on like a flare behind Maeve, and she felt

Loco jump away from her leg. She was horrified to see all the faces below twist upwards and catch her peering down at them. She yanked her face back behind the curtain.

"Sorry, hon," Gloria said.

"You caught me spying on your neighbors," Maeve said. Directness was always best, she thought. "The whole gang is in the back yard."

"Hmm. Do you like what you see?"

"I was just curious, that's all." She shrugged. "But not *that* curious. I've had my fill of gangs." She tapped her blouse over the scar.

"I dropped off to sleep for a while, I'm sorry," Gloria apologized. "I know you haven't eaten. Let me take you out. I don't think Jack is going to make it tonight."

"Can we go to El Tepeyac?"

Gloria made a face. "Too many cops. I know a better place."

"Sure, you choose. This is your barrio."

Three

The Gook Hater

"I'm not sure what it is you want."

Peter Kim had invited him to his cramped edit bay on the ground floor of MacGowan Hall, on north campus, UCLA, an oddly narrow room full of computers and monitors and video equipment, all set up along the long wall. Sitting in front of all the slide controls, with his red hair spiked up, he looked like a mad scientist who'd just air-pirated a 747. To make a little more room for his guest, he rolled his chair back until it came to rest against a rack of dozens of digital videotapes, each about the size of a cigarette pack.

"Where did Soon-Lin hang out?"

Jack Liffey was just getting over relishing the unexpected re-discovery of a great resentment that he'd fed and nourished years before. He'd parked way down Charing Cross Road just below Sunset and walked the half mile to campus past all the NO-PARK-ING-EVER-NO-NO-NONE-AT-ALL signs in front of the gigantic houses of Holmby Hills, a long stroll that he remembered from his days as a student from Long Beach State trying to use the

UCLA library. The rich homeowners wanted all the perks of living near a university except the students.

"Her bedroom at home was far too tidy," he went on. "At USC, they say she's been long gone."

The young man offered an ambiguous smile. At least at the moment he wasn't trying to redeem his life by recording it. "It is epistemologically impossible to have an authentic thought within hailing distance of one's parents. They give off a kind of force field that neutralizes any idea more weighty than See Spot run. That is why God, in his wisdom, gives them late-life hobbies."

Jack Liffey didn't quite follow the logic of the last bit, but he smiled to show he was a good fellow despite his own advanced age, then raised an admonitory finger. "I'm a parent. I have a daughter who's almost college age."

"And do you know the depths of your daughter's fantasies?"

"Jesus, man, why would I want to? My own scare me enough. Just give me a hint where Soon-Lin did her work. I could point to a map of L.A. and you could say 'hot' or 'cold.'"

The young man pointed instead to a second rack of videotapes and notebooks near the door. "Hot. Very hot."

"You let her work right here?"

"Sure. She's a night person, and I've always been at my best in the morning, so it works out fine. And who can afford to rent an edit bay for the stuff she does? I don't mean to diss political documentaries, but I'm just not into that sort of thing. If you come back at five, I'll set you up here and you can watch some of her camera tapes. She doesn't have much of her current stuff cut yet. Or if she does, it's not here."

"Can you tell me the subject?"

"She's got two things going. One's a pretty boring piece on the fight—*struggle* is the preferred word, I guess—to keep that old Y a home for a bunch of geezers. The other one's on the comfort women. You know anything about them?"

"Forced prostitutes for the Japanese army?"

"Uh-huh. Not a new story, but she thought she had some fresh dirt on the whole puking mess."

"What do *you* think happened to your sister?" Jack Liffey sprang the question mainly to see how he'd react.

The young man thought for a while, emotions flitting across his face like cloud shadows flickering over a small cabin on a windy plain. "She's always been a very sensible girl. Down-to-earth, maybe you'd say. I mean in her personal life. I'm the loose cannon in the family." He dug in a wide flat drawer and came out with a computer printout. He looked at it for a while as if wondering whether to pass it on.

"I don't know how important this is. But the USC administration said it wasn't. She got this last year when she was still on campus. And I think she got another one later."

He handed Jack Liffey a much-fingered printout of an e-mail:

Hear me, Miss Gook,

All Gooks must leave USC NOW or I will personally make it my life's work to find and kill every one of you fukers personally. OK? That's how determined I am. Do you hear me? You study too hard, you don't know how it makes the rest of us suffer. This place is for Americans. Will the last American to leave please bring the flag. Go now, while you have time.

Gook Hater

"They ever find who did this?" Jack Liffey wondered just what sort of person couldn't spell "fuckers," but could get all the rest reasonably cogent and grammatical.

"The administration just covered their butts. They all went down into the it-was-just-a-prank bunker and sealed it up tight. One of them said maybe an Asian did it, to try to stir up sympathy. You know, our famous Gook deviousness."

"I haven't even heard that word since Nam."

"Actually, I believe it came out of the Korean War—it's a corruption of Han-kook, which just means Korean. I've seen a few guys wearing 'I'm a Gook and I'm Proud' T-shirts. But that's not my style." The young man opened a loose silk overshirt to show what he meant: his black T-shirt had Marilyn Monroe standing over the famous sidewalk grating, trying to hold down her billowing skirt, but it was Peter Kim's own face grafted onto the legendary body, making that big embarrassed O with his lips.

"I want one of those," Jack Liffey said enviously.

"Sorry. You've got to come up with something original. That's the essence of the post-modern."

"I'll have to think, then."

"The curse of our times, dude."

He took a copy of the e-mail straight to his whiz-kid friend Chris Johnson. Chris and his wife had three children now and had slid downhill a bit from the big foothills house they'd had during the silicon bubble to a gentrifying part of Long Beach. It was an ordinary suburban block, with pleasant Spanish bungalows from the forties and bright-colored Big Wheels toppled everywhere. But only a few blocks away there was a busy highway of used-car dealers and bowling trophy stores, the kind of downmarket strip that let you know that not many yuppies had moved in yet. He was reminded of a line about Long Beach from *True Confessions*, by the late John Gregory Dunne: *But a classy bar in Long Beach was just a place where the bartender didn't have tattoos.*

"Hello, Wonder Woman."

At one time Barbara had been into collecting the old WW comics, and she could go on at length about the changes in the character over time or about the Eisenhower-era Freudian psychologist named Dr. Wertham who'd launched a national crusade against Wonder Woman as a castrating female, an obvious man-hating lesbian.

"Hi, Jack." A little boy and girl came running up and clung to her skirts where she knelt to dig a weed out of the crab grass. Barbara had been gay herself before Chris met her—but it wasn't something you ever asked about.

"How's the online nursery business?"

"Not great. I'm studying landscape design now." She was noticeably pregnant, too.

"Between children," he said.

She nodded, not in a particularly good mood. "Chris is in the garage."

"I figured." The detached garage at the back had been converted to a computer room and server farm, with scores of the latter parked where cars would never be, with enough winking indicator lights to make you fairly jumpy. He was a service provider now and designed complex applications for small businesses; his probation had been over for several years. He'd once been fairly naughty as a hacker and still went to the underground phone phreak conventions from time to time. Jack Liffey wouldn't put it past him to swipe some credit card numbers once in a while from members of the Republican National Committee, but now he was discreet about it.

"*Hola*, Chris!" Jack Liffey called as he opened the side door.

There was no answer and Chris wasn't immediately evident amidst all the electronica. The long desk area under the side window was unoccupied.

"Have you jumped to cyberspace?"

The grin ascended from among the servers like Mephistophe-les coming up a stage trap door. He was so blond that the flicker of one of the fluorescents overhead raised weird beats in his long hair. "'Jumped to cyberspace.' Not an expression I've heard you use before, Jack. Are you online yet?"

"Maeve sends messages for me if it's absolutely necessary. No cell phone, no DVD, no Blueberry or Strawberry, whatever it is."

"You're a true eccentric," he said, with an odd intonation, as if he'd just discovered the word and was experimenting with it a bit.

"But I do have an actual note in my hand. I was wondering what you could do about tracing it."

Chris Johnson high-stepped out of the maze of computers, carrying a coil of cable and a screwdriver. Jack Liffey handed it to him and he laughed. "I'm supposed to track an e-mail from a *printout*? That's a bit like trying to check out yesterday's weather by breaking into the thermometer."

But after he read the message, his face went grave. "This is ugly."

"It was on the system at USC, if it helps. You've got the date, the recipient, and the sender and some sort of data at the top."

"The sender's pseudonym won't help much. I doubt if *Gook Hater* is registered anywhere. Nobody there looked into this?" The Aeron chair at the desk creaked startlingly when he sat. Jack Liffey did recognize that icon of the techno universe, though it looked fantastically uncomfortable for all the money it cost.

"As far as I know, they treated it like a prank."

"No, they didn't. They may have said that, but it was just a coolout to get somebody off their backs. Everybody takes this stuff seriously these days. I'm sure someone tried to trace the guy, just not someone as good as me."

Jack Liffey could see the light going on at the challenge. "When can you get to it?"

"I have some other stuff on the front burner. Call me tomorrow."

"Sure."

"You know, our family is going to be six." He smiled proudly. "That's over the average."

"Don't talk about averages. If you go by averages, one of us has to be Chinese."

Her friend Karen was right: there really was something wrong with the Echo's battery. Maeve held the key cranked over through another feeble grunt or two, but the engine didn't catch, and then even the grunting ceased. Now the car was giving nothing but a single pathetic *chunk* when she switched on the ignition. She wondered what that *chunk* was—picturing a little overworked elf, trying to crank a Model T after getting a jolt in the ass from a cattle prod. She always did her best to humanize machines in her head. Gloria was at work, and her dad was off somewhere working, too, so she resigned herself to making a call to the Auto Club and waiting however long it took them to respond in East L.A. Down in Redondo it was rarely more than twenty minutes, but Maeve bet the wait got a bit longer over here, if not a whole lot longer.

There was a rap-rap on her window, and she looked up to see the face of Beto Montalvo. She made a helpless gesture and then pointed to the electric window switch to indicate the power was dead and she couldn't roll the window down. He didn't seem to understand, so she opened the door.

"I'm sorry. The window won't work."

"You can't start?"

"You heard that awful noise from the battery. I guess it's dead."

"I got no jumpers, but I got a trickle charger in the back."

She thought of turning him down in favor of the Auto Club,

but why not meet the neighbors? Especially this one. She couldn't deny she was curious about him. "That would be really kind. *Muchas gracias.*"

She got out as he stepped over the short hedge to his backyard and, predictably, dug into a corner of the *yonque* to come up with a little yellow metal box with some thin wires coming out of it that were attached to a cigarette lighter insert.

"Please wait. I got to get a cord."

He went up the back steps, and abruptly she was nagged by a suspicious simulacrum of her mom that she carried inside her, wondering what on earth she was doing encouraging him. But, really, there was never a reason to question friendliness, neighborliness. It was a nice cloudless day, and she could chat with him for a few minutes while the battery charged. She saw him slide up a small kitchen window nearby and toss out an extension cord. It took only a few seconds for him to find the capped cigarette lighter on her dash—she hadn't even realized she had one—and plug in the trickle charger.

"That's amazing," she said.

"It's slow as bad dope. My name is Alberto Montalvo Pérez. My friends call me Beto." He held out a hand, and she took it. He wore Ben Davis baggies and a superclean white T-shirt that didn't hide the tattoos leaking down his muscular arms.

"I'm Maeve Liffey." It was a little tough to get her hand away from him.

"I know. You the one got shot last year by Thumb from the Lomas. You want some payback?"

"No, no, it was sort of an accident. We're kind of friends. My dad made him come down here to mow our lawn."

"I know. I saw how your dad was. I got the word around, stopped people greenlighting him."

She watched him closely, trying to read what he was really saying.

"Does that mean somebody was going to kill him?"

He thought about it for a moment. "Come over and have a beer. The charger takes a while."

She stepped carefully over a low spot in the hedge, and they sat in the *yonque*, she on the old vinyl car seat facing him where she'd seen the other girls before. She didn't know why but she felt honored. He handed her a big-mouth bottle in a paper bag. She wasn't crazy about beer, but she could hold her own—though she only sipped when she pretended to chug. She presumed it was best to act severe and serious. So far, levity seemed to be a foreign concept to Beto.

"Thanks."

"Your dad a cop?" he asked.

"No. He finds missing children and tries to get them to come home. But he says he won't bring them home if they were abused."

"Like a detective?"

"A little."

"How come you ain't pissed off at Thumb? You was hurt bad."

"Are you a Catholic?"

He made a strange face. "Sure."

"You're supposed to forgive your enemies, like Jesus, aren't you? I'm not a Christian, but I think forgiving makes you stronger." She should have stopped there, but something drove her on to an absurdity that had just occurred to her. "Like an Indian eating his enemy's heart."

He smiled for an instant as if her odd idea had pleased him. Then he asked, "Where you at school?"

"My mom lives in Redondo, so that's where I've been going. I might transfer over here if I stay with my dad."

"The school's shit here, man. You won't like it."

"Call me Maeve, please." She was at such a strange place in the universe that she decided to go for broke. "Are you in a gang?" She knew he was.

"You don't really shouldn't, *pues*, you don't ask that . . . Maeve." He looked grave but not threatening. "You got to say, Who your friends? Where you live? You *rep*resent? We say *klika* if we got to say."

"You're an O.G. in Greenwood, aren't you?"

He brought both hands up and made strange signs with them, bobbing them a couple of times with his fingers in contorted shapes as if dunking them in nail polish remover. "Goes back to my dad. G'wood is really old. All that *cholo* stuff before the war. Zoot suits and switchblades, you know."

He was remarkably easy-going, as far as she could see. When she veered off limits, he didn't seem freaked.

"Were the tattoos the same back then?"

"The taks? This one was." He stripped off his T-shirt without any awkwardness, though she felt a bit of embarrassment. An arc of Old English lettering, like a stencil she'd had in fifth grade, ran across his entire belly saying GREENWOOD. She'd noticed it before when he was working out, and he pointed to it now, running his finger from the G to the D as if she needed help reading it letter by letter. On his shoulder he had a *Virgen de Guadelupe* with her unmistakable coffinlike aura of golden rays. And on the upper arm was the name LOCA CECI, and a spiderweb spreading from the elbow.

"That's my old girlfriend. Crazy Ceci. I guess I better find me another Cecilia," he said. It was the nearest thing she'd noticed to humor and she laughed. He was really quite handsome, if you could get over the air of menace that leaked off him from time to time. He seemed quite confident and secure, as if his chosen realm would never rise up to challenge him.

"What's the spiderweb for?"

He shrugged. "You're caught in the life, you know? Leopard don't change no spots. I ain't going to be no cop or no *chingada* priest. All I know is man business. Defend the *barrio*. We'll be right here in our place for a thousand years but all the *gabacho* cops get tired of hassling us, go home to whitetown, get burned out, eat their guns."

She felt a slight chill on her spine. *Man business* was open to a lot of interpretations, as was his hostility to the police. He had to know Gloria was a cop. "What do you do? I mean, your work?"

He grimaced for an instant. "There's not much for me. Last year I work up in West Covina as a fireman for the Forest Service. I did my job for the fire season, but they all stare at me, you know? Even the black guys. Prejudice is something, *ese*. They didn't want me to do good. Then I had to spend some time in *la pinta*. That's the jail. I came back home even though they killed my best friend here, Penguin, when I was inside. I heard them all—Hey, that's Pingüino's *compa*, let's fuck with him. But I stick through it. My homies help me out when I came back. You know, some people think it's all the time crazy violence over here, a big *desmadre*, but it's not. It's just guys trying to get over."

"I know a little about violence." She tapped her side where the scar was.

"Yeah, that was something. *Balazo*. Can I see?"

Why not? she thought. She lifted the side of her blouse as modestly as she could to show the star-shaped scar. Maybe it would give her extra props as a neighbor. Beto came across the intervening space and got on his knees as if for a closer look at the scar. "*Hijole*, girl! That's really something."

He bent forward without warning and kissed the scar tenderly. Her skin tightened all over her body and she could barely breathe.

"I better go," she blurted, not knowing quite what nonsense she was saying. "I'll call the Auto Club. Thanks for the help." He smiled and touched the back of her hand lightly where she was tucking in her blouse.

"You come over any time, Baby Girl. Meet the people. You got that virgin fever all over you."

She felt her face burning as she hurried back across the hedge. What on earth had she been playing at? Gloria was right. This guy was dangerous as a snake, and she knew perfectly well that you couldn't always walk away from snakes.

A small woman, KANG-LIM PARK, with snow white hair sits on a stiff chair with a limp calico cat on her lap. There is a birdcage with a parrot in it beside her. The woman sighs a lot, wiping her eyes.

KANG-LIM PARK

I keep a cat and a bird and a goldfish because I'm lonely. There are many other Korean women here, but to most of them I am completely disgraced. I could never have a family because of the diseases the men gave me and the beatings for running away. At the end of the war, the Japanese man in charge disappeared and a Chinese man took over because we were in Shanghai. I cannot speak of what was done to me before or after, but I managed to escape after a time and I walked all the way home to Anju in Korea. When I got

there my home was gone, it was now the
Communist North and my family had gone
south. A good Korean Baptist man brought
me to America in 1958. We separated after a
time but I worked as seamstress.

YOUNG WOMAN'S VOICE, off
Please tell us a little about your ordeal. I
know it's hard but it's part of the process of
bearing witness.

The old woman shakes her head.

YOUNG WOMAN'S VOICE, off
At least tell us who recruited you.

KANG-LIM PARK
My father did not own land in our village. He
sold baskets that he made for a living. My
mother hurt her leg, and I had to cook for all
the brothers and sisters. When I was fifteen a
man came to the village and said he had a
good job in a factory in Haeju. He said he
worked for a company called Daeshin.
(she wipes away a tear)
When my train left, my little brother ran
along the platform yelling my name. I don't
know how he knew I was on the train. That
was 1938.

He ejected the cassette and set it back in the gap between 28
and 30. There was only so much of this you could take, he

thought, raw or edited. Jack Liffey pulled over the notebook that Peter had said contained the start of his sister's paper edit for the video, but it was a bit too cryptic for him, just long strings of numbers, representing time codes from the tapes.

What he had just watched was about three minutes preceding—and a few seconds following—the time codes that she had written down for the tentative opening shot of the documentary. Roughly, it was meant to start where the old woman had said "When I was fifteen . . . " up to the mention of Daeshin. Then the outline said NARR: LIST DAESHIN SUBSIDIARIES. COVER WITH STOCK.

Even Jack Liffey had heard of the big Korean conglomerate Daeshin: shipbuilding, plastics, motorcycles, resorts, toys, you name it. And he wondered if "Gook hater" himself had ever crossed paths with Daeshin, its tentacles were so widespread.

Gook hater. What was it, he wondered, that made some people so incensed at a skin, or an accent, or a culture that was different?

And if they really felt that way, why, for god's sake, did they stay in L.A.? There would always be some redoubt in northern Idaho where white guys could still get chosen to play basketball.

Four

Serenity Requires Lubrication

It was somewhere near dawn and he needed a break after most of a night spent viewing Soon-Lin's interview tapes. He picked up a cassette that he'd noticed lying on the console on Peter's side of the room, provocatively labeled *Project X: Top Secret.* He entertained images of secret rocket experiments in the Mojave, but figured that wasn't really Peter Kim's style. The tape box opened to a typed set of complex instructions, and he almost put it back—but in the end all he had to do out of the ordinary was move one jumper cable on the big switching board to a new socket, and switch the audio output to channel 12 on the mixer. He figured he could handle that, so he set it all up and flicked Play and got the shock of his life.

The lights turned themselves out in the edit bay, and his attention shifted to a featureless canvas bag set up on a skinny stand about chest height in a corner. Now it was highlighted; before, he hadn't even noticed it. At first the bag was all aglow, and then, abruptly, it was the face of a man with a handlebar moustache. That sent his eye back across the room to a tiny projector TV that had been activated. The eerie face made a rude raspberry noise at him and began to talk:

> What the fuck are you looking at!? Did I say you could look at me? You're smug, you are. Know that your knowledge of the universe doesn't come from reality itself but from the social context that allows you to interpret that reality. Hey, if you're going to watch, *watch*.

It was the damnedest thing he had ever seen. It was impossible to get over the illusion that a disembodied head was speaking right to him. The head now licked its lips and spread its mouth, wider and wider, impossibly wide, until it morphed into a vagina and a woman's voice took over.

> I'm the Talking Pussy, Fuckhead. I'm a rupture in the social context of your reality. I create a gap that makes it possible to subvert your conventional responses to anything. But I don't think you're ready to play.

The vagina began to recede.

> 'Bye for now. But, remember, you're now responsible for your own text. Explain to yourself what I represent.

The mouth reappeared and then snapped shut, as if swallowing the image of the vagina. The mouth receded until the man's head was back, plus the male voice.

> Listen. High art is concerned with important issues, like moral content, and it is constructed according to well-established

rules of taste, elegance, and style. Transgressive art, on the
other hand—

Jack Liffey reached quickly over to the digital machine and hit
the blue button on the end that he thought was Eject. The pro-
jected light went out, and the tape whirred and slid out of its slot
in the player. That was about all the disorienting entertainment
he could take at five-thirty in the morning, having missed a full
night's sleep. The Talking Pussy, he thought. That was just what
he needed in his life.

"Has she got a cell number?"

Reluctantly, the boy in the tidy flannel shirt handed him one of
Jennie No's cards. There was no shortage of numbers: office, office fax, home, home fax, pager, cell, car, portafax and something
called LiveText. He sat at her beat-up desk and dialed "cell."

Jennie No worked for one of the successors to the *L.A. New
Times*. Consolidation and anti-trust shenanigans had just about
eliminated the old alternative press in L.A., but people kept trying. *The Big Voice* was run out of a storefront in Los Feliz.

Even on the cell, he had to leave a voice mail. He asked her to
call her desk number at the paper in the next ten minutes or he'd
be forced to sign over the subpoena to a really aggressive private
agency. This was nonsense, of course, but it was the kind of thing
that often confused the issue enough to get results.

An overweight character in a Hawaiian shirt kept a weather
eye on him from the desk next to Jennie No's, but Jack Liffey just
smiled back. The desks were all beat-up oak shorties, bought at
some fire sale, and there were a few wisps of cigarette smoke on
the air, like the good old days. It could almost have been a corner

of a real city desk from the '50s, at least more convincing than the
new carpet-hushed smoke-free cubicled city room of the *L.A.
Times.*

She called her desk phone in three minutes flat and berated
him angrily for a minute.

"My name is Jack Liffey, and Soon-Lin's parents have asked
me to look into her disappearance. I thought you might want to
be her friend."

"I met her. We're not pals. What's this about a subpoena?"

"You don't need to worry about that."

"You just made it up to threaten me?"

"I prefer to think of it as leverage. Could we meet this afternoon?"

She laughed, but without much humor. "And if I don't, you'll
trash my desk and burn my files and spread radioactive waste
around my back yard . . . For more leverage?"

"Just tell me where to meet you."

Over the phone he heard noises that made him realize she was
in her car. "Do you know Walker's? It's in San Pedro overlooking
Point Fermin. Actually, people call it Bessie's."

"I grew up there."

"Two o'clock."

She clicked off before he could demur. It was a long drive, but
more important, going to San Pedro would just about oblige him
to stop off and see his dad who lived there, and there wasn't much
he wouldn't do to avoid that. But life was full of things that you
had to avoid so as to go on living with yourself.

Jack Liffey had a bit of unmanageable midday time to kill. He
snoozed for an hour, cramped in his front seat, and then drove
southward on Western for a while, keeping to the surface street
just to give his skull a rest from the precariously imposed mo-

mentum of the freeway.[1] He had about twenty-five miles to go on Western, but any time he tired of the slower pace he could hop on the Harbor Freeway, as people who actually live in L.A. call the I-110. They were all still the Long Beach, the Pasadena, the Hollywood, the San Bernardino, and the Santa Ana to him.

Still passing along the northern reaches of Western, he saw an empty lot containing a three-way fistfight among men in business suits and red baseball caps. After a while he glimpsed a man stripped to the waist with at least two dozen metal rings surgically implanted in his chest and belly. Performance art? Some strange rite of bondage? Farther south, near USC, he saw an impromptu parade of a dozen ragged homeless people wheeling shopping carts loaded with nothing but mailing tubes, like a moving cardboard organ. At a stoplight near Century Boulevard a woman came up to the window and harangued him at the top of her voice, claiming he was someone who "only pretended to be a homosexual but really wanted to bugger little girls."

Perhaps, he couldn't help but think, traveling on a different plane from all this was the point of the precariously imposed momentum. The speed, the embankments, and the fences all conspired to shelter you from the city's ragged and unsettling strays, who colonized the flattest reaches of the city, the plains of the id.

He passed a shopfront advertising "pet colonoscopy" with a line of women cradling small restless dogs, but the city's raw nerve endings were beginning to make inroads on his own precarious momentum, so he gave up at Imperial. The rest was easy: a steady run to the end of the Harbor Freeway and then south across San Pedro on Gaffey Street to the southernmost point of the entire city at Point Fermin Park, overlooking the Pacific. The little diner was still there where he remembered it, facing

---

1. Joan Didion, for those who care from whom evocative expressions were stolen.

the old wooden lighthouse, with about a dozen Harleys and choppered Japanese bikes parked in front. He noticed the name on one Japanese model and was amused by the fact that some Japanese marketing team thought to name a big macho bike the "nagging woman"—the Yamaha Virago.

He wondered when Bessie's had become a biker bar, but he had long since given up any trepidation at dealing with bikers, so he parked across the road and sauntered inside to the sounds of Chuck Berry's "Hail, Hail, Rock 'n' Roll" on the juke box. Bikers were nothing if not up-to-date.

A denim-clad man about the size of one of the islands off the coast glanced up as he came in. "Hey."

"Hey," Jack Liffey replied, wondering if he'd just plumbed the irreducible minimum of male communication. He saw a slender attractive-looking Asian woman on a stool with a bottle of Anchor Steam. She wore a braid in yet another shade of red (before long he was going to assume all Asians had red hair) and she wore a bright green microskirt. Jack Liffey gave her credit for chutz-pah, coming into a biker bar with only an inch of upper thigh covered.

"Jennie No?" he asked loudly over the music.

"Yes." With a wry smile.

"You probably get that a lot. The yes-no bit." He slipped onto the stool next to her.

She put up a palm. "You don't want to ask what I get a lot. Jack Liffey?"

"I just drove twenty-five miles to prove it. Nice to meet you." They shook hands, though her grip was limp.

"Want a beer?" she asked.

Here's where it would have been so much easier just to go with the flow, he thought, but he beckoned to the heavyweight woman with butch hair behind the bar. "Do you have coffee?"

"It's a bit stale."

"Send me a cup, and if it's that stale, I'll pay for a new pot."

She nodded and ducked behind a partition.

"May I ask if you're Korean, I mean your ancestry?" he asked. "I'm sorry if it's offensive but I can't always tell Korean features from Japanese."

"There's no reason you should be able to. Yes. My folks came right after the war. I was born here, so I don't know Korea from Latvia and I don't speak more than a few dozen words, and I don't even like kimchee."

"I was hired by Soon-Lin Kim's parents to try to find her." He'd told her this on the phone, but it never hurt to make such information abundantly clear.

She made a face. "That was one really difficult girl. Downright rude, in fact. I grew up here and I work hard to get a story, but I'm nowhere near that pushy. She has some chip on her shoulder. And don't get her started about abused women."

His coffee came and it was just drinkable, so he nodded to the bartender. The music finally stopped, and nothing replaced it, so he could hear ambient sound all of a sudden, like a fever breaking.

"I've seen a lot of her footage on the comfort women," Jack Liffey said. "That must explain some of the squabble at International House."

They both looked up at a sudden sharp noise from a table nearby. Two heavily tattooed guys had their left hands splayed out on the table, and one was tapping the point of a switchblade in the gaps between his fingers, slowly speeding up the pace. Jack Liffey remembered it: it had been called mumbledy-peg when he was young, and only the loonier kids had gotten into it.

"One of the former comfort women was living there," Jennie No said. "To make the irony complete, if you believe Soon-Lin, she said that the developer taking over the building to turn it into some big resort hotel was part of a corporation that had been a pioneer in the comfort woman business."

The annoying tap-tap-tap of the knife point went on and on, accelerating and then decelerating on some signal, punctuated with hoarse dares and male guffaws.

"You don't believe it?" he said. Her tiny skirt kept creeping up her thighs as she swiveled restlessly and he had to keep his gaze up north.

"Not quite. As far as I know, the *chaebols*—the big Korean conglomerates—were all postwar. Korea was a poor agricultural society before the war. Nothing but rice."

He didn't mention that one of the women on the tape had mentioned Daeshin. "The company Soon-Lin mentions in your article is Daeshin."

"Uh-huh," she said. "That's the company that makes the cars with the weird names. They just started importing them last year—the Sumanitra, the Gadara, and the Wanda." She laughed. "Not that you could ever know all the stuff they make." She took a little digital voice recorder out of her shirt pocket and showed it to him: the name on it was The Cricket. "Made by Daeshin," she said.

"*Owww!*" The mumblety-peg game sounded as if it had taken a swift downturn. Jack Liffey glanced over to see the switchblade sticking up by itself, pinning a biker's finger to the table. He was hammering the table with his other hand.

"Pull it out!"

"Pour some beer on it first!"

"I wonder if Daeshin swats gadflies?" Jack Liffey said, turning back to the reporter.

"Like Soon-Lin? Why would they even notice? I spoke to that P.R. guy Fowler and he had the party line down pat: they're improving a run-down area of L.A., finding new homes for the residents, etc., etc."

"Run along, boys." There was a sudden clattering as the bartender helped two of the bikers carry the bleeder out the door, his finger tied up with a dirty napkin.

"Have you heard about this?" Jack Liffey said. He showed her a copy of the Gook Hater e-mail—which reminded him that he hadn't checked back with Chris about it yet.

"Old news. They had a run of that down at UCI, too."

"Racism doesn't get to you."

She hopped a little on the stool to tug at her skirt, managing to cover the forbidden zone pretty well at last—Jack Liffey had had one chagrined glimpse of fluorescent green panties—and he felt a wave of relief.

"It used to bug me," she said, "but now I figure that without the pointless violence of grown-up little boys . . ." She shrugged and jerked a thumb at the table where the bikers had been. "What would I have to write about? Good boys and girls don't make news. At least not front-page stories." She glanced again at the e-mail. "Anyway, if some jerk wants to o.d. on hate, it'll just end up poisoning his own life."

"I've tried working with that," Jack Liffey said. He thought of his father. "It makes some sense, but not for long."

"You don't drink enough."

"You're probably right."

"Serenity requires lubrication," she said, and she finished off the beer. He noticed there were at least four empties beside her.

As Jack Liffey drove up, he saw Maeve's little Echo parked out front of his father's peel-paint cottage above the harbor. It didn't surprise him, as the wizened old fuckhead had become a project of hers. The senior Liffey had been a self-made scholar-devotee of the whole bizarre universe of the white race theorists, all those bunkered Aryans on the western slopes of the Continental Divide, which had led Jack Liffey to write the old man out of his life for fifteen years and even deny he was alive. When Maeve had learned otherwise, she had turned her grandfather into a personal project and seemed to think she was making headway, but Jack Liffey didn't trust a bit of it.

Mariachi music was chugging away up and down the block, and he had to knock hard. He heard a half dozen deadbolts clack open noisily, and the instant she recognized him, Maeve sprang forward to hug him.

"Come in. We're just playing Scrabble. Jack, meet Declan, your dad." She was teasing a bit, doing her best.

The old man half rose, but Jack Liffey waved him down. "I was in town on a job and just wanted to say hello." He was almost jealous. She hadn't played Scrabble with him in years.

"She plays the way you used to," Declan Liffey said. "Cautious. She works you down into a corner with little words and suffixes so nothing opens up."

"It's a matter of waiting for the very best word," Jack Liffey said, defending their guarded style of play. He peered over the board. "No Japs or Spics. That's an improvement."

"Dad, stop it," Maeve protested.

"You could join us," Declan offered cautiously.

"Thanks, my mind isn't up to it. I've had a busy day on a job that's not really coming together."

"Do they ever?" the old man asked. "It's a strange job you've got."

The two men eyed each other for a time, with Maeve almost trembling in the tension of it.

"I do my best," Jack Liffey said.

"That's all anybody can do."

He figured they'd reached the limit of their civility, and he stood up and squeezed his daughter's shoulder. "Will I see you tonight, hon?"

"I may stay here for dinner, but I'll be back later. I can't go back to mom's yet."

"Take it easy," Jack Liffey said. "Thanks for letting her beat you."

"Dad!" Maeve said indignantly.

"I wouldn't think of it. She plays even better than my son."

Jack Liffey hesitated at the door, but they were both staring hard at the game board. He felt like he was on the edge of spoiling something so he went out into the salt air and walked away. He still didn't trust the old man, but Declan Liffey was obviously trying hard to stay on the good side of his granddaughter. How could he begrudge him that?

He returned to Chris's and survived a body block by all three of the kids at once on the crabgrass lawn. If he hadn't turned sideways at just the right moment, they'd have gotten him with the world's oldest sucker move—the bigger boy shoving on the backs of his knees while the other two pushed from the front.

"You kids are lethal. What if I had a bad hip?"

"You're not that old," the boy said.

"How old do you think I am?"

"Thirty-fifteen."

"Old enough to break a hip. I'm a junior G-man and I'm hauling you all in." He got out his wallet, facing away, and they ran off squealing as he whirled to show off the plastic badge, like De Niro in *Midnight Run*. He'd got the badge from a mail-order detective course at World Wisdom University of East Orange, New Jersey, a course that had consisted entirely of reading a pamphlet and then answering twenty true/false questions. *When hunting a skip-trace it is better to refer to the Internet than the phone book. TRUE FALSE.* He'd done his best to guess the wrong answer each time, and still they'd taken his money and sent him their "success kit." Though the kit was basically just another book—*Detecting for Fun and Profit,* along with a photocopy of the police ten-codes, the cheap badge and a black T-shirt that said *Bail Enforcement Agent,* which he had worn once, inside out.

Chris was back in the garage, and a wave of unusual heat met Jack Liffey at the side door.

"This can't be good for the electronics."

Chris shrugged glumly. "The big fan went down and Barb is out looking for a replacement. If I can stand it, they can." He got up, scraped away some cobwebs with his toe and opened the old swing-up garage door that looked like it hadn't budged in a generation. "That'll help."

"Did you find out anything about that threatening note?"

"Is the bear Catholic, does the pope shit in the woods?" He fumbled around on the messy desk and then handed Jack Liffey a manila folder of papers. "The guy is a pissed-off Latino, strangely enough. Socrates Estrada. He's dropped out of USC himself now. He may have had a special axe to grind for your girl—maybe she shot him down for a date—but as far as I can tell he never did anything violent. I might get pissed off, too, saddled with a name like that."

"Thanks, Chris. As usual, I owe you."

"And as usual, that's an exercise in fertility. No, wait, that's me." The three kids ran wailing in through the open garage door, arms outstretched like ground attack jets, as if to illustrate his pun.

· · ·

He had an urge to win Gloria's approval, or maybe just perk her up a little, so he picked a big chore at random. He tugged on thick rubber gloves and attacked the crusted old Gaffers & Sattler oven with Easy-Off. Loco had been especially affectionate for some reason, but he had to lock the dog out back to keep him away from the chemicals. Two applications and a box of Brillo pads later, it wasn't half bad, a real retro classic.

He heard her RAV-4 arrive in the driveway and decided to let her catch him at it, maybe earn some on-the-spot credit. He peeked once and saw her heading wearily for the side door, all suited up in her blue policewoman two-piece which meant some official function. The door came open noisily. "Jack, don't pull no jokes. I'm not in the mood."

"Just cleaning the oven," he said.

She stood in the kitchen door and they had a little pantomime for a time: he going on scouring unnecessarily, she watching him with her hands on her hips.

"We let it get away from us," he said lightly.

"Is that supposed to mean something?"

Uh-oh, he thought. "Not at all. You have a bad day?"

"That's the way they make them." She took a beer out of the fridge, snapped the easy-off and patted his head gently as she passed. "Thanks. I may keep you yet."

That annoyed him slightly, but he knew better than to reply just then. She disappeared into the living room and he began tidying up. In a while he closed the oven door and let Loco in. Then he got a ginger ale and joined her, sitting on the floor at the foot of her easy chair and resting his shoulder against her thigh. Her feet were up on the ottoman and her eyes were closed, but he could tell that she was awake and brooding.

He watched Loco struggle across the room, favoring his hips a bit, and he realized the poor dog was getting old. He'd had him for six or seven years, but he'd gotten him as an adult and had no idea what age he was. He looked arthritic, and Jack Liffey wondered if it was time to start grinding aspirin into his kibbles.

"I ran into Maeve at my dad's," he said. "She'll declare him saved yet."

"You were in Pedro?"

"I had to go down to talk to a reporter."

"You could have looked in on me at Harbor Station."

"You don't like it when I show up at your work. You told me it gives you a funny feeling, like you've got to be two different people at once."

"Yeah. But you could call."

"Ever try to find a pay phone these days? I'll get a cell, I promise."

Somebody revved an old Detroit car outside. You could always hear the low-end torque of those old oversized pushrod engines. Rubber burned, and the car sped away.

"Display of speed," she said idly. "23-109."

"Hard to avoid with one of those honkers."

"Are you *trying* to contradict me."

"Sorry." He simmered for a moment, then couldn't help himself and let a little spill. "You asked me to move in, sweet."

"I was resisting being fifty. It's in the textbook. This is my penance."

"Your penance is having to put up with me?"

There was an evil silence for a while, only the mantel clock stirring faintly.

"My penance is not living as a Paiute, I suppose. Always feeling something is wrong." She paused for a moment, thinking. "Maybe I'm just a rat, Jack," she said dully. "Have you considered that? You've been nothing but good to me. But one of these days, you're going to see that the only sensible thing is to cut your losses."

"I've done that too much already in my life. I'm committed to making this work. Will you marry me?"

"*No*. But I'll blow you if it'll make you happy."

He sighed. "Honestly, I'd rather make love."

"I'm too beat up for that right now, hon."

"Then let's just cuddle."

"I don't want to put any pressure on you," she said.

"No problem."

"I don't want any pressure on *me* then."

"Then let's just sit here and be us. Ten minutes after I met you," he said, taking a risk, "I knew you were going to be high maintenance—"

"I *hate* that expression."

He wished that she had let him finish. "But there's a hollow place inside me that always fills with something tender when I see you."

"Just tell me a story, Jack. Don't try so hard."

He forced himself to downshift into something like idle and rested his shoulder against her leg again. After a while, he told her about a young Korean girl who'd been recruited by a small company during World War II to go off and sew uniforms but instead found herself serving the Japanese army as a prostitute. In a very peculiar way, he told her, there was even a twisted kind of humanity behind it all. After the horrifying Rape of Nanking only a few years earlier—four hundred thousand Chinese civilians had been murdered and eighty thousand girls raped—the Japanese officer corps decided their troops needed a sexual outlet to prevent further outrages. But of course nothing could justify the enslavement of thousands of women.

After the war, shamed and alone, the young Korean woman had emigrated to the United States and worked most of the rest of her life as a shy and quiet seamstress. She'd never married because of the disgrace and also because of the diseases she'd contracted. Late in life, though, she found a comfortable retirement home with other elderly Korean women. She was finally happy, or, at least, content with her lot. And now the same company that had come to her village to recruit her into prostitution was shuttering her place of sanctuary to turn it into an exclusive resort hotel for Asian tourists.

"Stop, please. Is this all real?"

"It's beginning to look like it."

"They have a hell of a nerve," Gloria said.

He could see how distressed she was by the story.

"What's your role in this horrible story?"

"Somebody once wrote that the role of a detective is to restore the state of grace. I think it was Auden."

"I don't know who Auden is," she said, "but I don't see how you can do that."

"Me, neither. I just do my best."

Five

The Sun Also Rises

He was a little bleary-eyed and abstracted after a second sleep-deprived night, this one spent coaxing Gloria down from a monumental funk. Now he kept rereading the first paragraphs of a *Times* column-one feature that seemed to be about some new breed of strawberries that had both taste and a sturdy shelf life, though he wasn't extracting much sense from it. He'd ground up an aspirin into Loco's morning meal, but the dog had sniffed it and glared at him with those flat yellow eyes, suspecting something amiss. "It's not euthanasia, pal," he'd said. "I'd tell you, I promise."

As he tried to read the strawberry article again, Maeve brought it into focus by dropping a strawberry Pop-Tart into the toaster—her sole junk-food habit.

"Here's an article about strawberries that are supposed to actually taste like strawberries."

"I'm immune to your taunts, Dad. You eat animals. Big red steaks, ugh."

"Red meat—the *other* white meat."

"Huh?"

"Nothing. I like to feel like a cowboy. I eat grub I can really wrassle. Who wants to wrassle carrots?"

She stuck out her tongue and poured a big bowl of müesli—which seemed to be the Swiss word for parrot food. She stirred in plain yogurt, waited for the Pop-Tart to pop, then dunked and shoveled the cereal with it. He supposed the two cancelled each other out, like neutrinos and antineutrinos.

"How is Gloria?" she asked lightly.

"We weren't yelling, were we?"

"No, but her tromps downstairs for more beer went on pretty late."

"Then you must have been up pretty late, too."

"I have worries, too, Dad. It's practically the definition of being seventeen."

"You don't want to talk about them?" It was the first time she'd been secretive with him, at least obviously so. Though she wasn't a bit sullen yet, thank god. He wondered if that was in the wings. How sad it would be.

She smiled. "A woman's got to have some mystery, sir. But you're changing the subject. The subject was Gloria."

"Be kind to her, hon. She may look pretty solid, but under the skin something unruly is whirring away."

"Do you know what it is?"

He shrugged. "Pain. It never occurred to me before how much passion a human being can suppress. Sometimes it scares me. She really needs to go home, but there isn't one for her, and she knows it."

"Can't we build her one?"

"We can do our best."

Maeve wandered the kitchen restlessly digging at her cereal with the shrinking pastry. She stopped at the side window, then did a silent movie take. "*Jeez.*"

He waited.

"It's a good thing you came home before me," she said. "I'd be stuck."

They always parked nose to tail on the narrow side of the drive, so the cop and homeowner could get in and out easily.

He didn't even want to ask, but he got up to peer out over her shoulder. Her Echo was fine, but his pickup had four flat tires, looking as if it had sunk into the earth, plus a spray of graffiti on the door.

"Oh, crap!" He retrieved some shoes from the bedroom and went outside to look closer. As near as he could tell the weird angular letters on his door said LV X3. The doors were still shut, and no one seemed to have touched the old econo AM-FM radio. Each tire had a long slash in its sidewall, making it useless for a trade-in.

Back inside, he argued with Maeve for a bit but finally got her to clear out before he called the police. He didn't want her involved in any way, even as a peripheral witness. Her name would trigger too much fuss at the local station. Luckily, she said she had some sort of get-together with her Redondo buddies anyway.

He debated calling the Hollenbeck Station, but Gloria had shown him the substation on East Third where the gang unit worked, and he'd met Dean Padilla from there a couple of times, dealing with Maeve's drive-by the previous year. Padilla was a bit rough around the edges, but he'd seemed competent and decent enough. And Padilla knew that Jack Liffey was a cop's boyfriend, which could be worth a lot. So he called him directly.

About twenty minutes later, Padilla showed up alone, parking a plainwrap Crown Vic at the curb and going straight for the pickup. Jack Liffey came out to meet him.

"Good morning, Mr. Liffey."

"Good morning, Officer."

"How's your daughter?"

"Fine, thanks. This happened some time in the night. After Gloria got home at seven and before I noticed it this morning about nine."

"Any reason some *klika* would choose you out?"

"Not that I know of. I was friends with one guy from the *Lomas* until he moved away."

"We know. Thumb Estrada. I hear he was the guy that shot up your little girl, though nobody would say it." His eyes came up with sleepy menace. "Never figured out what kind of game you were playing with him."

"Let's say I either had to kill him or try to make something of him. Would you prefer the other?"

"Bangers just use up oxygen as far as I'm concerned."

"What can you tell me about this tag on the door?"

He squatted down to his heels to have a close look. "Something about it doesn't look right, but as it stands, the LV means Little Valley. Their territory's just outside the city boundary up around City Terrace. The X3 means 13. M is the 13th letter. *La Eme*, you know. It means they show the usual allegiance to the Mexican Mafia. There are a few tax-free gangs who won't pay up on principle, but not many, for obvious reasons. It could just be a kid with no affiliation screwing around, you see that on walls a lot, it could be a Little Valley kid hitting the *tierra* of Greenwood on purpose. Usually there'd be some banger's individual tag, too. Some derivative of his *sobrenombre*—his nickname."

Jack Liffey peered in the truck's window and experienced a little frisson of shock when he noticed an envelope on the driver's seat, addressed only: *Liffey.* How had he missed it before?

He went on talking to Padilla to try to distract him, but Padilla was taking notes and wasn't looking inside the vehicle. The policeman finished and offered the name of a discounter nearby that carried used tires, if Jack Liffey wasn't feeling flush enough to buy four new ones.

"How's your Spanish coming?" He somehow knew that Jack Liffey went to night school once a week.

"Not so good. This old brain doesn't absorb well."

"Well, if you ever get in trouble, just say, *Metételo en la cola.* That'll work like a charm."

"Thanks, Lieutenant. If I forget the Spanish for 'Fuck your mother,' I'll try that one."

Padilla laughed and sauntered away. Jack Liffey waited until the police car was around the corner before unlocking his door to get the letter.

"The book is called *Fiesta* in England."

David pushed his glasses up his nose with a single extended middle finger, a gesture that annoyed Maeve for its fussiness if not its unconscious message. "I used to have a whole list of movie titles that the British changed."

Amy had sent word she couldn't make it and the twins were out of town, so it was just her with David and Justin, only half their summer reading group. They were meeting this time in David's upstairs bedroom with some German techno CD going softly and hypnotically *beat-beat-beat* on the expensive stereo in its black rack—something that his engineer father had got him because it still had vacuum tubes and all the experts agreed that analog beat digital every time. Since it was just two guys and her, she was trying a little experiment, on herself as much as them. Her blouse was unbuttoned two buttons lower than where she usually kept it, and whenever she flexed her shoulder she knew she was showing off a lot of bra.

"It's so strange trying to identify with all this Lost Generation stuff," Justin said. Justin normally had his hair in blond spikes shooting out at all angles, but he had cropped it like a Marine for the summer and it was surprisingly attractive. "Like, it seems so dated and innocent. Imagine, they're actually drinking *alcohol* and running around to *parties*. How *naughty*, as the Pythons say."

The three of them sat in a circle on the rug in the middle of his bedroom floor. "I thought it was kind of artificial to have the guy have his—you know—his penis shot off. So he's automatically sort of an outsider and he can't *do* it with Brett and he sort of has to watch her flirt with all the other guys in the book. I didn't like her very much."

"Me, too," Justin agreed. "I mean. What was her problem?"

They both looked at Maeve—their only expert on women this day. "I liked her," she said. "She was so sad. She really loved Jake, but they both knew he couldn't fuck her and that was important to both of them."

"I mean, what's the deal? He could still go down on her, couldn't he? After all, they're in *France*. Where they practically *invented* head."

"Maybe, for some people, oral sex isn't enough." She flexed her shoulder, hoping for a little rush of her own sexuality; she could tell Justin was peeking. "Maybe some women *need* to be penetrated to feel they've really been possessed. That's a dumb word. I just mean they need to feel they've reached the peak of their passions. You know what I mean. That's what Hemingway was talking about. And whatever he did for her, Brett would know that she could never please *him*."

David looked a little embarrassed by the direction the discussion had taken.

"What about the anti-Semitism?" Maeve said. "I mean, why is

it such a big deal that this Cohen guy is Jewish? Somebody's always bringing it up."

They discussed *The Sun Also Rises* for another half hour. Only Maeve found much good to say about the book, and she wondered if, in doing so, she wasn't thinking of poor Gloria and her personal sense of estrangement. Or maybe her own grandfather, who was simply incapable—too old, too rigid, too lonely—of opening his door a few inches to any other culture.

Right after Justin said, "And those bullfights, that's just *sick*," she rebuttoned her blouse and gave up hope of feeling a thrill of desire for either of these guys. She couldn't believe she'd actually fantasized luring one of them into a little heavy-duty kissing and stuff afterwards. She wondered why the Hemingway turned her on so much, but he did. She felt like she was ready for something powerful and important, something Ernest would approve of.

Liffey,

What is real and what is not? Is a dream of a capitalist luxury hotel real? Is simple human suffering not? The people who did this to your car think you should mind your own business. Marvel at our reach, even in our weakness. Remember, you must distrust your senses, always.

Forget Soon-Lin Kim. She has gone away into a world of unending struggle and does not want you to follow her. Unfortunately we cannot waste time with another warning. If you ignore this, you will open the door onto a world of dishonor and pain.

The New World Liberation Front

This note confused and annoyed him. It was like a parody of the ravings of some '70s radical cell. It suggested an art school prank, too cunning and erudite, a forced lampoon of a radical screed. Perhaps it was the same feeling Padilla had had about the graffiti on the door—that something was a bit off.

He decided to pay a visit to Socrates Estrada, Soon-Lin's e-mail nemesis, and see if he'd had any strange visits from the NWLF himself.

A very old woman with a full head of curly gray hair juts her chin to look proudly into the camera. Her name is Kum Hak-Soo.

KUM HAK-SOO

I was born June 10, 1924, in KyongSang Province near Pusan in the far south. We were very poor in my family and owned no land and my father did small jobs for others. My mother worked in a shirt factory in Pusan that was half owned by Japanese and half by Koreans. It broke my heart when I saw girls going off to school. We could not af-ford school. When I was nine, my parents rented me to a landlord. I was supposed to be a maid, but he made me sneak under some barbed wire into a Japanese factory and steal rice. It was very dangerous. Twice soldiers caught me and made me touch them and then sing Japanese songs for them.

She looks down into her hands, which are clasped tightly.

I hated singing in Japanese more than any-thing. I knew I was Korean. I had never seen

a Korean flag—the Japanese who ruled us
forbade them—but I had heard what they
looked like. One day the landlord gave me to
a group of soldiers who came to demand all
spare young girls, and they took me to a
train and said I was going to work in a better
place. I cried and cried for my parents. I was
fourteen and this was 1939. There were many
Korean girls in my car, but we were forbidden to talk to one another. We had only rice-
balls to eat and they closed the windows with
black curtains for two days and then we were
all forced out of the car by shouting soldiers.
I asked an old man on the platform where we
were. He barely understood me, but I managed to work out that we were in Harbin in
Manchuria. It might have been Mars. I had
no idea then where Manchuria was.

It had only taken him two hours to follow Padilla's advice and
have four secondhand tires delivered by Ricardo's Tire Swap
Meet. But first Ricardo's tow truck had to come and yank the
wheels off right there in the driveway, leaving the pickup on jack-
stands, then bring the wheels back reshod. The used tires actually
looked like they had a lot of wear left on them.

As he drove down to Cahuenga south of Downtown along the
L.A. River—the memorable site of one of his first cases—he recognized several buildings that were now occupied by different businesses, which gave him a pang at the passage of time. For almost
a decade he'd been a half-assed detective. He'd rescued maybe
thirty or forty kids. He'd failed on a dozen or two more. His epi-

taph wouldn't have much more than that. But, presumably, it was better than writing tech manuals for launching nuclear satellites.

JACK LIFFEY 1945–2045
"HE ALWAYS GOT THE TECHNICAL WORDING RIGHT."

JACK LIFFEY 1945–2045
"HE FOUND A FEW MISSING KIDS."

Maybe it was enough. He played the wheel back and forth a little when there were no other cars nearby, just to reassure himself that the replaced tires wouldn't lose their grip on the road or simply fall off.

"Don't trust Mexican work, eh?"

"That's not it. I've just never resorted to secondhand tires."

"You think they're going to pop like party balloons?"

"Who knows? I know, in a day, I'll forget all about it." It was a bad habit, but he'd begun talking to himself in the car.

"Maybe you'll forget THAT, too." Mentally he pointed at a half-inflated black barrage balloon the size of a small house that was being towed slowly across the path of his pickup by a flatbed truck. Beside it, half a dozen walking Latinos were tugging desperately on their towlines to keep the breeze from whipping the thing up and away. It was painted like a shark or a whale, and it rippled and billowed in the wind. The single word ANATOMY was painted on it. He'd seen such balloons used to advertise car dealerships, but, somehow, he couldn't imagine a Chevy dealer called Anatomy. Just then, two of the men clinging to the ropes let go and began shouting at one another and then wrestling standing up in dead earnest, as if one had deeply insulted the other.

All of a sudden he was nostalgic for a much less frazzled world—the more orderly Eisenhower L.A. of his childhood—

and he had to remind himself that it hadn't been that great back then, and that the nasty machinery of nostalgia could only work on you when you let the original experience fade so thoroughly that the container of your memory could refill itself with wishful balderdash. That was the era when dissenters had all been forced to shut up or hide, women wore girdles, and blacks stepped aside. So he did his best to enjoy the Anatomy whale—the mark of a more complex world—as the wrestlers gave up their disagreement and ran for their assigned ropes.

Just beyond the intersection a vertical fin of the balloon caught on the power lines overhead and its handlers became frantic to free it as cascades of sparks fountained down around them. He hurried on through the intersection before something worse could happen. Christ, he thought, life can wear you down.

It was a small shingle bungalow the character of which had been altered drastically by a general spray of stucco, right over the shingles, and a big Spanish arch at one side that didn't belong. There was a definite arts-and-crafts skeleton that had been desecrated, but on the whole he didn't really blame people for making their homes more homey to themselves. The whole Westside was dotted with mansionized bungalows that now had pompous two-story front doors that were flanked by giant columns and fanlighted windows, apparitions known to the realtors as Persian sugar cubes. People a long way from their roots did what they had to to feel at home.

This was the last known address for Socrates Estrada, only a few blocks from the L.A. River's course southward. Jack Liffey had been through the manila folder of information that Chris Johnson had given him. Socrates had been lucky enough to be attending 38th Street Elementary School when USC chose that inner-city brick fortress of a school as one of its urban partners. Any student from 38 who kept his grades in the top ten percent through high school was guaranteed a scholarship to USC. But after that they had to keep up a C average through college, and apparently Socrates' beef was with those who dragged up the average by doing things like studying their textbooks and turning in term papers.

Of course, Jack Liffey was reading between the lines. Maybe Socrates was a perfectly ordinary kid who just couldn't hack it in college and lost it one afternoon and sent around a bunch of threats that he didn't really mean and immediately regretted.

He came up the walk through a shaggy and browning front yard and knocked on a door beside a worn sticker that said *Orgullo Mexicano* under the red-white-and-green flag with the eagle killing the snake. His feeble attempts at language lessons at least enabled him to translate Mexican Pride. A short brown woman opened warily, holding a chubby and placid infant in her arms.

She said something that came so fast it flummoxed his handful of nouns and verbs.

"Socrates Estrada. *Quiero verlo,*" he replied. It probably wasn't idiomatic but it would do.

"*Nomi!*" she called. Then there was the pudgy young man whose picture he had seen in the folder that Chris had downloaded from somewhere. He wore a paint-specked jumpsuit and held a second infant.

"Mr. Estrada, I need to speak to you." He knew perfectly well that Estrada spoke English.

"You found me." He looked crestfallen.

"I'm not the police. But one of the girls your e-mail went to is missing. I'm trying to find her."

The young man studied the infant's face, as if some reply might be revealed there, then gave up. "I don't know noth—anything."

"Can I come in? You might know more than you think. I mean you no harm."

He had obviously been taught somewhere along the line to be polite and his instincts forced him to nod Jack Liffey in. The young woman skedaddled without introductions.

"Please sit down, sir." It was clearly Salvation Army furniture, wearing thin. Socrates was apparently doing his best to make a home, Jack Liffey guessed, on some kind of housepainter's wages. Already two babies behind the game, he could be respected for his efforts.

"Thank you. I'm not here to cause trouble, and I'll go soon. Could you tell me how you chose Soon-Lin Kim to send your e-mail to?"

The young man sat, too, and his eyes searched the room, as if for some quick escape. "She was in the student directory, and she had an Asian name." He shrugged but seemed to be thinking things over.

"She was in my history class," he admitted. "I knew her. She was with some Orientals who made fun of my ideas, and she was a radical. You could see she was a leader. I know what I did was stupid. Real stupid."

"Did the school ever track you down?"

He shook his head, but there was something he wasn't volunteering. The baby in the other room snuffled and cried for just an instant, but its mother must have intervened, probably with a breast. There were flying ducks on the wall above the sofa that were so acutely Anglo working class that Jack Liffey had to assume they were left over from another tenant.

On a hunch, he took out his note from the Liberation Front and walked across the room to show it to Estrada. "Have you ever seen anything like this?"

The young man's eyes went wide and he recoiled as if slapped.

"You get something like it?" It seemed clear that he had.

"It was the same name, the Front thing," Socrates admitted.

"And did you get out of Dodge when they said?"

"Huh?"

"Forget it. Just tell me about it."

He shook his head once, as if trying to clear it. "It's like a bad dream, man. I know it was them. They came and got me from my apartment. They tied me up in a van and took me to some place that was maybe a half hour drive. Talked all the time in some Oriental language, like squawking."

He stopped and ran a finger in circles in front of the infant's face. Its eyes followed the movement greedily.

"What happened?"

"Nothing, man. They just scared me bad. They had guns. I don't want to talk about it."

He got up and carried the infant out a side door. A couple of sirens passed on a street nearby, and there was either a backfire or a gunshot. Jack Liffey perked up, but heard no sequel. Human life seemed to have passed out of the world, and he wondered if Estrada was ever coming back.

The short woman came quietly into the living room. "You go now," she said.

There was no lock on the bedroom door, but this time Maeve moved a chair in front of it to give her some warning if Gloria decided to barge in. Cautiously, she worked her head between the curtain and the cool glass. The whole gang seemed to be hanging out again in the semi-darkness of the backyard next door. She counted—seven girls and nine guys. The girls were mostly apart, drinking beer from tall bottles. Beto did not seem attached to any of the girls. She studied the way the girls dressed, the restless way they held themselves as if they would leap into motion at any moment, the way they related to the men, like small magnets aware that huge powerful magnets were just over there, just a few inches beyond the range of physics that would spin them around. One girl with a lot of earrings sat next to her man, and he had an arm locked around her neck as if he expected her to try to make a break for it at any moment.

Maeve felt this inexplicable longing to be among these outsiders, impossible as it was, and to belong to one another the way they did. She felt a terrible emptiness inside—a consciousness that life was poignant and full of true, deep, soul-defining emotion, and that she had no idea how to get in touch with any of it.

Six

All My Babies

"So I'm in this, too?"

"Hold your horses. I was still living with Becky then, but you came along pretty soon. Hell, you know as much about this as I do." He wriggled around to get a little more light on the book. It wasn't actually a book but something called "bound galleys" with a plain cover and a lot of typos. He'd gotten it in the mail today, with a note from the author.

"*Rebecca Plumkill lowered herself gently beside him,*" he read aloud, "*and ran her fingers lightly on his arm. 'You've got an appointment with Auslander at two.'*

"That's Beck talking. Remember that quack Auslander?" He didn't really like reading aloud, but Gloria said she found it soothing, and she was up on one elbow now, her chin cupped in her palm, and highlights from the reading lamp doing wonderful things to her bare olive skin.

"*'Can I have a wisdom tooth out instead?'*

"That's me."

"*She chuckled and ruffled his hair. He closed his eyes and pressed his head against her hand like a pet.*

"'I really appreciate you, Beck.'"

It was making him a little nervous here. He hoped there was no sex. The guy who'd interviewed him on the Terminal Island case had done a pretty fair job of writing it up, after several weeks of talking into a new-fangled digital recorder, but from what he'd seen so far, the writer wasn't above including the embarrassing bits that Jack Liffey would rather he'd left out.

"The calamity that had left him with a collapsed lung and as weak as a kitten had also reinforced what seemed to be a slow-burning nervous breakdown, and he was astonished Rebecca had stayed with him through it all."

"Hah," he said. "She cleared out soon enough when the going got tough."

"Shut up and read."

"Auslander was a shrink and Jack Liffey didn't get along very well with him, but he was an M.D., too, and the only access to the pills that kept him from a lot worse. His normal life, for whatever that word was worth, was tracking down missing children and he hadn't been able to get back to that in several months now.

"'You're still pretty good in bed, even if you're not much good for anything else.'

"That's gotta be Becky. Uh-huh."

"'I can make a farting sound with my underarm,' Jack Liffey boasted.

"'And you still make me laugh,' Rebecca said. 'No woman asks for more than that.'

"'A lot have, believe me.'"

"Yeah, I want a bit more than that, too." Gloria let her hand rest softly on his half flaccid erection under the sheet.

"Can I stop reading now?"

"Have you got something else in mind?"

"Oh, yes."

"Does it involve me?"

"Intimately." She was in a much better mood tonight.

"How much are you getting for all this?"

"The guy promised to split any royalties above the advance, but I asked around and they say there never are any."

"So he ripped you off. But you'll be famous. That's worth something for your business."

"Not if this guy stays an unknown writer. Probably about ten people will buy the book. Oooh. That feels good."

"Maeve's home, so don't get loud." They were her last words as her head disappeared beneath the flowered sheet.

The old woman makes a hush gesture with one finger to her lips as she considers something.

KUM HAK-SOO

Then they took me to a barracks inside the Japanese army compound. It was called a Comfort Station, and I did not understand the cruel meaning right away. A Japanese couple were our chaperones, to teach us hygiene and make us learn some Japanese. After about three weeks, this couple brought an officer to me. I even remember his name—Aritomo. "Nothing to fear," the couple said. "It is nothing." I crouched in the corner of the little cubicle. He tried to force himself into me and I bit his hand, but in the end he called some friends and they tied me up. Then they all had me. This continued many days and I was beaten for resisting. I pretended to be dead and they poured cold water on me. While I

resisted, they gave me only water and one
small rice ball a day. After about a month,
I was so weak I gave up and did what they
wanted. I even sang and danced at banquets
they held. At least the officers usually wore
condoms. I have not been able to speak of
this before now, but the record must come
out.

The old YWCA building was beautiful by any standard. Red brick and four stories tall, it had dormers along the roof, was colonnaded and set back from the street, much like a cloister. Now it was surrounded by a temporary hurricane fence and idle hulks of heavy machinery—a backhoe, a small crane with a wrecking ball on it. A silk banner across the front of the building screamed: SAVE INTERNATIONAL HOUSE! PEOPLE BEFORE PROFITS!

He parked across the street and tried to imagine the building in its glory, in a time before the lawns and shrubs had been scraped down to the bald clay slopes and before the rose bushes had been flattened by machinery. It must have been something, the big welcoming cove of garden drawing you in off the street. And if any city in the 1920s and '30s had needed an oasis of peace for arriving young women, this was it—the big tinseltown magnet for the implausible dreams of stardom that infected girls everywhere. For decades the Clark had been a residence for young women coming to try their luck in the film industry, and then, at the end, it had become a single-room-occupancy hotel—the euphemism for a welfare hotel.

A chainlink gate creaked open and admitted him. He'd had to ignore the warning sign from Tunic-Semba Construction Company that the property was condemned and he was risking some undefined penalty by entering. Tunic-Semba was the same giant contractor that had constructed the subway walls several inches too thin under Hollywood, which caused the immense cave-in at Hollywood Boulevard, so their demand for rectitude did not impress him.

A commercial-size Yuban can by the door was filled with sand and cigarette butts, and he pushed in the fancy frosted glass door that had seen better days—some leafy tracery was overlaid now by scratches and rag-ends of Scotch tape from dozens of old notices. The front desk was in the same condition. A sign said NO GUESTS IN ROOMS and another said WEEK-MONTH. No one was there, and he tapped the zinc bell on the desk.

A bald man with a cauliflower nose emerged from a back area and leaned on the far side of the counter, as if short of breath. It was disconcerting that his misshapen multicolored beezer actually whistled at each inhale. Were those breathing whistles called rales? Jack Liffey tried to recall.

"I'm a friend of Soon-Lin Kim. I'd like to talk to Mrs. Hak-Soo Kum. Or Kum Hak-Soo."

The man nodded toward a room behind French doors. He appeared quite short of breath. Jack Liffey had a spare oxygen cylinder at home and felt like offering it to the man. "She'll meet you in the garden room."

He made no move to call her.

"You'll let her know? This week?"

"Sure."

The linoleum on the floor had once suggested a Persian rug, but along the heavily used paths the design had been abraded away to a pale orange underlayer—one trail from door to desk, another into the garden room, and one more branching toward the sign that said NECESSARIES. Jack Liffey had never seen that one anywhere outside Texas.

He wiggled the latch until the French door came open, and a blast of humidity hit him. The place was full of ferns and lovingly tended tropicals. All it lacked, he thought, was Major Sternwood in a wheelchair, blanket over his knees, but Jack Liffey figured he'd be along any minute. He looked out the back at what had once probably been an ordinary lawn, but now held a portable office trailer that said Tunic-Semba. It didn't look like anybody expected the delaying tactics to succeed much longer.

Now six incensed people filed into the room. Each of them seemed to be pushing eighty or beyond. One was a man, his skin so dark and wizened it was hard to tell his ethnicity. Undoubtedly they took him for yet another agent of the enemy, a lawyer bearing a veiled threat, a city inspector, a contractor's front man offering something—probably not a very far-fetched assumption given their experience. Jack Liffey had never put himself in the path of a hundred-million-dollar project, but he decided he would feel incomplete if he died without giving it a shot some day.

The old people actually linked arms and faced him, as if to stop a sudden breakthrough for a touchdown.

"Ladies and gentlemen, I hope the International House goes on, just as it is, forever. I work for the parents of Soon-Lin Kim and all I'm doing is looking for her." He couldn't read their expressions. "She's the girl from USC who came here to make a movie. I am not from Tunic-Semba."

One woman spoke up, "Tunic-Semba is not the problem. They are only builders. West Lake Partners is the problem, and behind them, Daeshin."

Judging by the video he'd seen, this looked a lot like the woman he'd come to talk to, but he wasn't certain. All of the women were Koreans, or at least Asians of roughly the same age. "Are you Mrs. Kum?"

"Why should I tell you?"

"You shouldn't. I've just seen video testimony by a woman of that name and I was very moved by it."

She turned away and covered her face to make a muffled noise. He guessed it was shame.

The male resident seemed ready to square off, as if about to challenge Jack Liffey to fisticuffs.

"I'm sorry. What I saw was mainly dignity and courage." He faced the old gent, whose fists were up more or less. "Please don't hit me, sir."

The man let his hands sink slowly. "People use even the sublime to degrade one another," the old man said.

"Is that a quote?" Jack Liffey asked.

"Ortega y Gasset. I am Spanish." He launched into a lecture on the superiority of Spanish ethics, and Jack Liffey let him rattle on about Neruda and Lorca until he simply ran out of steam and sat down on the divan.

"Let's all sit down and remain calm. Mrs. Kum, please. Could you tell me about Daeshin?"

They all sat on the sofa and wing chair, which left him nothing but a short piano stool, which was just fine.

"They are the company that wants to transform this building into a luxury resort."

"I understand that. I also understand from a friend that the big Korean conglomerates like Daeshin were founded well after the war, mostly after the Korean War."

"All except for Daeshin," the woman insisted. Her English seemed very good, almost unaccented. "I remember it vividly. There are very few opportunities for an energetic criminal in an imperial colony—except serving the occupier. One way is to be a labor recruiter. With all the men off to war, Japan needed a lot of labor. I believe Daeshin started by setting up labor recruiting offices in every Korean city. Our own block organizations were sometimes given quotas. There were many oppressive laws then. You know, Korean language was forbidden, and then they banned even our names. We all had to go to the prefecture to register Japanese names. I was Kuno Haruko. Or Haruko Kuno, as I would say now. My, I haven't spoken that name in a long time." She seemed a little shaken.

"That's all right Mrs. Kum. Take it slowly."

She turned to her friends. "I'm all right now. This man is no danger to us. You could leave me with him, thank you."

Each of them said good-bye and touched her lightly as a kind of moment of solidarity before they left. Jack Liffey and Mrs. Kum waited patiently until they were alone.

Mr. Kum continued. "Yes, Daeshin had an office in Pusan, and a branch right in our village. I clearly remember the sign on it. Let me translate. My Japanese is rusty." It was as if she had to screw up her face to think: "*Your labor serves the Greater Co-prosperity Sphere for all Asia.* What a terrible time that was for us. But you can see that it didn't seem so odd to us when they started recruiting young women. They said it was to work in factories that made army uniforms in Hokkaido. In fact, I was already an indentured servant to a foolish Korean landowner and he sold me to the recruiters to protect his own daughters."

She sat in silence for a while. "I think you know what happened next."

"No, ma'am, I don't." In fact he wanted to have her tell the tale to him in person. He needed to be able to ask questions, check details.

"Then I want you to see something, young man. Please come with me."

The "young man" surprised him, as he was pushing sixty, but

he decided all things were relative. Taking very short steps, she led him to an old-fashioned manual elevator, with a sliding triple-layered glass and brass door. He slid the outer door open and then the accordion-grate that was attached to the car itself and let her punch the worn brass button for the third floor. The elevator alone should be in a museum, he thought. All it lacked was a big Bakelite crank handle and a deferential black operator on a fold-down seat.

"Third floor," he announced. "Sporting goods and ladies clothing."

She looked a little puzzled.

"This elevator is like the ones in the department stores of my youth."

"That's one of our differences, Mr. Liffey. For you, nostalgia is harmless, even positive."

Her comment impressed him. He wasn't sure why he had expected an elderly Korean woman, a woman without education who had suffered so much abuse, to have a dull mind. It was both stupid and racist, he thought, to think that way.

"You're exactly right," he said. "No matter what's gone wrong in my life, and sometimes it seems to me a lot has, it's very little compared to yours."

She nodded. "There is so little I can remember with fondness."

The excruciatingly slow elevator finally jarred to a stop, a few inches below floor level. As he opened the doors, he warned her, probably unnecessarily, of the stepup. The accordion-door crashed shut behind them as they entered a dim hallway that emanated a vague odor of urine. Two doors away from the elevator, she let him into a tidy one-room apartment, with a Murphy single bed pulled down and made up and a tiny kitchen area of hot plate, basin, and waist-high fridge. There was no TV that he could see, nor a radio, but a small stack of books sat beside the bed. She indicated a worn easy chair next to a hump-topped steamer trunk, and he sat while she hunted for something in a china bowl she lifted off a shelf. Her search, swirling a finger in the bowl, made sounds like sifting through a collection of nuts and bolts.

She came up with an old-fashioned key and knelt quite nimbly at the old sea-chest to unlock it and flip open two brass clasps. "I want you to see this, Mr. Liffey, but I don't want you to judge it."

"I'll do my best."

The top came up with a faint squeak. It was hard to appreciate what he was seeing at first, it was such a jumble of yarn, about half of it flagrant pink and the other half baby blue.

"A great Korean writer once said that we do not see things as they are. We see things as *we* are." She picked out one item and held it up. It was a set of pink booties for a baby girl, obviously hand-knitted and linked by a single string of yarn. Then another: a little blue jacket that would just fit a newborn, presumably male. A tiny dress, then pajamas with feet, more booties. The entire chest seemed to be filled with hand-made baby clothes, hundreds of them, none of which seemed to have been used.

"Is your wife of child-bearing age?" the old woman asked.

"No," he answered. "My daughter from an earlier marriage is seventeen and getting close to that point herself, but she'll be holding off a while for college. At least I *hope* so."

"You know where to come when you need baby clothes." She paused a moment. "If you can't guess, these are for all the children that I cannot and will not have. The Japanese soldiers gave me so many diseases—deep inside my body—that, after the war, your doctors had to take out most of my . . . organs."

"I'm so sorry."

"No man in Korea would have had me anyway. I was dishonored. It's why I came to this country as soon as I could. But I had no skills. I ended up working in what you call sweatshops for forty years. I had a good boss at the end, a kind man, and after a while he agreed to let us all join the needle trades union, so it was better then for a few years."

She fumbled on the shelf where she'd found the key and then showed him an old photo in a gilt frame, a young and pretty Korean woman with bobbed black hair, who looked glum and downcast. "I think a man might have had me if I had been intact. I was not bad-looking. That is my passport photo in 1948."

"You were and are a beautiful woman."

She waved the comment away and glanced down at the knitted garments. "All my babies. I cannot forgive what was done to me, because the Japanese government has never even said they are sorry. That is what Soon-Lin said to me. My testimony might help make them apologize. It's the only reason I agreed to talk about my shame."

"There's no shame in what is forced on you. Never," Jack Liffey insisted.

She shrugged. "Live in my skin. It knows shame." She stood up and closed the trunk.

"Do you have any idea where Soon-Lin might be?" he asked.

"I was always worried about that girl. She was so . . . rash. So explosive. Her emotions were always too much. It frightened me. They claim we Koreans are that way, but this girl was . . . beyond all saying."

"Do you have any reason to think Daeshin would harm her?"

The old woman made a sound of puffing out a breath, as if trying to clear herself of any memory of that corporate name. "All of what the world chooses to do to us goes on behind a screen, Mr. Liffey. How can I know?" She looked at him, almost coyly. "Silence is sometimes the only answer."

. . .

Her skin tingled as she started with the earrings, working the little training studs out of the piercings she'd just had done at the shop on Chavez and replacing them with the big hoops. She looked in the mirror and tried to imagine how it would look when she dyed her hair a lustrous black. She undressed and tugged on the cut-off Levis, then fastened the bright red brassiere and pulled the spaghetti strap top over it and tugged it down so about a third of the bra cups showed. The lower seam of the top didn't cover her midriff but it did make it over the scar.

She looked at herself in the mirror, posed sideways and did a little breast shimmy, almost laughing at herself. It would take a couple of tattoos to make it complete, maybe a butterfly peeking out of the bra. Maybe a big PROPERTY OF GREENWOOD across her navel. And then she clapped a hand to her mouth to stifle a giggle. She thought of adding an arrow from the PROPERTY OF GREENWOOD pointing straight downward toward her vagina, and how her dad's eyes would go wide and he would go ballistic and immediately wrap her in a thick blanket, trying to staple it to her body so it could never be removed.

But, within a few minutes, the novelty had worn off, plus the humor, and she imagined actually getting some tattoos, men's eyes on her, and felt almost woozy with the whirl of forbidden emotions. "It's all for you, *mi amor*, all of me," she said aloud in a throaty voice and almost fainted. She had to sit hard on the bed.

You're delaminating, she thought, using a word she had read only that morning.

"Want some dinner, hon?" came from outside the door, and she went rigid. "I picked up some of those great tamales from Juanito's over on Floral. And here comes your dad."

Instinctively, as she heard the rattle of his truck coming up the drive, Maeve got up and set her back against the door and began tugging out the earrings.

Seven

Libros de John Brown

Walking up to the UCLA campus from the one spot in the Holmby Hills where he could park legally for an hour, he could have sworn he heard a coyote's howl, plaintive on the spring air.

Loco, if you've followed me here, I'll have your ass, he thought. But it could be a full-blood coyote. A survivor might have trotted down from the hills through the mansions of Bel Air, posing as a stray housepet, perhaps showing fake ID to the private security patrols. He'd read that the coyote was the only North American mammal resourceful enough to extend its range after the arrival of the Mayflower and they had gotten as far as Long Island now, kicking over Eastern trash cans and chowing down New York housecats. He felt he had a special bond with coyotes. Not just that his own pet was half coyote—and it was the better, less subservient half—but that these feral beasts represented something that had been scrawled outside the margins, peering in at our self-important doings with their flat yellow eyes, a little disdainful, ready to take the whole place back if we dropped the ball.

He came out across Hilgard into the vast sculpture garden that marked UCLA's north campus. He'd read recently that it was one of the world's great sculpture gardens, though he'd never paid much attention before. Yet there was a Rodin he recognized, there a Lipchitz, and, over there, one of those horses seemingly made out of driftwood by somebody or other who was probably famous.[2] And right here was Peter Kim, spiky red hair and all, trussed up like a roast where he sat on the grass, picking among a half dozen little bowls of food with chopsticks. What he was strapped into was some sort of standoff framework that held his little video camera a few feet in front of him, pointing back at his face. He seemed quite unself-conscious about it, as did various other students on the grass nearby who were napping or reading or getting in a furtive bit of canoodling.

"Peter, hello. I was on my way to hunt you down."

"Hello, Mr. Liffey. You have hunted me down."

"Call me Jack, please."

"Sure." He reached out and rotated the camera for a moment, as if to grab one identifying shot of his visitor as Jack Liffey squatted and then sat on the grass. Then the filmmaker aimed his camera back at its one true subject. "If you had some sticks, I'd share lunch."

"That's okay. I had a pretty awful sandwich on the way over. I stopped at something called *El Pollo Demente* and had a thing called *el mero mero*. It had some distant relation to chicken and probably battery acid."

Peter chuckled, then carefully picked out a greenish morsel and held it out. "Here, Jack. Kimchee covers the flavor of anything."

Jack Liffey swallowed obediently. He'd had the spicy sauerkraut before. "That'll clear my sinuses. You know, I saw your film

2. Deborah Butterfield, if you're interested.

project." He wasn't quite sure whether to repeat its name aloud. The Talking Pussy, words that could drift disconcertingly on the wind.

"I know you did. It has a counter on it. Did you like it?"

"I don't think I saw all of it, but it gave off a nice sense of transgressive whimsy."

The young man's expression was a bit dubious. "Whimsy. As a fully serious post-modern artist, I'm not sure I can take that as a compliment. Art is an arena for the combat of quite equal texts. Disney's *The Little Mermaid* is just as authentic as my piece, and they are all serious."

Jack Liffey noticed he wasn't invoking the title either. "Okay, your project comes up to the standard of *The Little Mermaid*."

Peter Kim laughed good-naturedly. "Just remember, we try to cultivate a quite *non*-ironic engagement with the popular culture."

Before this banter could go any further, Jack Liffey reached out and rotated the camera to face himself. "Earth here. I have some detective business. Quite non-ironic and rather confidential. About the New World Liberation Front."

He rotated the camera back just in time to catch the young man's face go as guardedly neutral as a boxing referee.

"I don't know them," the boy said.

"But you've heard of them?"

"It's an atavism. It's like Ford rolling out a brand-new car that—*chogot poseyu!*—looks just like the '58 Edsel. The Front doesn't make any sense today. 'The people united will never be defeated.' *What* people? I always wondered. A handful of angry kids?"

"Could your sister be that angry?" Jack Liffey thought of a girl her age filming Mrs. Kum, as the wrecking ball swayed out front, and knew the world could seem a cold and violent place, utterly lacking justice. It was a wonder the kids didn't all join some crackbrain rebel outfit.

"Soon-Lin's got her . . . enthusiasms, that's for sure," her brother said. "But as far as I know, the New World Liberation Front is by and large a big myth. Maybe they were six kids who took Mommy's station wagon up to those demos in Seattle. Maybe they went to a vigil against Iraq somewhere." He almost smiled. "Maybe they're just shadow puppets up on the big-walled estates of the rich. You know, this country would love to have only 'the festive immigrant.' Give every group one national holiday, then slow down traffic a little for the parade—as long as it's not *that* inconvenient. One more way to marginalize us. It's the nonfestive immigrant that's a bit more trouble—the guy who cuts your lawn for half what you used to pay the kid down the block. The illegal making fifty dollars a day smoothing concrete."

"I had no idea you were so angry, yourself."

He shrugged. "We're not like the Plains Indians, burned out of our homelands. We can hold our liquor and we can get good jobs, but they still colonize our psyches. No one I know wants to tear this country down; we merely want to be part of the big inclusive conversation that this country is supposed to be having."

He liked Peter Kim: he seemed to have found some kind of militant peace through his art, and he was obviously clutching it around himself for protection. Now he started transferring his little bowls into a big plastic box, preparing to go.

"Could your sister be caught up with a band of . . ." Jack Liffey didn't want to say terrorists—it had become such a cheap, all-purpose denunciation. ". . . angry radicals?"

Peter stared out across the grassy knolls that were sprouting their sculptures, as if an answer might appear on one of the jutting forms. "I don't know. I didn't like some of her friends, but I

didn't know them well. Somebody important at USC invited her
. . . no, *told* her to take her documentary films off campus. That's
why I gave her the edit space. Other than that, she and I didn't
mix much."

"Thank you for continuing the conversation," Jack Liffey said.

"Derrida's Rhetoric in the third," Jack Liffey suggested. "He's always good past six furlongs and does well in the dry." The out-of-
place pigtailed girl in the betting lobby, who was clutching a
yellow legal pad, seemed quite puzzled.

"Where's Mike?" he asked.

She led him out the door and nodded to a lower tier of seats
and sidled away quickly, clinging hard to her yellow pad.

The class was called "The Social Science of Risk," or something ridiculous like that, and after a few calls he'd found them
out on a field trip to the Los Alamitos racetrack, all fifteen of the
students filtering through the sparse weekday crowd of punters,
clutching their clipboards and questionnaires and flashing out-
of-place, clean-scrubbed smiles.

Having to compete with L.A.'s two big tracks—Hollywood
Park and Santa Anita—Los Alamitos was at the far downmarket
end of the racing scene, catering to a blue-rinse and reversed-
baseball-cap crowd, and the track ran mainly quarter horses and
harness rigs and shortish claiming races for nags that had been
bred in urban Anaheim next door. It was good to see Mike
Lewis—back in town and with a respectable (though nontenure)
lectureship at UC Irvine. This was despite the *Times* and the real
estate interests having done their damndest to run him out on a
rail over a book that pointed out just how much it cost the city to
subsidize and protect all the cliffside and beachside and forestside
homes of the ultrarich. The sociology of risk.

His long, swept-back hair was now silvering up like a Porsche, but it was him all right, sitting by himself halfway down the sparse stands, actually studying a *Racing Form*. Jack Liffey hadn't seen him for two or three years.

"Mike, who's a good bet in the second?"

He looked a bit startled. "Liffey, I'll be damned. I didn't think you gambled." They shook hands, a bit of one of those complex sixties things until they both gave up halfway, but still punctuated it with a fist pop at the end.

"I don't. But I'll bet you know something about it."

"The obvious. I know that all gambling emporia, without exception, are designed so that their customers, in the aggregate, lose. Everyone knows that. To circumvent that, the great trick is to make every damned one of them think he or she has an edge."

"Did you just bring a bunch of suckers from UCI here to bet?"

"Oh, no, no. That *would* be wrong." He grinned. "We're studying just what it is that folks *think* is their edge. Of course, at the end of the day, if my kids turn up the fact that people who bet on gray horses with even numbers tend to win, I'm not above coming back and trying to apply it."

Jack Liffey laughed. A man in checked trousers and white shoes walked past them muttering. There was cigar smoke on the air, something he hadn't smelled in a long time in a public place. "So, basically, your kids are social scientists doing research on assholes."

Mike Lewis frowned. "One difference between us is respect for the human condition."

"Yeah, but which of us has it?"

Mike Lewis smiled, and his eyes made a circuit of the immediate area, on the lookout for something and obviously intent on letting the verbal sword fight fade away.

"It's good to see you back in town, Mike. They didn't find a way to stop you at the California border."

"I flew in. It won't last, but if my books make enough money, they can't very well shoot me."

"Hell, that last book—the *Times* assigned a hit team of about thirty people from editorial to find every typo."

He shrugged. "You kick a big bear, it's what happens. I have no complaints. I get to be acknowledged as one of the city's leading bear kickers. It's what we always wanted, isn't it?"

"I have another theory about bears," Jack Liffey said. "It's a very old one. Don't kick a bear unless you can kill it."

An old woman in a motorized wheelchair whirred her way down the ramp, juggling a drink, a sandwich, and a handful of betting slips.

"We're in different businesses, Jack. I imagine that's a pretty sensible rule for yours. Which reminds me, you knew Jim Sefh, didn't you?"

The name stirred a chill on Jack Liffey's spine. "Roomed with him for a year at Long Beach State, before he went to UCI in graduate chem."

"Uh-huh."

What neither of them were saying was that Sefh had gotten himself so incensed at the fuel-air-explosive invented at UCI in the last days of Vietnam that he had torched the chem lab late one night and unfortunately killed a janitor sleeping in the basement. He'd been on the lam from the FBI ever since.

"The rumor is he's back in the country, after hiding out in Europe for thirty years. And some of the feds would badly like to find him."

"I'll bet they would. But I knew him long before his picture went up in the post office." With the Weather Underground all caught or surrendered, Sefh was about the last big fugitive from that era.

"Just letting you know some guys with shiny black shoes may come see you."

Jack Liffey shrugged. "What can I tell them? Jim liked to play Crazy Eights. He had an uncle he really loved who was some kind of environmentalist, probably long dead now. Funny you should mention him though. I came here to ask you about the New World Liberation Front."

He and Mike Lewis had been in an ad hoc antiwar committee right after Jack Liffey got back from Nam, but he had dropped out fairly soon. Mike, however, had kept tabs on the Left through all its ups and downs and then the *real* downs.

"I didn't know any of them were still around."

"Don't be coy," Jack Liffey said.

"I try not to waste my time on microbiology. When these grouplets get small enough they tend to disappear behind the paramecia."

One of Mike's students came trotting toward him, a young woman with an earnest look and a long blond ponytail that swayed innocently like a model-train semaphore. "Mike, what's a trifecta?" she asked. "I got a guy over there who doesn't do anything else."

"It just means you pick the top three finishers in order. Not every race allows it. A *boxed* trifecta is the top three, in any order, but they don't do that here. In an exacta, you pick the top two in order."

"Thanks!" She headed back eagerly.

"Been to the tracks a bit, eh?"

"I made a living long ago at Del Mar, for a summer. You've got to figure your money's in a big pool against a bunch of stumble-bums and the superstitious who bet horses because the names remind them of something. That was my edge."

"NWLF. Do you like that name?"

"Not a lot. At the end of the last really meaningful period of rebellion, there was a brief hysteria of what people called party building. Everybody seemed to want to found a new Communist Party, less tainted than the old one and all that, and they cobbled together about five of them. Your pals were the rainbow one. Collectives of a number of ethnic groups got together in Chicago and formed their own party—the Chicanos from the August Twenty-ninth Movement, the Black Liberation Army, the Samoan Freedom Fighters, the Puerto Rican Marxist-Leninist Party, and I think . . . something from the Native Americans. Not AIM. That's what the New World Liberation Front was way back then. I can't imagine what would be left of that after twenty-five years. A few acolytes, some geezers, a runaway from a reservation, one kid smart enough to fix a printing press."

The horses for the second race meandered skittishly down the chute with their jockeys looking bored, and Mike watched them carefully.

"You sound pretty scornful for a guy who was part of all that."

"Somebody ought to do a serious study of self-deception, Jack. It'd probably fit right in with horseracing. We told ourselves there was a rising tide of revolution—just when the sentiment for revolution was collapsing. We said we wanted state power and we didn't have the support—or the competence—to run a small bus system in Dubuque."

The horses were milling around on the track now, a few of them trotting, and the starting gate was being motored into position.

"I don't really need edifying abstract lessons, Mike. I'd like something concrete on the Front."

"They used to have a bookstore in the MacArthur Park area. The area's about as mixed-race and poor as you can get, mostly

Central American. It was called Libros de John Brown. It might still be there."

"Thanks. I hope you get a winning system out of all this."

"The only winning system is to exploit other people's labor," Mike Lewis said, though it was an open question whether he meant capitalism or sending your college students out to gather data for a private betting scheme.

Jack Liffey raised a thumb, just as the PA announced that the horses were in the gate.

"Horseracing is such dumbshit," Jack Liffey said as he got up to go. There was a roar as the gates clapped open and the horses took off, but how on earth could anyone care?

If it's really a sport, he thought, forbid the betting for a week and see how many people show up.

The old woman's eyes are closed. She shakes her head once, as if chasing off an insect, then opens her eyes.

KUM HAK-SOO

I must tell you this, but without embellish-
ment at all. Because we tried to escape so
often, one day the Japanese soldiers marched
us to a factory yard nearby. They brought in
many young Chinese women all bound with a
long rope, and they disrobed them. Many soldiers waited in line for their turn. After taking their pleasure, they tortured the poor
Chinese women with knives and then they
threw red pepper onto their wounds to make
them cry out. The soldiers seemed to enjoy it.
Some soldiers even poured oil on the women

and lit them on fire. Many of them died before our eyes. One very brave woman did not
make a single sound. Afterward we stopped
trying to escape.

It wasn't a bookstore that invited casual browsing, that was for
sure, embedded in a block of sweatshops and car body shops. In
addition, it was upstairs and there was a substantial steel door at
the street, beside a very small sign for LIBROS DE JOHN BROWN/
JOHN BROWN BOOKS, as if anybody in L.A. needed the bilingual
gloss. Another sign said to ring for entry. He rang and a disembodied voice asked what he wanted.

"*Libros, por favor.*" He tried not to sound sarcastic.

Jack Liffey watched through a wired-glass window the size of
a playing card until a gangly young man in a blue Pendleton shirt
hobbled down the stairs into sight. A couple of heavy bolts
snapped back and the door swung open.

"Thanks." He stepped in before the doorman could change his
mind. "What if I were somebody you don't want in?"

"You'd be in trouble." The young man locked the door and
nodded up towards the top of the stairs, where a heavyset Latino
sitting in a wheelchair held a shotgun.

"I wouldn't suggest a scattergun, *compañero*. It'd take out both
of us down here."

"We're not unfamiliar with martyrdom," the young man said,
as they started the climb up the faintly mildewy-smelling concrete steps. "Some Cubans—*gusanos*—came in a few months ago
and put us all on the floor and shot up our stock with automatic
weapons, probably supplied by the CIA. Is there something special you want?"

"Yes," Jack Liffey said. As he climbed, he raised his hands and then opened his jacket in a protest of innocence and weaponlessness to the gunman. "I don't go armed."

The young man he was accompanying patted him down a few steps short of the top to make sure and the wheelchair backed away. Jack Liffey came up into a dank room with makeshift pine bookshelves everywhere. There were no other browsers, but a Latina and an Asian woman worked at desks to one side. "I haven't been in a place this paranoid since the seventies."

"We try not to destroy ourselves with our passions," the Latino said. He seemed the boss.

"I should think loneliness would be enough to do you in," Jack Liffey said.

"You're not really after a book, are you?"

"I've been hired by Soon-Lin Kim's father to try to find her. Do you know her?"

"What makes you think I might?" The wheelchair angled about deftly, and the man slid the shotgun back into a diagonal holster beneath a desk, like something out of an office Western.

"I've been told she might be a friend of the New World Liberation Front." That got their attention all at once; he could sense it from a tremor of electricity on the air, though all they did, each one, was focus their eyes squarely on him.

"That's the problem with outsiders," the guy in the blue shirt said to the gunman, as if Jack Liffey didn't exist. "No frame of reference at all. Why would a neo-Trotskyist with nationalist tendencies hang out with real Marxist-Leninists?"

"Go dust the shelves, Marty."

The man in the wheelchair held Jack Liffey's eyes as his younger comrade sauntered away. "We aren't the New World Liberation Front, friend. We're a bookstore, as of today a very progressive but purely commercial enterprise. There have been a lot of fights over who would end up with the real estate, but Marie and I won." He seemed to indicate the Latina who was still staring fixedly at Jack Liffey. He could see now that she was older than he'd thought, in her late fifties, with generous stripes of gray in her lustrous hair.

"Good for you and Marie. I'm not the FBI. I don't even like the FBI. I find missing kids, and her dad hired me, probably just to see if she's okay."

"I've met Soon-Lin. She's a typical adventurist—somebody who got stuck in Lenin's *What is to Be Done?* and never outgrew it. I always preferred Bakunin as a starting point. Good old-fashioned anarchism. You know what he said?"

Jack Liffey could tell he was about to find out, and saw no point in resisting it.

"'I can never ride in a coach past a man setting a fire and not want to jump out and help him.'" He grinned. "I can get behind the simplicity of that, the pure bring-it-on." His eyes went to the telephone and he leaned slightly that way. "But it would be *wrong* to start fires or any kind of violence," he enunciated distinctly, as if for posterity. He glanced back up at Jack Liffey. "Just in case they're taping today," he explained. "We believe people should have the option of reading the great radical thinkers that you won't find in Barnes and Noble. It's not the same thing as putting any of it into practice."

"I'm not accusing you of anything."

"Yes, you are. It's periods of political quiescence like today that breed the most pointless terrorism. It's pure frustration when people see no hope. That's what Russia was like at the end of the nineteenth century. There was just no popular movement to engage anyone. We aren't part of that in any way, but we wish something real did exist. A whole generation of children is growing up not knowing the satisfaction of political engagement."

"Look, I was in Nam, and then I was in the antiwar movement just like Kerry. You know what I hate now? I hate people making loud noises and spectacles. I like nice quiet days—people who barbecue and build family rooms on the back of their houses. All these ghosts just make you old. I want to talk to the girl, I sure don't want to argue with her about the Great Helmsman or Pol Pot or anything else. Could you give me a break?"

The bookseller cocked his head, as if actually considering. "Snitch on her? I don't run in that track, *ese*. No fucking way. You're free to browse in here."

"You wouldn't know how to get a message to her—I mean, very indirectly—or to the Front?"

The man thought for a moment. "I'd say, if she's in this group you talk about, and if you've been looking as noisily as this for more than a day, the message has got through already. They may be crazy, but they're not idiots."

Jack Liffey suddenly felt belligerent. It didn't happen to him very often, but right now he wanted to punch someone. "You guys are such geniuses, I don't know how you ended up running a bookstore where you have to know a password to get in." He left his business card, which luckily didn't have Gloria's address, but referenced his old Culver City condo which he kept as a kind of office and storeroom. And, of course, a just-in-case bed, if Gloria didn't work out—but he didn't like to think of it that way. "Soon-Lin drops in to browse, give her that. Can you let me out?"

"No problem, *ese*."

She'd had the dye job and snuck back into the house fast before Gloria or her father got home, and now she stood in front of the mirror admiring how rich the color was, how glossy, like a

thousand million strands of the blackest silk. It looked a little odd
with her skin tone, but she could sure get used to it. And she'd really fit in a lot better over here. But how was she going to get
through dinner?

She put in the big gold hoop earrings, and she almost couldn't
recognize herself. She turned to study the new clothes all laid out
on the bed and almost lost her nerve. You go, Baby Girl, she ad-
monished. You can do this.

She'd swiped two of Gloria's Coronas from the fridge and carried
them out back, over the hedge and up to his back door, where she
could see him inside working at writing something on the
kitchen table. There was a long moment of hesitation—terror really. She was almost peeing in her pants. Finally she pinched herself and knocked softly. So softly that maybe he wouldn't
hear—but he did. He smiled when he looked up and saw her and
then made a quizzical face when he got a good look. He waved to
come in, and she did. She held out one of the beers as an offering.

"What you done to yourself?"

"Don't you like it?"

"You look like one of the sheep."

"That's not nice. The girls just want to look good for you and
your friends."

It was probably not possible to get any more self-conscious,
Maeve thought. Two buttons were undone on her top and a lot of
the new red bra was showing, plus her midriff and just about all
of her legs below the cutoffs.

"*Chido*, you look real good, you do. *De pelos*, man. Baby Girl,
you real something." He took the bottle she held out to him
and uncapped it, then took hers, touching her hand on purpose

as he did—which almost made her faint—and opened her Corona for her.

She took a sip when he handed it back, and the beer taste hit her hard. She wasn't used to it. "I saw you working on something in here."

He gave a grimace and took a long swig. "It's for a job. At County General. I got a *carnal* there who turned me on to it, but I don't know. They want an *essay*, Why I want the fuckin' job. It's not like I'm asking to be a fuckin' *doctor*."

He was applying to be an escort, one of those entry-level guys who were dispatched to take patients from place to place. A small part of her was amused by the disparity between this and the jobs she knew her Redondo pals would end up applying for, but what right did anyone have to be snobbish? Someone who worked eight hours, put in the time, did a good job—it was all the same.

"Can I help?"

"*Sobres!* You bet. You a good friend, I was about to give it up. I mean, why do I want to push somebody in a wheelchair a mile across a hospital?"

"Because it's the only way they can get the treatment they need. Getting them there is the critical link in their medical care."

"*Padre!* That's perfect, *mijo*. Here, you write."

He tried to hand her a pencil, but she refused. "No, it should be in your handwriting."

"Sure, I see. *Claro que* yes." He stood for some reason, took another long pull on the beer and sat again, and she was mesmerized by the muscular grace he had in simply sitting down in a chair. This is your last chance, she told herself. You can scram right now.

"Say what you said again, Baby Girl. Come here."

She stood next to him and he put his left arm around her waist, and all her vision went pink. It was a struggle to concentrate, but she led him word by word through a four-line essay on the worth of simple labor.

"Really good, Baby Girl! You got me the job, I can see it! I gotta do you a favor now."

She was pressing the length of her body against him, and he caressed lightly across her bare belly. Then his hand wandered up over the front of her bra, setting her nipples on fire. "You know what this is in Spanish?"

Her eyes were closed, and she shook her head

"*Chichonear.* And this?"

He rubbed his hand softly in the crotch of her cutoffs, and she moaned. It was as if her head wanted to shoot off like a rocket, just rip off her neck and blast straight up.

"This is *dedear,* Baby Girl."

"I want you inside there," she said, and she could feel her voice break. "Please."

Eight

Doc Feelgood

It was about then that he began to have especially revolting nightmares. He'd always hated telling people his dreams, and he didn't now—they were always so drearily emblematic of everyone's childhood fears—but Gloria noticed anyway, commenting on how restless his sleep had become. It was as if he'd been hexed in some way by the Korean case. The recent encounters—Peter Kim's unremitting peculiarity, the video interviews with the comfort women, the stranded-in-time paranoia of the Liberation bookstore—it all contributed to the same vertiginous sensation, a strangeness that threatened at any moment to drop him through the thin ice of reality into a scalding bath of something else.

It reminded him of a vivid memory of sitting in the back of his father's car, his forehead to the cold glass and a jacket over his head to shut out even the weak light of the dashboard. They had been driving through the rain in some darkened countryside that they did not know, and far off he saw the bright smudge of a town—suggesting hundreds or thousands of individual bedroom lamps, porch lights, headlights—each of course a story, part of an endless tapestry of dramas and melodramas that he would never have the least access to. That drive coincided with a brief religious period of his youth, but already he'd felt himself losing his faith, and he realized that these thousands of people would never know of his fall from grace and no one would ever be redeemed. He abandoned his vigil out the car window and experienced his first sensation of diminishing.

It was quite visceral, the sense that everyone and everything nearby was retreating from him and he himself was shrinking, contracting toward a miniature being and then a spot that might just blip out of existence. It had been pure sensation, pure overheated teen imagination, of course. Inadequacy writ large. Probably just like that dream of finding yourself nude in homeroom or intractably lost on the way to the final in French, a class you had forgotten all year to attend.

These days he'd sit in Gloria's living room, looking up from a magazine he'd picked up at random, and expect the old *diminishing* to come again. But it didn't. Just some fuzzy analogue of that phenomenon, probably left by the nightmares—a dread, deep inside, that things were about to go wrong. He wondered if it was a side effect of the anti-anxiety drug he was still taking from time to time and he decided right then to drop it.

"I'm worried," he said, as Gloria relaxed across from him with a gin and tonic.

"About what, *querido*?"

"I wish I knew. Don't you have some ancient wisdom about fears that come over you without warning?"

"Sure. It means a bunch of guys in blue coats is about to ride horses over the horizon and slaughter all the buffalo and kill everyone you know."

He smiled. "These days it's an army of geologists in Jeeps

looking for some mineral that the army needs so badly you'll all get kicked across the border into Nevada."

"Since we're a little ways off the reservation, honey, do you know what's bothering you? Is it me? I know I bother myself."

"I don't think it's you. I keep having this premonition that something is going to go wrong just when I'm needed and I wont be there for you."

"Don't forget your daughter. Be there for *her*. She's getting pretty hormonal, after all."

"How do you mean?"

"You're kidding, right? If you could actually take a good look at her through that sentimental haze you throw up, you'd see a girl who's working herself up to get herself laid."

He wasn't entirely surprised, but he protested, "She's seventeen. I didn't have sex at seventeen."

"She's almost eighteen, and that was a long time ago, Jack. Life's accelerated a bit since you were singing the Mickey Mouse Club song."

They could hear Maeve moving around in her room upstairs. "Maybe I should go have a talk with her?" He sounded dubious, even to himself. Especially to himself.

"Maybe you should." Gloria took his hand. "Jack, remember . . . whatever she does, it's not the end of the world. Right? This is the twenty-first century. She's already been badly wounded and fixed. We can fix most wounds when people are good at heart."

That only made his fears worse. "She's got such a streak of sympathy in her, Maeve. I have this image of her getting into a car with some crewcut guy who says he needs help and then being driven off toward the vanishing point by a serial killer from Nebraska. All the neighbors said he was the nicest boy."

"Jack. Come in, Jack." She mimicked speaking as if to someone far away. "Woman to dad—forget Nebraska. You haven't been around a lot recently. Your daughter is pretty starstruck by Beto Montalvo right next door, like a moth and a flame. He's no serial killer, but he's not anybody's idea of Mr. Goodbar."

"Jesus fucking Christ."

She couldn't stop grinning at herself in the mirror on the back of the bedroom door, staring intently to see if it showed: that great melodramatic passage that was universally understood—*she was a real woman now.* Beto hadn't been quite as gentle with her as she'd fantasized, feeling, perhaps, that a bit of the rough was what was called for, snapping orders and squeezing her breasts a little too hard. But, still, it had been about as thrilling as she could take, especially having him strip off her clothes until she was shamelessly and awkwardly naked before him in his bedroom, every inch open to him. Then later she'd got a kick out of hurrying out the back window, still dressing herself, as his mother came home from work and called "*Beto, mijo, mi guapo,*" from down the hall. Maeve couldn't help but anticipate how she'd tell her grandchildren some day about her close call this first time.

In her mind she went over and over the act itself, squeezing her eyes shut to picture it better, that very moment he got on top of her on the tufty bedspread and then entered her, the squeezing feeling and sharp pain and then the woozy abandon as he started to move in and out. She hadn't even known that she went in that far. By now she'd relived it so many times, she wasn't sure she was even remembering the act itself or just remembering remembering it. As soon as she'd gotten back in her room at Gloria's, she'd taken the spaghetti-strap top off and the cutoffs and the hoop earrings, and she'd tied her new dark locks into a ponytail to try to subdue her new *chola* look a little. But sooner or later, she'd have to go down to dinner.

She thought of the other possible consequences with a pang of worry. She hadn't made him wear a condom—though she'd always planned to do so her first time, always planned to be smart—but it would have been like trying to stall a race horse in the stretch. She didn't know anything about the statistics for AIDS in the Latino community. Pregnancy was another question, of course, but she was pretty sure it was the wrong time for that. She should probably douche now—if she only knew how and actually had the stuff. There were rumors about using a shaken Coca-Cola, but that didn't sound like a great idea. Her mind was such a whirl of thoughts and feelings. Then there was a tapping on her bedroom door that was much too tentative to be anyone in that house except her father. *Did he know?*

She glanced once, quickly, in the mirror—it had to show!— and then sat down at the little dresser and clasped her nervous hands together to still them.

"Yes?"

"It's me. May I come in?"

"I haven't piled up the furniture."

He opened the door and the instant she saw him, she could tell that something was up. He hadn't registered the hair dye yet and he took a little time studying her as he stood there. "That color's darker, isn't it. And the piercings are new, I think."

"It was about time I did it. You *think*?"

"Well, guys are notoriously unobservant, but I don't remember those little studs in your ears."

"They're trainers to keep the holes open."

He sat at the end of her bed. "You look like you've switched to Garfield High," he said.

He seemed to think he'd made a joke, but she didn't take it that way. "Would that be so terrible?"

"Well, it would be unusual. With all that Irish DNA squealing in panic."

"You never really want to claim being Irish," she challenged.

"Sorry, I didn't mean to joke. You know I'm not against Latinos. Not after Marlena and Gloria and almost a year of Spanish classes, despite my clogged old brain."

"That's okay. I know you're not like Grandpa." She knew, despite all her efforts to soften him, that the old man remained a horrible racist at heart.

She was now hoping that her father would just stop prying, pat her once and go away.

"Remember when you promised to tell me the truth always?" he said.

It had been after she'd misled him badly and got herself into a lot of trouble for it, a couple of years earlier. She remembered it all vividly. But a promise like that was about as meaningful as one to stay healthy, she thought. It's all beyond your control, and you do what you have to do.

"Sure, I remember. That was a while ago."

"Okay, but that doesn't mean it's canceled. Is there anything I should know?"

She stared at her hands for a while. "If I tell you the truth, will you promise not to get upset?" She thought of coming clean and tried to imagine his reaction. *Dad, Dad, try to be calm now . . . I just fucked that gangbanger next door, and I'm going to do it again and again, as often as I can.* She knew there would be a little trouble at first, maybe a lot of trouble, but eventually he would soften.

"That's asking a lot, hon. If you've joined the Nazi Party, I'm going to get upset."

That helped, because she could feel him avoiding what he

was really worrying about, and she took his lead. "No Nazis, I promise."

"Whatever happens, I'll love you. I hope you know that. And I'll be here for you. I'll protect you and support you if you need it. I love you, Maeve Mary, with everything in my being. I promise not to yell or fume."

She looked up at him. His earnest face was like a terrible reproach. She teetered on the edge of weeping. Here it came: "You have nothing to worry about, Dad."

But there were worries aplenty. The next afternoon, the backhoe parked at the old YWCA was set on fire and burned to a blackened hulk, and, after dinner, Jack Liffey abruptly had the cops to worry about, a pair of them showing up, asking angry questions about the Koreans. It wasn't the gang guys from the substation, but detectives from Rampart itself, both overweight, like pretty much all detectives, and looking more like journalists in their rumpled Penney's suits.

He went with them voluntarily to the station, just to keep any unpleasantness away from Gloria and Maeve. It didn't seem to count much with these two that he was a cop's boyfriend. They settled him into an interrogation room that was a bilious green, and ostentatiously hit a switch that turned on a red pilot light on a video camera fixed to the ceiling. He couldn't see the microphone, but the lead cop announced the time and date and all their names in a normal enough voice so he knew it was sensitive.

"You visited a woman named Hak-Soo Kum at the building known as International House on Loma Drive near Downtown." The lead interrogator had draped his jacket over the chair and the sleeves of his white shirt had already been rolled to just below the elbows, making him look even more like a journalist. His

name was something Sandos and he was a lieutenant of detectives, but he hadn't said what his specialty was. Jack Liffey was
guessing Anti-Terror, formerly the Red Squad, a branch they
were supposed to have done away with by court order long ago
but which everybody knew had just changed its name once again
and was never talked about. Sandos had olive skin and stony
black eyes with no centers to them.

"The older Koreans in this country keep their names in the
traditional order, the family name first," Jack Liffey said. "Kum
Hak-Soo. That's how I know her."

Sandos glared at him, then read off the amount of time that
Jack Liffey had spent at the old Y, pretty much to the minute, as
far as he remembered.

"Sounds right."

"Why did you visit this woman?"

In the movies he wouldn't have told them who his client was,
would have insisted it was privileged information or something
like that, but this was the real world. "I'm looking for a missing
Korean girl named Soon-Lin Kim. Her father hired me to find
her. She'd filmed Mrs. Kum extensively for a documentary about
International House, and I thought she might know something
about where the girl was. She didn't."

"Took her over an hour to tell you she didn't know anything.
Is that your story?"

"I first met with all the residents. They're very suspicious and
protective."

The second detective took off his coat and sat now. Jack Liffey
was surprised to see old-fashioned suspenders holding up his
trousers, real button ones, not the cheesy clamp-ons that kids
wore. He had such a belly that a belt wouldn't have helped much
unless he'd had it riveted to his hip. This one's name was O'Brien,

if Jack Liffey remembered right, just to make the noir-cop caricature that much more perfect.

"What do you know about Daeshin?" O'Brien now put in. He'd pronounced it Day-ee-shing, as if trying hard to get it wrong.

"I'm told they have companies making everything from dump trucks to diapers. One of their subsidiaries is redeveloping International House. And they make the famous Wanda that's slightly more reliable than the Yugo."

"Picky for a guy with a beat-up Toyota truck."

"Runs fine. Lousy mileage though. Come on, my car isn't the issue here."

Neither of them spoke. Jack Liffey saw no point in holding back the obvious. "You think I'm hot on the trail of the New World Liberation Front, don't you?"

There was no reply. He could see that O'Brien badly wanted to smoke, touching the pack in his breast pocket from time to time like a talisman. Jack Liffey decided to goose them a bit. Finish what he'd started.

"I don't even know if they exist. I got a note signed by them, warning me off, but it could be anybody. It seems pretty implausible that anything is still around from the bad old seventies." Sandos rested his chin on a fist, his elbow on the armrest of the only chair in the room that had them. Settling in for the long freeze.

"Speak right up, any time you want," Jack Liffey said. He was letting them get to him. He always hoped to be better at it than this, able to handle the pressure of the Big Silence. "I think about that time a lot. Southern California spawned the Manson family—a bunch of lost kids who were really looking for fame in the music biz, and San Francisco had the SLA, who were a little brighter and wanted a revolution."

Still, no one said anything in reply. Whether they were interested or not, Jack Liffey found it hard to tell.

Now Sandos consulted a printout he unfolded from his pocket. "You were in Vietnam Veterans Against the War, weren't you?"

"So was John Kerry. I lasted about three months. I think half our chapter was FBI agents, to be honest, guys always trying to get us to do something really stupid so we could be busted."

"Why did you leave it?"

"Eventually all the things that were making the other people angry just ended up making me sad and lonely. I went up into the sequoias for a while and recharged my batteries."

"What batteries?" O'Brien demanded, and Jack Liffey thought he caught a flicker of annoyance on Sandos's face.

"That was an expression." *Metaphor* might be a bit deep for his end of the gene pool, Jack Liffey thought. "Most Californians need to touch a sequoia every few years just to remember what a glorious thing life is."

"I don't."

"Pat, go have your smoke and get us both some gum, would you? I can see you're dying for it."

"Sure." O'Brien left the room, and Sandos seemed to relax a little. Jack Liffey decided there was no question who was the bright one. The policeman glanced at the printout again. "A couple years ago you were mixed up with terrorists and a dirty bomb. Right?"

"Jesus, man, I *stopped* the attack. I got a collapsed lung to show for it, thank you, and somewhere I've got a nice piece of paper from the mayor with a gold star, calling me a hero."

"Yeah, well, we can never be sure how it went down, can we? Last-minute change of mind. Who knows? Don't kid yourself, Liffey, things have changed in America. I could have you on a plane to Guantánamo in a half hour, for more thorough questioning. What are your feelings about social justice?"

"I think I want a lawyer."

"You're not under arrest. You're cooperating."

"That just stopped. I have nothing more to say."

"Don't count too much on your girlfriend. Some of us don't like lady cops much, anyway."

O'Brien came back in but it wasn't with a pack of gum. He carried a small black old-fashioned doctor's bag and set it down on the table. "Recognize this?"

Jack Liffey said nothing, as he'd promised.

"I'll bet your prints are on it," O'Brien said.

"I want a lawyer." He repeated it loud enough for any microphone to pick up, but O'Brien reached up on the wall and switched something off.

Their threats grew more extravagant, and then, as if they had crossed some sort of line and now had to follow through, they seemed to call a halt and led him downstairs. When he saw it was the parking lot, he relaxed and assumed they were driving him home, but instead they locked him into an empty concrete closet off in a corner of the lot. There was no light and no furniture.

"Hey! Stop kidding now!"

All he could hear was their footsteps diminishing.

For most of the time Jack Liffey lay on his side in the damp dark, clutching his knees and trembling from the chill. He may even have slept a little. The sound of footsteps halting outside the door brought him alert.

"We gonna have trouble with this guy?"

"He's a pussycat. But you can give him a little Doc Marten if you want."

"Doc Feelgood is better."

It was two men but no voices that he knew. He sat up when he heard a scratching at the door lock. The door swung open fast, as if they were expecting him to leap out, but it was almost as dark outside and he saw only suggestions of men in dark clothes and skimasks. One of them jacklighted him suddenly with a blinding light.

"I want a lawyer!"

A man laughed.

"Think of yourself as a volunteer. In an experiment."

Another form passed in front of the dazzle, a woman, and he could have sworn she carried the black bag the cops had shown him earlier.

"Bring him out," the woman said.

He was tugged to his feet and hauled out of the closet into an overpowering smell of cheap cologne.

"Oww!"

A needle had jabbed his thigh straight though his clothing.

"Which airport?"

"Hawthorne." The woman's voice. "The old Northrup Building 4. Look for a LearJet 45."

He was starting to grow faint and the men holding him were bearing more and more of his weight. He heard a vehicle approaching. It sounded hollow in some strange way, a van. Then a racehorse was watching him, breathing hard, and things became too odd to be reality, and strangely, he was aware that he was dreaming.

She thought of Beto, and how serious he had been and she wondered why Mexicans were so taken with melancholy. She wanted to leap and squeal for joy. But things had changed forever, and even the air in her bedroom was different now—it had both risk and promise in it. Then the cell phone on the little desk started ringing, bringing it all home; she was pretty sure who it was.

"Hello."

"Baby Girl, *que tal?*"

It was that wonderful baritone voice. Even his secondhand presence made her giddy. "I'm completely crazy, that's how I am," she said. "I can't eat. I can't think straight. I want you I want you." She couldn't believe what she was saying.

"You come on over to Greenwood Park, meet the *cuates* and *chicas*. We sittin around."

"I'm a little worried. My dad's not home yet tonight."

"Hey, Baby Girl, who's the boss?" It was amazing how fast the menace had entered his voice. "You come see us."

She knew she was going to acquiesce. She wasn't even sure why she had demurred at first. "Can I bring you anything?"

"Sure, you bring me proof you my girl. You wear a short skirt and don't be wearing nothing under it." His voice was now complacent.

She had to close her eyes. In record time, she had not just gone woozy, but become so wet she was afraid it was about to start running down her leg.

"I'll do whatever you want, *Beto*."

"Don't make me wait."

The room spun like the Teacup ride at Disneyland. She flopped on her back on her bed to keep from fainting dead away. How could half of you be scared to death and the other half feel like a merry-go-round on turbo?

The transformation was a whole routine now, and she hurried to get it all done—the hoop earrings, the extra eye makeup, dark lipstick, musk perfume, the new denim miniskirt, and of course the bright-red bra.

As bad luck would have it, Gloria saw her coming down the

stairs in the full East Los getup. Gloria sat in the living room still recovering from work, sipping at some drink. Her eyes narrowed at the sight on the staircase.

"You're going out like that?"

"Yes." She tried to sound challenging, but she liked Gloria and hoped she wouldn't have to defy her. Maeve tugged hard on the tiny skirt.

"I'm not your mother, so I won't try to stop you. I had my wild time, too. I hope you use protection. You can get over a mangled heart, Maevie, but there's some other stuff out there you don't get over."

"Thanks for caring."

"Your dad's not home. I'm a little worried. Did he leave you any messages?"

"No."

"Okay. If he calls, can I tell him when you'll be back?"

"Not too late." She hesitated. "I'm just going to sit with some friends in the park."

Gloria looked her over carefully. "Hon—all the hair dye in the world, you're still a *rubia* on this side of town. *Cuidado.*"

Nine

Jumped In

Uphill, Greenwood Park had a big retaining wall alongside a row
of raised barbecue fireboxes, and over time the wall had been so
layered by graffiti that in the diffuse evening light it appeared a
long abstract expressionist mural. Between the picnic area and a
distant baseball diamond was a large expanse of scabby grass that
got used mostly for soccer. At least two groups of people were inhabiting the park that night and as Maeve drove slowly past the
one sitting out on the grass she could see they were younger
wannabes, taggers. Her group, the real Greenwoods, sat on the
lower tier of the baseball bleachers, maybe fifteen of them, most
about twenty years old.

As she walked over to them in the fading evening light, she
could see three girls at one end of the bleachers primping and
making up. Several of them were smoking long brown Shermans
and drinking bottles of Modelo. Beto sat in the center, com-
manding the rapt attention of all. She waited respectfully a few
feet away as he finished up, as if wanting an usher to show her to
her seat.

"... This guy was hard to take, *qué bárbaro*. You go to the *pinta* you get no choice in your cellmate. Romo had no dignity, no *hon-radez*. He insisted on talking about whacking himself in the john, and just how much stuff went all over the floor and how the screw came in to check up and slipped on it and fell on his *nachas*."

A couple of the guys laughed.

"After about ten times hearing about his *chaqueta*, I had to tell the guy if he mentioned whacking his dick one more time, I'd make it a whole lot shorter. Lucky, he got 'roled out and I got a guy who could tell ghost stories. That was *padre*." He noticed Maeve standing politely near the bleachers.

"*Orale! Carnales*, I want you to meet Baby Girl, my new little lady." He patted the bench beside him and she walked over and climbed up. "Be good to her. She's new to town."

"*Aquí estoy*."

"Hey, Baby Girl."

"Hey."

"Esa."

"You ain't Mexican."

"*Disculpe*. It's not my fault. I tried to be."

One guy laughed, but none of the girls did. Beto draped his arm heavily over her shoulders, and she did her best to sit with her legs tight together so as not to advertise her lack of under-pants. "That's Spanky and Pony and Chilango, and there's Ruby and Tiny and Ivana . . ."

He introduced them all, but the only ones she could remem-ber were Ruby, the girl with the blond hair, and Pony, who was very muscular and wore a Chargers cap. All the guys had mous-taches, but there was no single distinguishing trait for the girls, except a lot of makeup and jewelry. A younger guy with stylish sunglasses leaned over to hand her a bottle of beer. One puff of a Sherman that was passed along had her light-headed. Either it was too strong for her or it was laced with something. She handed it on to Beto who drew deeply and held his breath.

"Where you from, Baby Girl?" It was a guy with a big square jaw, looking about ninteten.

"I live next door to Beto."

"I mean before."

"Redondo Beach," she said warily. "My parents are split up." She thought somehow that might win her some consideration.

"Yeah, mine, too," said the guy with the big jaw.

She was starting to notice the homemade tattoos, peeking out of sleeves and at the neckline. Part of her was anxious about finding herself so far out of her element, but she was also quite proud of being there. This was a line no one she knew had ever crossed over nor were likely to, not even her father.

She huddled closer to the solid trunk of Beto as he retold one of the ghost stories he'd heard in jail—a tale about a mop that cleaned the floors all by itself at night. The slim Sherman went around again, and now she was sure there was something more than tobacco in it because little tingles danced on her cheeks. But so much was going on that it was hard to know. His body touched her from hip to shoulder, like a huge burning coal, and she had never imagined sexual desire could be so intense. All she could think of was the evening before and wanting to be alone with Beto again so he could push himself inside her. Every confident laugh of his turned her insides to mush, and her head was drifting in a haze of craving. When one of the others was talking, she whispered in his ear, "Beto, I want you so bad."

"*Trucha!*" somebody warned. "*La jura!*" Two big men were sauntering toward them across the infield. They wore dark suits and carried flashlights.

"*Nadie se mueve, pendejos,*" one of the big men called.

"*Pinche* cops."

Maeve had come alert, and, looking down, she could see small transparent plastic envelopes fluttering away like butterflies beneath the bleachers.

"Shit, it's Padilla," Beto said. "Sit up, Baby Girl."

She straightened and felt something cold and hard pressed into the back waistband of her skirt. It took her a moment to realize that Beto had just passed her a big pistol, and he tugged her top down to try to cover it.

"Be cool," he said.

She recognized Lt. Padilla from the couple of visits he'd made to the hospital a year earlier after she'd been shot. She'd been pretty doped up back then, but she was sure. She hoped he didn't recognize her, but she knew she didn't look much like that old Maeve Liffey any more.

"A guy can get sick and tired of you bad boys. Hello, Beto. Pony. Spanky. Digit. Girls."

The other policeman went under the stands and collected the little envelopes and the remains of several Shermans.

"I don't suppose none of you know nothing about all that speed and dust down there," Padilla said.

Maeve had a terrible urge to correct his grammar.

"We just got here," Beto said. "No bullshit. That musta been there. You and your girlfriend welcome to a *cerveza*."

Padilla waved a hand as if chasing off a fly. "We could fingerprint your baggies, but none of this is sell-weight. Know anything about somebody shooting up a *quinceañera* on City Terrace earlier tonight?"

Maeve was deeply and intimately aware of the pistol in the small of her back. The odd bulging shape made her guess that it was a revolver, and she had uncontrollable images of being led away in handcuffs.

"Ah, *hombre*, that's *Lomas*, we *like* them."

Padilla's finger began a tour of pointing at the faces staring back at him. "*Tú reconosco*, and I know you, I know you, I know you." The finger stopped directly in Maeve's face. "*Tú.* You're new, little sweetie pie. Please cover your brains, *señorita*."

Maeve felt herself blush as she tugged her skirt down discreetly, trying not to dislodge the pistol.

"What's your name?"

"Baby Girl," Beto said for her.

"Your real name. You don't look Mexican. I think you're a *güerita*."

"Gloria . . . " Maeve almost added Ramirez. "Smith."

"Wiseass, huh. Come here, Baby Girl."

Beto held onto her shoulder to keep her seated. "You got no business with Baby Girl, Padilla. She's staying with my family. She's a cousin from up north."

Padilla gestured with more force for her to come. "*Caiga.* Got some ID?"

"No."

Beto still held her down. "She stays with me, man."

Maeve was nearly paralyzed with fright.

"Have it your way, big man," Padilla said. "I'm not going to hurt her." Padilla took an old-fashioned Polaroid pop-up camera out of his jacket pocket and sprang it open. "This is just for our rogue's gallery, Baby Girl. You run with the bad boys, we gotta know about it."

But first he knocked away Beto's protective hand and looked her over, examining her shoulders and chest. "Got any tats?"

"No."

"How about some I can't see under there?" He grinned as if threatening to disrobe her.

"No."

"Just stay there."

Padilla lifted the Polaroid camera and fired it straight into her face, blinding her with the flash.

She wondered if it might get passed around, division to division, until Gloria would see it.

"*Qué viva la LAPD*," Padilla shouted. He pumped a fist in the air. "The blue gang rules, you know it, we're *rifa*." Padilla and his partner walked away, and Maeve was grateful that Beto wrapped his arms around her to hold her still. Her whole body was trembling and her mind no longer controlled any part of her.

He swam back toward consciousness because he heard a snore that reminded him powerfully of Kathy, and he hadn't slept with Kathy for a dozen years. He wondered if maybe they'd shot him up with something that put him outside his own body a little and he'd been listening to his own snore, because he was lying on his back alone on a plastic-covered foam pad in the aisle between some fairly posh airplane seats.

The painful whine that filled the air said it was a jet and the bouncing that they were airborne. There were tiny holes through the white plastic arch over his head, breathers or just design. Next to him, he saw a leg in camo fatigues.

"Where we going?" Jack Liffey said.

"Anothah county heard from." A man's voice, a broad Southern accent, maybe Louisiana, but the man leaned the other way and did not come into view.

"What's happening to me?"

"You, sir, have an amazing biological resistance to hypnosedatives."

Quick as a wink, there was a syringe in his arm.

"Ouch!"

The man grinned in a friendly way. He had the most amazing bushy black beard, and he began to croon in a soft Delta baritone:

> *"Fais dodo Colas mon p'tit frère*
> *Fais dodo, t'auras du lolo*
> *Maman est en haut*
> *Qui fait des gâteaux*
> *Papa est en bas*
> *Qui fait du chocolat."*

Jack Liffey was just drifting off again when he realized there was a blues club in L.A. called *Fais Dodo."*

Gloria had finished her gin and tonic and then another one, and neither Jack nor Maeve had come home or called. She wondered if she should do something. It was remarkable to her how much she missed him. Before he came along, she'd grown quite accustomed to being alone, thank you, the peace of it, the sense that she was the total master of her time and could do whatever the hell she wanted. She hated answering to anyone for what she did; she didn't even take orders well on the job, and she knew it. Now it was as if there wasn't quite enough air in the room to breathe. Everything had thinned out to leave her staring at things she didn't want to look at. She hated her own possessions that were all around her.

There was a trashy dream catcher on the wall, a thing somebody on the job had given her after finding out she was Native American, though as far as she knew, dream catchers were specifically Navaho and this one was gas station art anyway. But to most Anglos all Indians were the same. It was like giving a Russian doll to a Czech. What did the damn thing mean to her? Beads and feathers. Commercial nostalgia.

She could feel herself getting frustrated and angry. Jack, Jack—what are you up to? The damned man refused to carry a cell phone, the jerk, the idiot. He hadn't left a note. Soon she'd be calling police stations, hospitals.

Beto had taken the pistol back and praised her cool. "What you say, Ruby?"

"Real *loca gaba*." It sounded like sarcasm to Maeve, but all she really cared about now was the comforting feel of his body against her again.

"She done good. I want her in the *klika*," Beto said.

"Naw, man. She a *ruquita* but not for that, homes."

"I say yes. We jump her in right now."

"You don't got to bring her in just to fuck her, *ese*. Look at her, she so *caliente*, she do you right here."

"¡*Así es, así será*! You want to fight me about it?"

"No, man, but this *ruca*, we don't know shit about her."

"She's my worry, *carnal*." Beto picked her up under one of his arms, like a big loaf of bread. He was so strong it startled her. He carried her out into the infield and dropped onto the sandy baseline, skinning her knee. "Oww!" she cried out.

"Girls, do your thing. I want it proper."

Maeve looked up, with only a vague idea of what was happening. She'd heard of the concept of *jumping in* where an entire gang piled on as an initiation rite, but she didn't know if they did it to girls. It was the bottle-blonde who started off.

"Bitch!" She grabbed Maeve's hair and yanked her head up so

she could slap her hard across the face. There was a lot more cursing, mostly in Spanish. Then they punched and kicked all at once, making Maeve curl into a ball to protect herself. She tried to say something about her reattached intestine and the sutures not being completely healed, but when she tried to talk Ruby slapped her again across the mouth, which was like being hit by a flame. She felt her blouse tear, then more blows. Somebody kicked her between the legs and another fiery pain filled her insides solid so she could hardly breathe. There were sudden scratches and the smell of blood as she felt rings cutting her cheeks. Then a kick on the point of her chin made the whole park go.

The old woman makes a small steeple of her fingers in front of her face and then lets her hands drop.

KUM HAK-SOO

We were examined every week for venereal disease. Mostly it was those who had to entertain the enlisted men who suffered from it. The officers were more careful. We were all given a potion against getting pregnant, but one woman—Michiko—I don't even know her Korean name—did get pregnant and gave birth in our compound. The child was already dead and decayed due to some disease, and they took Michiko away. It was hard to keep friendships because they moved us around and changed our names. I had several names I don't even remember. When I was alone, I began to curse the farmer who had sold me to them, I even cursed my father for not

coming to rescue me and take me home, and
for the first time in my life I felt an anger
that I could not make go away. All I could do
was sing the Korean songs that some of us
made up. I will try to translate one of them:
                    (croons softly)
I'm going up the hill, don't cry. I work hard
day and night, so don't worry about me,
Mother. Just say good-bye to me. The train is
leaving. The coal smoke makes me cry. When
can I go back to my hometown? Where are
my mother and father, where are my brother
and sister? I am far away and worthless.
Can't you bring me back, can't you just bring
me back once more?

There was a shriek like a longish fingernail scraping down a blackboard, a sound he had dreaded all his life and figured could only be the Jungian memory of the cry of some predator that had hunted early man. The light seemed autumnal, the air blood temperature as he woke in a wire cage, like a panda, expecting to be poked by sticks. An olive green tarp was over the top to protect him from the elements, but the rest was pretty basic. A rubber mat on dirt, with one blanket. An open-air shithole.

A voice somewhere nearby was speaking some guttural language with a lot of coughlike and spitlike sounds. This fit right in with the nightmares he'd been having, but he knew the difference. He reached out and rattled the chain-link just to convince himself this was all real.

Could they really have flown him to Guantánamo?

"*Allahu akbar!*" he cried out. It was the only Arabic he knew and he hoped it would get somebody's attention. There wasn't even a change in the cadence of the rat-a-tat discourse he was overhearing, like a prerecorded sermon in some Turkic language. He decided the voice was just beyond a gray concrete block wall that he could see outside his cage.

A young woman came finally to his chain-link fence. She wore army camo fatigues and carried a Bakelite tray, presumably of food. She was not unattractive, a little pudgy, with short blond hair, but no really distinguishing features. In fact she looked like one of the notorious jailers from Abu Ghraib.

"Are you going to make trouble, if I open up to feed you?" she asked from the other side of the chain-link.

"Am I making trouble now?"

"The day is young." She actually seemed frightened of him.

"I'll look away." He hadn't noticed a door, but he rolled onto his side and heard a key in a lock behind him, and then a gate creaking open.

"Okay, Z3-221, you can eat." He heard her set the tray on the ground.

"My name is Jack."

She brought her palms up when he looked at her, as if to fend off something unwanted, backing outside quickly and locking the gate. "Don't tell me. It says right here—" She pointed to a plac-ard on the fence, of which he could only see the back. "Zee-three-two-two-one. That's you."

"What's your name, hon?"

"Call me Guard."

"Where am I?"

"In custody."

"Is that Arabic I hear?"

"I don't hear anything."

Suddenly the disproportion of it all struck him as hilarious and he had trouble choking back his laughter. "I was only trying to look for a missing Korean girl, for Chrissake."

"I don't know anything about that. It doesn't seem very likely, does it?"

"No, it doesn't."

"Eat hearty, Z3."

She walked away. Z3, he thought. What a strange new nickname. He was a BMW. For some reason he almost liked it better than Jack. He found he was terribly hungry, and he crawled to the brown tray. A plastic dish held a mound of rice and a similar bowl contained a stew of overcooked vegetables. There was a plastic spoon and a plastic water tumbler.

Abruptly someone beyond the wall shouted as if he had been hurt, really screamed for a few moments, then fell silent. The monotonous guttural chant had stopped, leaving only a susurrus of wind in trees, though he could not see any trees. There were gray concrete-block walls beyond the chain link, hiding who knows what.

He mixed the vegetable glop with the rice and ate it all with the plastic spoon. He was famished, and it was tasteless but not disgusting. In fact, he chased down the last fugitive grains of rice with a fingertip and lifted his fingers to suck them off. It was a nutty basmati rice, the kind you'd find in the Middle East and India, not the sticky rice of East Asia.

After a while she came back for the tray. "Step back, sir."

"Of course." He backed to the far side of the cage and sat cross-legged to try to seem unthreatening.

The young woman retrieved the tray and then locked up again and unfolded a sheet of paper from her pocket. "I am to read something to you."

"Fine."

He expected rules and regulations, some local code that would border on the insanely exacting and remorseless, but it was nothing of the sort.

"'There are many masks that God wears in our normal life,'" she read.

A laugh burst from him, but he covered his mouth to suppress it when she glared at him.

"You must not be disrespectful." She seemed hurt and waited a moment before glancing down again at the paper. "'You have grown up in a permissive society that has allowed you to become inured'"—she pronounced it *in-ERRed*—"'to attitudes of disrespect for religion, for your country, for your community, and for your fellow man. Many Americans believe that this is an entitled expression of individualism, but any man of the East would tell you that it is an almost wholly self-defeating proposition when applied across an entire society. In the coming century, it is going to be necessary to make compromises with the Asian worldview in order to compete with China. We are in the century of Asia now. Please think over this imperative before we question you.' That's what the paper says."

"Guard, hon, I haven't got the slightest desire to compete with Asians on the question of giving up my freedoms. They can out-give-up me any time they want."

She looked crestfallen. "That's so sad, Z3. I feel sorry for you."

"Where am I, dammit? I want a lawyer."

"Oh, there aren't any lawyers *here*."

Ten

The Letter G

He must have dozed, but not for long, as the gray half-light suggested it was still evening, and now three men were on their knees, just beyond the hurricane fence that enclosed him, elaborately miming the act of Christian prayer. One had some sort of flowing black religious garment, bookended by two in fatigues.

The priestly one intoned: "God showed me his vision that the Middle East wars would go on until they became a nuclear war." He pronounced it *nuke-you-lar*, as you might expect. "I saw the nation of Iraq and it said *Iraq* on it and it had a circle around it with a slash through the circle, and I saw the nation of Iran and it said *Iran* on it and it had an X through the circle."

"Yea," one of the bookends said.

"On the fourth day of the Endtime tribulation, all the oxygen will disappear from the atmosphere."

"That won't be any fun," Jack Liffey said softly, but loud enough for them to have heard if they'd been listening.

They seemed to ignore him, as if he wasn't the point of their prayer vigil after all. "And on the fifth day, all the Red Chinese will die."

Jack Liffey wondered what all the Red Chinese had been breathing for the balance of the fourth day, but obviously nobody asked questions like that. He noticed now that the gaunt priestly figure had some sort of foreign look to him, maybe Turkish or Middle Eastern. "Hello, hello. Gentlemen, I don't want you to pray for me. Assuming I have a choice."

"I had another vision and saw a bomber plane bombing the nation that said *Iran* on it and I was high above the earth and then suddenly I was running with two little girls, telling them we were about to get nuked and I told the girls about a vision of world economic collapse. . . "

"Stop!" Jack Liffey yelled.

"I was on the interstate in Indianapolis and I saw a Speedway gasoline sign that said $5.09 a gallon, and then I saw an Indianapolis newspaper that had a headline that predicted Indianapolis was about to be nuked by the Red Chinese. Praise be."

Mercifully the priest stopped then and passed into a nodding phase.

One of the bookends took up the lecture: "And on the sixth day, the seven buckles of the seven seals will be undone."

"Thank you for your concern for me, all of you, but I am going to go into the earth to be eaten by worms, and that's the final word on the matter," Jack Liffey said.

The priest stopped nodding and cleared his throat. He talked now about writing the words New Jerusalem on the prisoner's flesh. The suggestion made the hair stand up on Jack Liffey's neck.

"May the Red Chinese parachute down through all the remaining nitrogen," Jack Liffey said forcefully, "and fuck you three *pendejos* in the ass." He had been working hard on his Spanish for several months and that word, which he loved to let slip, just blurted itself out. And, to his astonishment, it worked. They not only fell silent, they looked up at him in horror.

"I had a vision, too," Jack Liffey said. "This is the last day of your wretched lives. Small red men with spears will come for you."

"I pity you," the priest said, and all three men stood. They walked away, chatting in normal voices, as if nothing had happened.

"Have a nice day!" Jack Liffey called. He pinched himself hard on the forearm, just to make sure he was awake. He was.

"Dean," Gloria Ramirez said. "You the man, *ese*." His feet were up on the desk, as usual, and he was studying some report in a buff folder, one ear clamped to the telephone by his shoulder.

"Hang on, Sarge," he told her, and his eyes went back to his folder.

She was in the gang unit's storefront a mile east of the Hollenbeck station on East Third. They had a new homemade poster up that said THE SECRET TO COMBATING GANGS IS . . . followed by a mock blackboard that said CLICHÉ OF WEEK HERE.

The big map was still on the wall, with colored pins here and there, and shaded areas keyed to Marianna Maravillas, Eighteenth Street, Greenwood, Little Valley, Sangra, Lomas, etc., etc. Gloria Ramirez knew her neighborhood was deep in Greenwood's sway, and she was afraid Maeve might be, too, but she wasn't the girl's mother and Jack would have to get back to get on top of that problem.

Beside the gang map was the homicide board that changed from month to month: thirty or forty Polaroid photos of the heads and shoulders of young Latino males, mostly looking bloody and glassy-eyed. The new feature was a board called WANNABES. There were only six Polaroids under a hand-scrawled notice: WHO IS THIS? LET'S "INTERVENE," GUYS. Gloria felt a chill tiptoe all the way down her spine. There was Maeve, ghastly pale and wide-eyed in the flash, with long dark hair, big *chola* hoops in her ears and bra straps showing. A typed note said: "BABY GIRL." GREENWOOD PARK. MAYBE 18. ANGLO? APPARENTLY BETO'S GIRL. SHY. NO TATS. CAN WE SAVE THIS ONE?

Shit, Gloria thought. It had gone farther than she'd thought. She was amazed Padilla hadn't recognized the girl from the shooting last year, but Maeve sure didn't look the same in the photo.

Dean said something angry on the phone and hung up. He looked up finally. "*Ruca, qué tal?*"

"Hi, Dean. You took the report on Jack's car, didn't you?"

"Sure. Gang stuff, I guess. Maybe. It had a kind of counterfeit look to it, as if some other gang was throwing the wrong *plaka* on purpose."

"Did he tell you what he was working on?"

"Why would he? But I did try to teach him a nice useful phrase in Spanish—'Stick it up your ass.'"

"Jack's never going to be a linguist, but he's no dummy."

"If you say so." Dean Padilla stared at her for a while. "You really like this guy?"

"I like him a lot. How about some professional courtesy?"

He chuckled. "Professional courtesy is when sharks don't eat no lawyers that fall off the Malibu Pier."

"I've heard it."

"Okay, here's something you haven't heard. Sandos and O'Brien from Central's antiterror Boy Scout troop picked your Jack up last night—real hush-hush. They work out of that warehouse that nobody's supposed to know about, the one off the freight yard where there's nothing but noisy trains and *they* ask the questions and *you* wear the burlap bag over your head."

"What did he do?"

"With these guys, you ask me that? Maybe he said something

nasty about Rumsfeld. Who knows? But you're not going to get any answers out of them. Why not ask him?"

"He never came home."

"Ah, shit." He dug in his desk and came up with a card, then wrote something on it. "*This* is professional courtesy."

It was an ordinary LAPD business card, but without designation of branch or division. She knew the phone number as well as her own—it was simply the switchboard Downtown. The name on it was Joe Malafina. Dean Padilla had written: HELP THIS LADY. DEAN P.

"Dean, in another life I'll reward you."

"*Ay te miro*, there's plenty of ways still open in this life."

Maeve lay on her stomach on a musty-smelling sofa in a strange house, the tatters of her blouse crumpled into a ball beside her. Ruby and Ivana were dabbing at her cuts with some stinging solution that slowly took the pain away. Even though they were tending her wounds, they didn't really seem to have softened their attitudes much.

"Ay, girl, you bruise easy."

"I always have. I can't help it."

"*Mija*, you got to toughen up." As if to start the process, Ruby punched her in the small of the back.

"Ow!"

The house belonged to the parents of somebody in the *klika* who were away visiting relatives in Mexico, or so they'd told her. All Maeve could see from where she lay was a pair of easy chairs reupholstered in bright green. She winced but kept her mouth shut as she felt a knuckle digging and twisting hard in her flesh.

"Just so you don't think we're going soft on your white ass, girl." The digging stopped. "You got the big eyes for Beto, eh?"

Maeve didn't answer.

"He the one makes you go zoom, eh?"

Maeve just stared at her. Politely. Tolerantly. She didn't owe them anything. It wouldn't change what was happening, anyway.

Ivana seemed to be stronger than Ruby and she boosted Maeve onto her side to look for any more cuts. "Hold yourself up like that, Baby Girl."

"Beto used to be my old man," Ruby said, "but it's okay. I'm with Chilango now. "*Orale*, that's one *pinche* scar you got."

"I was shot. They put my intestine out a hole and into a plastic bag for six months." Let them think about that.

"No shit." Ruby took her hand away quickly. "So that was your new asshole."

Maeve looked at her. "No big deal," she said.

"Well, I'll tell you what Beto really likes you to do." She was leaning close, the wind of her voice in Maeve's ear. "He learned it in jail. When he's about to come, whether you're doing it with your pussy or your mouth, just stick your finger up his ass. He goes crazy for that. I used to make him buy me expensive things with this finger."

She held up her index finger as if she needed to demonstrate.

"Baby Girl," Ivana said. "Where you want the tak?"

"Tak?"

"Tattoo. We got to put a G on you. It's either on your tit or your ass."

Maeve stiffened. Tattoos were pretty much forever. All at once the idea of marking her body with a gang logo brought home to her how far from home she had drifted. What *was* she doing anyway? Disfiguring her body with some blurry letter that wasn't even a good tattoo. She knew she was way out here, all alone, on some kind of freewheeling emotional trip that she couldn't control. Was this going to be the end of college for her? Would she have to turn her back on her father?

But it wasn't likely that her dad or Gloria would see the tattoo in either of the places they planned to put it—so there was no immediate danger. She knew she was crazy in love with Beto and she guessed that he'd be really pleased to see the Greenwood G on her. In fact, she imagined showing it off to him, pulling down her bra or her pants, and got excited immediately.

"Which one, Baby Girl?"

"What do you think Beto would like best?"

Ivana hovered, considering, the ballpoint pen and sewing needle poised.

He woke and something was wrong, really wrong. He soon realized his head was covered by what must have been a burlap bag tied around his neck. He tried to pull his chin and mouth as far from the cloth as possible to give him room to breathe. He thought he was sitting on a hard chair, with his arms and legs tied so he couldn't do much about the rough hood. It was probably daylight because some light penetrated the cloth.

"He's awake."

Air, he couldn't get enough air. He started to panic and hyperventilate, but he forced himself to calm. It was a real struggle, and he kept as still as he could, instructing parts of his body to relax.

"Hello, señor," said a second voice that was definitely Latino.

Someone else was moaning nearby, and that didn't help. The air in the hood was hot and he knew it would be laden with carbon dioxide and if he got too much carbon dioxide in his blood . . . what? He couldn't remember what would happen. Pass out?

Wasn't it too *little* carbon dioxide that triggered hyperventilation panic? And there was something about bicarbonates in the blood chemistry, too . . .

"Are you a registered member of a political party?"

Why were they asking him *that*?

Very slowly, he said, "I'm registered in California as an Independent."

Then the other voice said, "Are you a registered member of a political party?"

He had no idea why they needed to repeat the question, but there seemed no point in answering a second time. A hand slapped his ear through the burlap and it stung, the abrasion of the rough cloth hurting more than the concussion.

"No," he said.

"Do you know *Señorita* Kim?"

"I was looking for her. I never met her."

The moan nearby came again, and then he heard the slap of a blow. His imagination was starting to go wild, building a picture of a torture chamber, or a person nearby being forced to endure worse than he was. He fought off another bout of hyperventilation.

"Do you know Señorita Kim?" It was that other voice, parroting.

"I do not. And fuck you."

There was a blow to the other side of his head. He had braced himself for one from the same direction as before, but this was so unexpected and so strong that he toppled off the flimsy chair. They righted him immediately, actually quite gently.

"Mustn't do that, Liffey. Disrespect will change our mood."

"Disrespect will change our mood." The echo again.

"I don't give a damn about your mood."

This time he was struck on both ears at once, and his head rang with it. Tinnitus began to squeal in his right ear, an affliction that had plagued him on and off since the army. He hoped it wouldn't last long.

"You will give a damn."

"Oh, you will give a damn."

The moaner nearby offered a plea in some other language. What it was was hard to tell.

Jack Liffey opened his mouth to speak and, abruptly—was hit square on by what must have been a bucket of water. It felt like he was drowning, and he changed his strategy on the burlap instantly, sucking it toward his mouth and trying to draw air directly through the wet cloth. It helped a little, but the panic hovered only an inch away.

"You are for all practical purposes stateless at this moment of time, Liffey. You must forget the illusion that you can wait us out and some form of help will arrive. You have entered another world that you are not going to like very much. There is no race here, only the prize. How you do here depends entirely upon your level of cooperation."

"Think of yourself as a voyager who has lost his passport and must accept the hospitality of strangers in an unknown land. What happens to you where you are going soon will be determined entirely by your level of cooperation."

"What happens to you where you are going soon will be determined entirely by your level of cooperation."

"On this trip I'm taking, will there always be morons repeating everything? *Jesus!*" A fiery pain stung his upper arm, and he had no idea what had caused it. In a few seconds he felt the arm going numb. Why had they numbed his arm?

"Bon voyage." The man had pronounced it as if they were two English words. Bone voy-udge.

"Have a nice trip."

This time he recognized the pressure of a second syringe going deep into him through numbed skin. Soon bright colors began to wash up behind his eyes. Whether they were bright colored lights glaring outside the burlap or only hallucinations, he could not tell.

She found his office up on the ninth floor of Parker Center Downtown. This was where they housed assistant chiefs and a few other loose executives with special responsibilities—such as the captain they'd appointed to try to find a way around the more onerous requirements of the federal consent decree while pretending to carry them out. Thus, the job titles up here ran to the intangible. Director of Permanent Force Realignment. Assistant Chief for Community Outreach. Proactive Deployments. Special Projects. But Malafina didn't have a title even that elusive. The little inscribed plaque in the slot by his door just said, JOSEPH MALAFINA, DEPUTY ASSISTANT CHIEF, PRO TEM.

A uniformed junior officer sat in an anteroom, writing on what looked a bit like one of the loose-bound murder books she knew well. "Ramirez?"

She nodded.

"Go on in. Joe's free."

There was a frosted-glass door, and she rapped once before opening.

He was a silver-haired old man, the front swept straight back in a style made popular ages ago in L.A. by Pat Riley when he coached the Lakers. Malafina was clearly one of the good old boys. He stood, revealing quite a paunch, and offered his hand, without much of a smile, but she never expected smiles on the job.

"Sgt. Ramirez. How can I help you?"

She handed him Padilla's card with the scrawled *help this lady*, but he gave it hardly a glance before indicating she should sit in an old wooden chair. "You work out of Harbor Division Detectives, don't you?"

"Yes, sir, three years now. Ken Steelyard was my T.O."

He raised his eyebrows but made no other comment on Steelyard, who had died in a shootout eighteen months earlier. "You like it in Harbor?"

"It's okay. I live in Hollenbeck. But the commute's against the flow."

He smiled coolly. "I live in Beverly Hills P.D., myself."

"Great response time, I hear."

"Plus everybody's got those little shields on the lawn, the rent-a-dick companies. You know, your poodle sets off your motion alarm and a half hour later a teenager shows up in a Ford Focus waving a little can of pepper spray. You got a substantial pair of Winnebagos there, Sergeant. Made for love."

She'd been dealing with this all her career, and though it did get easier, it never made her any less angry. "You got bad teeth."

He seemed to be masturbating a felt pen that he held erect on his desktop. He smiled again. "But they're all mine. The green stuff is just extra benefit for somebody I go down on, like you, perhaps."

"I don't think so. It's a well-known medical fact, guys with green teeth get a lot less pussy. Anyway, Captain, I got a steady boyfriend. That's why I'm here. I'm told O'Brien and Sandos picked him up and he didn't come home last night. They work out of that unmarked building in the Cornfield."

"Uh-oh."

"What does that mean?"

"Is your old man into politics?"

"I think he votes. That's about it. Jack Liffey. His job is finding missing kids and runaways."

"Oh, yeah. Liffey I know. He's been on the radar. Couple guys I know actually like him. Many don't."

"I like him a lot."

"I expect no less from my officers. Wouldn't have respected you if you'd gone down on your knees right here to aid your boyfriend. Still . . . "

Jesus, the guy was nonstop bad news, she thought. For an instant, she was tempted to take out her pistol and just shoot him. It would be terribly satisfying.

"Can you tell me where Jack is?"

"Not exactly, but if he's not still being held in the Cornfield and if he doesn't come home this evening, I can tell you his ultimate disposition."

"*Disposition?*" It was as if Jack had been caught up in some well-worked-out grammatical conveyor belt to hell.

The man slapped the felt pen down and ran his hand through his slicked-back hair, as if she'd finally got his attention.

"We don't actually interrogate certain kinds of prisoners so much, not any more. They just play with them, as far as I'm concerned. The Cornfield boys don't like it much when certain terrorist bells go off, and Homeland Security says to turn them over. The actual expression is 'extraordinary rendition.'"

"Let me get this straight . . . the FBI has him?"

"No, we seem to be putting a lot of our faith these days in private enterprise. Since he's a citizen, he probably can't be sent to some country full of torturing greaseballs. There's a company called ISOC that will probably end up talking to Liffey."

Intercontinental Security something something—she knew that much. "Not the company that supplies all the mercenaries for Iraq?"

"*Contractors* is the preferred term. I've heard they send bodyguards to a lot of client states—places like Afghanistan and Liberia—and army trainers, plus ex–Special Forces teams and interrogators and such."

"Shit. Where would they take Jack?"

"I don't have a clue, he might still be in the Cornfield. But for a little consideration, I could try to find out."

"If you're thinking of touching me, I'll shoot both of us. You're lucky I don't report this."

"Nobody'd give a shit."

She knew he was right. The old boys were going to win every time. She slammed his office door behind her, and Malafina's gatekeeper looked up from his paperwork.

"You keep your pecker in your pants, too," she snapped.

She found she was weeping inconsolably—she couldn't quite work out why—clutching a sheet up to her neck, when Beto came in the bedroom.

"Baby Girl, don't cry so. You okay now."

He sat on the edge of the bed and rested his calloused hand on her forehead, but she couldn't stop. The pain involved in the tattoo hadn't been all that great, but there had been something utterly undoing about the beating. Even though she knew they'd all gone through it, the sense of shame and humiliation was overwhelming. She even felt guilty about it as if far inside there was a voice saying: Doesn't everybody deserve it, if they get hit?

"*Güerita*, you gonna be okay. Everybody is disturbed up like that when they go through the jump. You *rifa*. You can't let the girls upset you. You a Greenwood now."

She pulled down the sheet on the left side, to show him the G on her inflamed left breast. She had thought she'd get a sexual charge out of showing it to him, but now all she felt was something like spite: see how they've mutilated me. She wished that at least it had been an M that she could pretend was for her own name.

"*Ay*, that's nice. Maybe you get some more taks later." He didn't try to touch it as if he knew how screamingly tender the breast was. "*Calma, calma, querida.*"

"Oh, Beto, please protect me." She rolled and hugged his thighs awkwardly.

"Of course, Baby Girl, you my little *gaba* now. *Me quieres?*"

"Of course, *mi héroe.* I want you all the time." She'd just as soon let it go right then but she knew enough not to deny him.

"Then show me, Baby Girl. *Chúpame.*"

She knew what it meant: suck me.

He unzipped his baggy pants and took out his penis, which was already half hard. She took him in her mouth, remembering what Ruby had told her that Beto really liked his woman to do, but she couldn't quite get herself up for that.

Eleven

Con Safos

The trees were bigger than any he had ever seen—bigger even than sequoias. Yet the bark was shaggy and the leaves were lobed like mountain oaks. Between the trunks the land was choked with undergrowth, impassible. Growing up in the West, spoiled by the elbow room of evergreen forests, this tangle of brush and thorn made him appreciate old textbook accounts of the rigors of "clearing the land."

He was also perfectly aware that he was dreaming. It was remarkable, a phenomenon that he thought was called lucid dreaming. To remain utterly aware that he was handcuffed and strapped into an airline seat and at the same time soar through imagery that evoked awe, then frustration, guilt, shame, rage. He had some success changing and redirecting what he was experiencing, but it was a constant struggle against what must have been his darker urges. This can only be the effect of a drug, Jack Liffey thought.

Unfortunately, the lucid dreams left in their track no clear sense of the passage of time. Each scene that played out could be an instant or an hour. He could tell that later he would not be able to work out the length of the air flight. He could be on his way anywhere.

The old woman gives a faint bitter smile, as if it requires quite an effort.

KUM HAK-SOO

I stayed with the troops when they were moved to Manchuria. The comfort station there was managed by a Japanese couple, who I curse with all my soul. Once, when I refused to do what they wanted, they had me tortured and put me in the base prison. But one night, I heard a "scratch, scratch," and I thought maybe it was a rat. Soon a brick was pulled from the prison wall and an old Chinese man who did odd jobs for us talked to me through the hole. He was named Mr. Lee and he helped me escape. He did it purely out of sympathy for my miserable life. He hid me with his family for a while and then gave me a little money and told me to run for the mountains. I met two other comfort women running away and we ran together, but as there were three of us, Japanese troops discovered us and chased us. The other women were shot and I was wounded in the hip by shrapnel from a grenade.

I was tortured again and taken to a new Comfort Station in China where my life remained the same for two years, but then we followed the troops down the coast to Hong

Kong. It was in Hong Kong that I actually
met Japanese comfort women from
Hokkaido. As the Allied air raids began to hit
us, the troops and comfort women all became
very pessimistic, and we all hid in shelters.
In the confusion of this time I made an escape again as we were leaving the shelter
one morning, when the guards were all
frightened. I made my way to a Kuomintang
army unit, but, unfortunately, they were the
Ryushesan, a unit known for collaborating
with the Japanese.

She parked the RAV-4 in a faculty lot on campus. If they tick-
eted her, she'd just give it to her captain. There were a lot of
questionable perks to being a cop, but this one made sense. You
couldn't have someone responding to an armed robbery worrying about feeding the meter. Pretty good rationale, anyway. She
grinned as she locked up. Damn few people gave up privileges
out of some purist impulse. Jack was the only one she knew who
insisted on doing everything in life the hardest way possible—
though she had a certain respect for that.

In fact, with Jack gone missing, she had a lot more of a yen for
his presence in general, if only so she could bump against his
foibles as a way to help mark her own boundaries. She missed
him in bed, too. And, in practical terms, she missed his help with
Maeve. The girl was about to get into real trouble if she hadn't
already; she'd have to call the mother soon, and this she dreaded.
After Maeve had been shot in a pointless drive-by in the front
yard, Gloria had caught the unspoken disapproval in her
mother's eyes. Mexicans. And who could blame her?

There were sculptures all over the hilly quad, but the only one that interested her very much was a horse that seemed to be made out of sticks. Remarkably, it had the magical feel of a real horse. She had only ridden horses briefly on visits to the reservation, but she had cottoned to the experience of it fast, all that intelligent power between your legs. One kick and you were away, galloping, a sensation like flying. Maybe she should go up to the rez for an extended period and try to see what it would mean to her. The times she'd spent there had been the least sour interludes of her life.

She rapped on a door from which were emanating weird sounds that stopped abruptly.

"Peter Kim?" she asked the young man with bright-red hair who opened the door. He had an apparatus strapped to his chest with what might have been a tiny video camera suspended a few feet in front of him. He reached up and rotated the camera toward her.

"That is I. Are you Sergeant Ramirez?"

She showed him her badge wallet. "Is that a camera?"

"Yes, I'm attempting to journal my life, fuckups and all." He hit a few switches on the gigantic editing console in front of him so the sounds in the room shut down. She relaxed a little, realizing how nervous it had been making her.

"Turn it off." She pointed to the camera.

"The space here is still available for critical exchange."

"Turn it off or I'll break it."

He reached up and a red pilot light went out, but she didn't trust that. She knew about the ones in the interrogation rooms.

"Now turn it sideways so I know it's off me."

He did better. He unstrapped the apparatus and climbed out of it. "Remarkable how few people insist."

"You probably haven't tried it on a lot of cops."

"It's true the project makes me something like an angry god-infant. Play my game, or I'll destroy the earth and go home."

"You really don't have the power. But I can do stuff like that to you. On a whim I could run you in for a 148."

"What's that?"

"Interfering with an officer. Or a 314, indecent exposure, how about that, or how about a 244?"

He held up a palm. "I get it."

"I'm glad. Now, listen. I'm in a bad mood because a friend of mine is missing, and you know him and didn't give him much help. Jack Liffey."

Recognition filled his face, and no hostility, she thought. "Hey, I liked the guy. He mostly let me tape him with no complaint. And he was trying to help my sister. That's all cool."

"What did you two talk about?"

"He asked about her, if I knew where she was, and I said no."

"Anything else?"

"He was interested in that old YWCA Downtown they're demonstrating about. I don't pay much attention to that stuff. It's not that I'm apolitical. It's just that my own world is so de-centered I can see every point of view. They all create their own validations."

He seemed to be working himself up to some familiar lecture, and it irked her. "So it's equally important to feed starving kids and build luxury hotels?"

"They each have a reality. But, no, I don't say the world is flat every time somebody says it's round. It's better to feed the poor than kick them. And science is a much more useful truth than magic."

"What did you tell Jack that he didn't already know?"

"Not much. Oh, wait." He dug into a big flat drawer under the editing table and came out with a sheet of paper.

She read a threatening note that started out: HEAR ME, GOOK. "You think he could have tracked this guy down?"

"I don't see how. If you had the actual e-mail online, maybe. But a printout . . . ?" He shrugged.

She wasn't quite sure what she was doing here. She already knew she should go directly to the Anti-Terror guys or ISOC, even though they probably wouldn't tell her a thing. She felt it was important, somehow, to pick up Jack's trail independently. Maybe it would take her to him through some back door, or maybe it would just tell her something about him. She was curious all of a sudden, now that she was deprived of him, just how his mind worked. She admitted to herself that she was a lot more infatuated with him than she'd let herself acknowledge.

She questioned the boy for a while longer in a desultory way, but got no further, though he scanned and printed the e-mail for her.

"Has anyone come to ask you about Jack?"

"You."

She offered a flicker of a smile. "A couple of men, say? Wearing shiny black shoes."

"I'm not sure how shiny." He swung around to a rack of tiny videocassettes and put one in a player. After a moment of fiddling with the console in front of him, a picture came up on a big flat monitor against the wall: the door she recognized as being behind her came open, and a grim-looking Sandos and O'Brien entered, going through an approximate pantomime of the same tantrum she had thrown until the camera was turned off. There was no sound.

"Forgive the silence. Believe it or not, that's known in Hollywood as MOS, for—honest-to-god—*mit-out sound*. I've heard it was a joke on all the German directors working over here before the war. I'd have to swap a patch cable to get their voices. Do you want me to?"

"That's okay. It's fine." She wondered if there was any way to get him to stop explaining things to death.

"Real cops? Or was I taken in?"

"If you haven't noticed, we ask questions. We don't answer them."

He laughed softly. "Yes. There's a remarkable consistency to police behavior. Somehow I took their threats more seriously than yours, though. Something about being made to eat my own liver."

She smiled now, remembering that Peter Kim had said he liked Jack. "Sorry. You've been pretty much okay with me. Those two are real cops. No need to get worked up."

"That's a comfort. As a conspicuous *other* in this country, I've always known that it's all too easy for me to land in situations that privilege the exercise of power over permission."

"Does that have a meaning?" she asked.

He thought for a moment. "Probably not. Sergeant . . .?"

"Yes."

"What's a 244?"

"Throwing acid with intent to disfigure."

"Jesus. That happens enough for a *number*?"

"I've seen it twice. Though once it was a real problem in court because a clever lawyer brought up the fact that the substance was a household caustic, not an acid."

Outside she sat on a wall near the horse sculpture. *Privilege*, she thought. What a strange way to use that word. He was a strange kid, into some weird stuff, but not a bad one. She looked up from the copy of the racist note to the sculpture. The horse was comforting somehow, unruffled, grazing, unthreatening. The world contracted around just her and the horse. She wondered if she were multiple people. A cop, for some pig-headed reason, and going on being a cop on her day off. A Native American whose nature she knew so imperfectly that that person was almost an unknown quantity. And a girl raised as a rough-tough Latina by unkind fosters in Boyle Heights. She remembered a lot of undifferentiated time in her youth sharing bedrooms with a rotating supply of other angry fosters who were brought in mainly for the county money, and the schools that she'd tried to ignore because nothing that had gone on there seemed to relate to her.

She admitted to herself that there had been one time that stood out from all that, when Arnulfo, her foster-dad, had been laid off. He'd worked in a little bucket shop in Pico Rivera not far from the big Ford factory, tending a machine that wound miles of nylon floss around hot rubber bladders so somebody else could cover them with vinyl shells to make them into basketballs, or so he told them all. He'd had the job for years until the company just picked up its skirts one day and moved to China. They'd been really hard up then, and for the summer the whole family—Arnulfo, his wife Aida, and three fosters—had piled into the beat-up Dodge station wagon with the cloth headliner ballooning down from the roof and driven up to Los Banos to work in *el fil* for an old family friend. However, he wasn't enough of a friend to pay more than ten cents an hour.

At first, she'd resented working on *la nuez*, walking behind the shaker with his long pole and collecting fallen walnuts into a long canvas sack that she dragged behind her. Very soon it had started roughening her hands and cricking her back. But after a few weeks, at fourteen, she'd had her first boy out in *el fil* at night, and in the end she had actually grown to enjoy that summer in the canvas cabin. It was as if it had been just a special sort of vacation, a little like the kind the other kids got at Yosemite, which, after all, was only eighty miles to the east.

She had tried to forgive her fosters and just get along, since they were under so many pressures themselves, but finally their constant talk about the dirty Indians—*los Indios sucios*—turned her into a sullen teen and then a rebel. Her last memories were of out-of-control slapping matches with both of her fosters.

"Excuse me, madam. Every time I am privileged to visit this sculpture I am devastated by the sheer vivacity that I encounter in the simulated animal."

There was a booming quality to the man's voice and a dreadful earnestness. He had a lot of gray hair and carried a briefcase so tattered that it looked like it had been used for centuries. His tweed suit was worn, too, and gave off a kind of musk of old book.

"It's nice," she said. My god, she thought. Is this old man trying to pick me up? Something told her that he didn't teach here, though he appeared to have come from the Research Library which was just across the lawn.

"Do I detect a fellow mature student who is returning to the halls of academe to perfect an *educatis interruptus?*"

She nearly laughed, but didn't want to hurt his feelings. "Something like that. Maybe."

"Truly, coming late to the wonder of knowledge gives one a sense of awe at standing on the shoulders of so many progenitors. I find that it's a feeling that one is unable to appreciate before arriving at what the French so delicately call *un certain âge.*"

"I don't know where that age starts, but I bet I'm there."

"On the contrary, you appear astonishingly youthful, madam," he protested, and she realized that she had to get away before he self-destructed, simply went up in flames in some wildly excessive eruption of flirtatiousness.

"I'm sorry, sir, I have to go," she said, as she stood. "I'm looking for my husband." Which was true enough, in its way.

"Forgive me, gentle lady. I saw no ring on your left third finger that would have denoted such."

"Our religion forbids it." She nodded once and walked away, feeling sullied by the lie. She didn't think Jack would have lied. She wondered what he would have done with the sad old man—or an equivalent sad old woman. Probably chatted for a while, honored him in a way. Yes, okay, I miss Jack a lot, she thought. More than I would ever have expected.

She strode across the grass to the faculty lot, wondering again what on earth she was doing here. It was her day off and she was wasting it, not just on police procedure, but inefficient police procedure. She could have gone straight to the Cornfield and talked to Sandos or O'Brien or looked up Intercontinental Security something something in the Rolodex, but somehow she just didn't want to.

Maybe, she thought, it was just a fear of hitting a brick wall right off, thwarted before she even got started. And she liked the idea of stepping in Jack's footprints, the way she had once, literally, placed her fifteen-year-old foot on Bacall's shoeprint at Grauman's Chinese. Pretty big, really, but not as big as hers, even then. Bogart's foot was a *lot* smaller. Gloria was about an inch shorter than Jack, so she figured his feet were a tiny bit larger, though there was always that old saw about foot size corresponding to penis size. She'd never given it much thought. Men were so thin-skinned about that.

One thing she was doing, she knew, was putting off her immediate duty to Maeve.

. . .

Beto took her up to a small apartment on the second floor of one of those beat-up 1950s buildings that had a sort of runway past all the doors. It was called the ATHENS GARDENS, but the A was hanging down and about to fall off, and soon it would be the THENS GARDENS. Inside, there was an adequate supply of Danish modern furniture, too worn and cheap-looking to have any retro value, and she wondered if the place had been rented furnished. She was only about six blocks from Gloria's—still in the Greenwood barrio—so she didn't feel too cut off.

"This yours, now, Baby Girl," Beto said, as if he was offering her a palace. "Make yourself at home. I got to go out. I see you later."

"Wait a minute. You're just going to dump me here? Do you live here?"

"Sure. I got to have more than one crib so my enemies don't find me."

"But your enemies can find *me*."

"That's *con safos*. They don't mess with girls. And you leave that room alone." He pointed at a bedroom with an ostentatious security door and padlock. "Guy stuff."

She went up to hug him, but he held her away from himself. "Not now. I'm in a hurry."

"When will I see you?"

"Soon." He peeled off some money and left it on the sagging coffee table. "Check the stuff in the *refri*. Go to the *mercado* so you can make us some dinner for later."

Feeling teary and abandoned, she wanted to cling to him. But the urge was too much like the emotion of a corny character in a soap opera, or one of those hideous nighttime sitcoms where all the minority characters screamed at one another and continually had tantrums like wayward children.

"What's your favorite menu?"

"I dunno. Surprise me."

How about sauerkraut and pigs' feet? she thought. She wanted to be good to him, but this wasn't starting out well. Then he turned back and wrapped his arms around her and gave her a passionate kiss, pressing his whole body against her.

"You're the best, Baby Girl. Tonight, I make you squeal."

Twelve

Captain Midnight

"Mr. Liffey, it would be much better for you if you paid attention."

He looked up at the bank of men. He was seated alone on one side of a metal table in a dingy room, facing four questioners, a job interview from Hell. One of the men wore a ski mask, ominously, but the one who had spoken had wavy receding hair and a tidy Walter Cronkite moustache. In fact he looked astonishingly like either Cronkite or Walt Disney. Beside him, another middle-aged man wore a yellow Mr. Rogers sweater. They did not seem comfortable in their casual clothing, as if they were high-level diplomats temporarily acquiescing to the dress code at Camp David. The fourth, beside Ski Mask, seemed younger than the rest and much fiercer.

Everything was new to Jack Liffey, as if he'd just dropped into his chair from outer space.

"Might I ask who you gentlemen are, and how I came to be here?"

"It would be much better for you now just to be attentive."

Cronkite. Jack Liffey always distrusted people who said they knew what would be better for him. But the voice was so soothing and the resemblance so startling he had to think of him that way.

"That's the way it is, *today*, pick a date," Jack Liffey said, doing his best to mimic that grand reassuring voice of the '60s, but nobody seemed to get the joke.

They waited silently for a few moments. "Tell us about your political activity."

"Pardon?"

"What groups have you belonged to?"

"I'm not much of a joiner. I assume you don't want to go back to my childhood."

"You could start with the Vietnam War, if you like."

"Okay, I was in the U.S. Army. They didn't give me a lot of choice about that. Signal Corps, Thailand. Then for a few months I was in Vietnam Vets Against the War. I found I really hated demonstrations. They're too much like parades. And I didn't have any medals to give back—not counting the theater ribbon and Good Conduct."

Mr. Rogers tugged on the lapel of his cardigan and interrupted. "Do you realize there were many known Communists in that group?"

"I suppose they'd have been crazy not to join it."

"Even some ultraleftists."

"If you say so. I always assumed the guys who talked all the crazy shit were FBI agents trying to get us in trouble."

"Why did you leave them?"

"That's easy—too many meetings. Look, if you believe in democracy, you really ought to put up with meetings, I know that. But a lot of people mouthing off—it just makes me nuts. I'm not proud of it, I know it sounds elitist, but I have a terrible time listening to people who don't know what the hell they're talking about."

They watched him in silence for a while before the ball seemed to return to Uncle Walter.

"Let's try a different tack, Mr. Liffey." He offered a gentle smile, as if forgiveness were only a few words away, contingent on Jack Liffey's trying a little harder. "Bear with us. Use your imagination now. Say there has been a severe worldwide depression for some years, and the United States is nearing a point of social breakdown, something like the thirties. Millions of people are jobless. Street-corner philosophers are recruiting mobs to loot the stores that remain open. Then terrorists assassinate the president and vice president. In this terrible state of affairs, technicians and engineers and soldiers organize a Party of Order to bring back stability. The acting president declares martial law. Given this scenario, do you support the Party of Order?"

He couldn't suppress a spontaneous laugh in response to the preposterous question. "Which answer gets me shot at dawn?" Jack Liffey said. After a moment, he added, "But no hard feelings."

"Take this seriously, please. Our interview is being recorded."

"Well, if all that shit happens, I certainly hope somebody shoots you and all your pals, too." He thought he caught a wolfish grin through the dark mouth-hole of the ski mask. The rest remained impassive.

"You realize, it's no longer a choice between a world of nonviolence and a world of violence. Given the social breakdown and disorder, we must all search for a norm of violence, one that we can assume will recede with time."

"Sorry, guys, I just don't know what you want. Do you really want me to say I choose fascism and I'll learn to goose-step, or is this an elaborate test to see if I have fascist tendencies? I think, really, you'd be a lot happier with my dad here—he's the one who's been into all that save-the-white-race stuff."

"Don't be snide, Mr. Liffey." This was Mr. Rogers again. "Perhaps you should have stayed with your friends of the Left in the VVAW."

"Perhaps he did," suggested the younger one.

Walter Cronkite silenced them with the mildest of gestures. "Try to pay attention here. In this world we're talking about, we are not implying that military rule is necessarily the right thing in any absolute sense. Simple success does not make something right, of course—but to be right in the end, you must be successful. You must have order. Then a better society can follow."

In the best of situations, Jack Liffey would have avoided this discussion like the plague.

"Fine, super, great," he said. "Have it your way. I vote for order."

"I don't think you're taking us seriously."

"You know, I've been kidnapped and I suspect I've been drugged. I don't know where I am, and I don't know who the hell you are. But you can forget the Stockholm syndrome, or whatever the hell it's called. I'm not going to fall in love with my captors."

Walter Cronkite didn't seem to know what to say, so Mr. Rogers leaned forward again. "We're trying to have a rational discussion with you, which you keep resisting."

"If you want a rational discussion, let me out of here and meet me in a bar tomorrow. Anything else is pure bullying."

"You are under detention, Mr. Liffey. I hope you appreciate that."

"Am I? Then I want a lawyer, and I want to know the charges."

"You're perhaps thinking of the country as it existed before the Patriot Act. As an act of courtesy, I can tell you that you're being held as a material witness to the activities of a terrorist cell and we can keep you indefinitely, if we wish."

"You mean the New World Liberation Front? Good god, man.

I haven't got a clue about them. I was hired to find a missing girl, and I never got close."

"Let's start over," said the avuncular Cronkite, soul of reason. "Erase everything that's been said so far. We all know that the human condition may be such that there is no truly satisfactory organization of the state to cover times of great civil stress. All law is ultimately based on coercion—or bullying, as you just named it. We simply wonder if you would be willing to accept a democratic state that's struggling to find a new means of validating itself while it's under attack."

"I don't know what the fuck you're talking about."

"Or would you prefer," his interrogator went on equably, "to be alone and naked in a world of strife and chaos?"

"I would prefer a bus ticket to L.A. Unless we're still there somewhere. But I seem to remember an airplane ride, and the climate doesn't seem right for L.A., does it?"

He looked from one to the other, but nobody spoke. In fact, he had no idea of the climate since he had no way to tell what had been real and what hallucination in the last few days.

"Well, I couldn't trick you into telling me. Would someone tell me where I am out of simple human decency?"

It came around to Mr. Rogers again. "You are *here*, Mr. Liffey, right here. Where we make the rules."

Jack Liffey tried to stare them down for a while, but they all stared back, and it was too creepy.

"You know—just to be clear, I don't do drugs—but back in the sixties a lot of my friends took acid to try to make the world weird and wonderful. Maybe they succeeded."

Suddenly there was a hair-raising buzz, like the alarm of a submarine that was about to submerge. All but the man wearing the ski mask looked up.

"It's not a test," Mr. Rogers said equably. Then three of them filed out to leave Jack Liffey facing Ski Mask.

"Prison break?" he asked.

"Martians," Ski Mask said.

"Is there anything at all you can tell me with the Apostles gone?"

The alarm cut off abruptly. "Base-10 logarithms were more or less obsolete as soon as handheld calculators became widespread."

"I'll remember that," Jack Liffey said. "I must be the last human being to have learned how to use a slide rule." He hoped a little chattiness might get to the man. He was the only one to have shown the slightest emotion at all. "What if—"

"Just shut the fuck up and sit there until this is resolved."

She'd shopped for hours and then cooked for hours, and she thought she'd come up with a passable version of a Mexican feast—or a Mexican-American feast. Store-bought tamales, admittedly, but the ones from Lucy's were supposed to be super. The *molé* chicken she'd made herself, even melting down cinnamony Mexican chocolate in a double boiler and stirring it up with one of those weird wooden-ringed devices (nursing the feeling all the while that this device was just a practical joke that they played on gringos). She had fresh tortillas in foil ready to heat up and some refried beans ready to go into a dab of lard. She'd never even seen lard before—a whitish block of grease in wax paper.

She wasn't old enough to buy beer, but she'd sneaked back to Gloria's and borrowed two more of her Coronas. Now they were chilling in the old fridge, the kind with rounded corners and a handle that pulled out like a lever. She'd changed the sheets on the bed—who knows what'd gone on between the old ones? There was no dryer, but she'd figured out how to work the 1950s vintage Kenmore washer—not so hard, really, except you had to yank the old rotary knob straight out to get it to come on. At the moment it was noisily thrashing around the sheets and a pair of towels and she was feeling pretty domestic.

Several times she'd grown curious about the padlocked room, but, short of using a fire axe, she wasn't going to get in there. And she'd snooped in all the closets that she could open. There were a few women's items, but nothing like a bra that would have been discarded in heat. A soiled apron that said *Kiss Me I'm a Chilango*. One lacy black glove like something left behind by Madonna, and a box of bobby pins. It was almost as if Beto had inherited the apartment from some old aunt.

Presumably because of the unusual new noises Maeve had been making, a neighbor had knocked at the door at about four. Maeve had greeted the extremely short, round woman in formal Spanish and invited her in, and they'd had a very limited conversation, as the woman spoke a Spanish that was chock full of *Indio* words. When the neighbor heard her mention Beto's name, she rattled off an impenetrable lecture to which Maeve had nodded like an idiot. Thus collapse two and a half years of high school Spanish, she thought, as the woman made a number of broad gestures of helplessness and left.

In an act of penance, she'd turned on the old TV and watched Spanish-language Channel 22 for a while. They were showing a vintage black-and-white movie about drug dealers with big American cars that sped over dirt roads with guns blazing in what was probably Sonora, and then she'd tried Channel 30, which had a colorful soap about large-breasted blonde women weeping uncontrollably in front of handsome dark men.

At about 7:30 she started to get upset, and by 8:30 she was really angry. She turned off the simmer under the *molé*, though it was already pretty much ruined. Was this the way it was to be? she wondered. Waiting up every evening, not knowing if her lover had just been killed, or was out with another girlfriend—or what? Still, she longed for the feel and energy of him. Inside, some part of her realized this relationship probably couldn't last: it was all so alien that it seemed like a dream, but, still, she wanted to throw herself wholeheartedly into it while she had the opportunity. Was it her dad who had said, What you end up regretting is the things that you *don't* do? And she really was crazy about Beto. All she could think about was playing with him on the old bed and letting him do whatever he wanted to her.

Then the door slapped open. "*Qué tal*, Baby Girl, what a night!" He sniffed the air. "*Fíjese!* Check this out! I could eat a whole Buick and you gone and cooked me a Buick!"

All the angry things she'd planned to say evaporated in the face of his vital presence.

"*Qué tal*, Beto. I missed you."

He wrapped her in a big hug and kiss and hopped her around in a circle; she could taste the whiskey on his breath. Then he stepped back and ran his hand over her breasts. "I gonna want some of this, too, Baby Girl. You got some fine *melones* for a skinny little *gabachita*."

"I'll do anything you want," she heard herself say in a throatier voice than she knew she had.

He laughed and tweaked her nose. "First, I got to eat something or I'm gonna die. Here, wash this off for me."

He took a metal rod of some sort out of his back pocket and handed it to her. She could see it was a fully collapsed car antenna, and the knob end appeared to be bloody. "Did you get in a fight?"

He wagged a finger at her and opened the fridge, finding the

Coronas. "Uh-uh, uh-uh, you don't ask me about that stuff, Baby Girl. What we got here? I'm thirsty."

She dropped the antenna in the sink, wondering if she would be destroying evidence of some crime, and he opened the beers, one after another, with a slap against the lip of the Formica dining table. She swallowed a moment of pique that was like acid indigestion coming up unexpectedly—she'd waited all day!—and started to fix him a plate of food. She put the tortillas in the oven and started the lard frying. "Dinner'll just be a minute. I hope you like it. I did my best to make a *molé*."

"I hear you had a talk with Señora Jutiapa next door." He laughed.

"I couldn't understand much. I think there were a lot of *Indio* words."

He made a funny mannerism beside his temple, like two fingers unlocking and relocking a door with a key. "She's a little bit loco, Baby Girl. You're lucky she didn't ask you for your spare cement mixer."

"It's hard to know if someone is crazy in another language," Maeve told him.

He finished off the first beer and without a pause started on the second, which by rights was hers. She saw it start to go and decided she didn't really want it, anyway. In fact, nothing much was working out the way she'd anticipated, and she put some refried beans on the melted lard. He came up behind while she cooked and unbuttoned the back of her blouse and then unhooked her bra, which almost made her faint. Then he slid one hand around and cupped her right breast.

"Beto, oh god . . . ." But he took his hand away restlessly, and she had to find some way to calm down enough to fix the rest of the meal.

The *molé* was scorched, but she took out the tortillas and put together a semblance of a meal, hoping he'd be okay with her effort. He dug in without a word when she put the plate in front of him, and she served up a little for herself, though she doubted she'd be able to get down more than a few mouthfuls. Sitting opposite him, she toyed with the gritty sauce.

"When you were in high school, did you like it?" she asked, attempting to make contact on a new level.

He glanced up, as if a chair had spoken to him all of a sudden. He seemed surprised to notice that she'd sat down. "What kind of question is that?"

"I just wondered if you were happy there."

He still seemed puzzled and went back to eating.

"What did you want to be?" she tried.

"I wanted to be *out* of there, *ruca*. I couldn't waste time with sissies while my homeboys were out representing." He swallowed down the last mouthful of his food and then emptied the beer bottle.

"*Arre, chica!*" He scraped back his chair. "Sit here." She came around the table and straddled his lap, overcome with desire for him at his touch, and began to kiss him as he tore at her clothes. Her head whirled with longing, and before long he lifted her up as if she were weightless and put her down on the carpet in the living room where she let herself make far too much noise, pushing her cries self-consciously a little, as if in all her life there might never be another occasion like this.

The old woman gingerly sets down a glass of water she has just sipped from.

KUM HAK-SOO

I was working in a hospital for the Kuomintang forces but once the Japanese were

defeated, the civil war started. The Ryushesan were quickly defeated, and the Communists captured me and moved me to Struggle
Hospital in the rear. In 1946, all Koreans
were given a chance to go home under the
plan called "Koreans return home to render
allegiance to the motherland."

(she pauses)

The Communists always have big names like
that for their ideas. Unfortunately, on the
way home I was wearing a Communist uniform from the hospital with a big Mao button, and when I had to change trains I was
captured by another unit of the Kuomintang.
They charged me with espionage and took
everything I had. One driver in the army
took pity on me and ransomed me out of jail.
After a while I married him so he would keep
helping me. I was happy, too, for a time, following him, but he was captured in the final
defeat of the Kuomintang in 1949. Because
he was only a driver, the Communists let him
go, and we returned to his village in Soo Len
Sen where the government gave us a small
plot of land to grow tea.

My husband's parents did not like me because I wasn't Chinese, but we were comfortable until the Korean War started. Then my
husband went away to drive for the volun-
teers and his parents started to treat me like
a slave. I found out he had an affair and I di-

vorced him, and then his parents threw me
out in the street, saying I was barren and
useless anyway.

It was after midnight, but Gloria Ramirez could still hear box-cars trundling back and forth with an occasional serial crashing of couplers in the Southern Pacific freight yards across the L.A. River. Or maybe there was some new post-merger name for the railroad. Ken Steelyard would have known. The long low cinderblock building in front of her was due to be demolished before long to make way for the Cornfield's urban renewal as thirty-two acres of Downtown state park. Only a half mile north of City Hall, the urban waste had tempted a lot of developers over the years. She'd be perfectly happy that Anti-Terror would be kicked out. She had little affection for the cowboys and ideologues who were attracted to Anti-Terror. A lot of regular cops didn't like them much, either, and Steelyard, her rabbi, who was no bleeding heart by any means, had once sent around an anonymous memo sponsoring a benefit drive to send AT old bedsheets with eye-holes cut out.

The cricket orchestra started up again out in the field after adjusting to her watchful presence. Their relentless buzz was audible over the white noise of traffic from the bottom end of the Pasadena Freeway in the distance, where it entered the Stack to become the Harbor.

The narrow Cornfield was sandwiched between northward extensions of Broadway and Spring in the no-man's-land north of Chinatown, but they were pretty quiet this late. All the lights were out in AT's building, and all the cars were gone from the parking lot. Hard to believe that any police agency shut down at night, but they seemed to have that luxury. Apparently, terrorists only worked by daylight.

When she was satisfied that none of the AT officers were home, she walked calmly across the scrubby field, through abandoned car parts and old campfire rings and the cheapest of half-pint bottles of fortified wine, then across the parking lot to the unmarked door under a canopy. She had called in a lot of favors to get an all-purpose door card and she wondered if it would do the trick. At worst it might set off a honking alarm, but laying it flat on the polished metal surface of the card reader caused a buzz in the door that allowed her to pull it open.

She stopped to listen for any suspicious noises and then turned on the lights. Something would be tripped sooner or later, she figured, but she had a cop's confidence that there wasn't really anything she could do so wrong that she'd have to answer for it.

There was an inner door beyond a receptionist's lobby and the card key got her through that, too, into a big room with an empty holding tank, a bank of powerful-looking computers, a bunch of beat-up but obviously unused desks and filing cabinets, and around the perimeter, offices and interview rooms. It looked like a dumping ground for unused furniture from the Glass House— the nickname for Parker Center.

She found O'Brien's office, and the card key let her in there, too. She stood still in the entrance for a few minutes, looking around, trying to get a read on him. There was a picture that might have been some inspirational corporate-type print, with a big eagle on the wing, except that this one said *Eagles may soar, but weasels don't get sucked into jet engines.* A hat rack by the door held a navy blue cardigan and a spare white shirt on a hanger. There was a row of tiny teddy bears taped to the top of his flat-screen computer monitor, but there wasn't a single piece of paper on his desk, nor on the tall bookcase on the side wall. All the books in it looked to be about radical politics, though so pristine she guessed they'd never been opened. A lower set of shelves under the venetian blinds held loose-leaf notebooks with only numbers on the spine, but she continued her preliminary survey before pouncing on anything.

Leaning in the corner was a tall leather cylinder that she guessed probably contained a fishing rod, and there was a marmalade jar holding cigars in aluminum tubes. Enough, she thought. She could have made some surmises about O'Brien's personality but she preferred not to. Now she opened the case file notebook with the highest number. They were the kind that flopped open on a desk and lay flat, and this one was for somebody named Thompson. She only had to go back six notebooks to find Jack Liffey. It was not a thin book.

They had collected information going back a good forty years, mostly recent cases he'd worked that crossed the path of the police. Thumbing through, she noted that at least two former girlfriends had been among the informants. She frowned at a somewhat compromising telephoto shot of Jack with an old movie star she recognized, but the caption pasted under it said she was deceased. She read a little of each entry. He'd once been mixed up with some Iranian kids who had themselves been mixed up with terrorists, but it seemed he came out of that one with a plus, isolating a dummy bomb which he thought was real. Growing impatient, she flipped to the last page, and found a discharge paper. Disposition: ordered to surrender custody to Captain Midnight, who had actually signed off on receiving Jack using that very name. So they were playing games even on their own books.

She was just settling in to go over the folder more thoroughly when the outside door burst open and O'Brien hollered, "Freeze!" into the building. She could see him through the glass of the office door. He was crouched down aiming a little show-off assault rifle straight toward her, something high-tech that waved around a red laser dot, and he was backed up by two blue suits with their pistols out.

"Aw, shit."

"Let's see your hands!" shouted one of the patrolmen.

"Calm down, gentlemen. I'm a sergeant in Harbor Division," she called. Holding up open palms and without making any sudden moves, she stood and torqued her body around to show the badge wallet clipped to her skirt. O'Brien figured it out at the same time the first patrol officer was flinging open the inner office door.

"You two, beat it," O'Brien said.

"You're gonna take the collar?" one said, disappointed.

"Yeah, I want the collar. Amscray."

They left, looking uncertain, and O'Brien lowered his laser sight.

"Captain *Midnight*?" she said, incredulous.

He shrugged. "How'd you break in here? That's a real no-no, sweetie. This place is strictly off-limits. We won't forget it."

"You picked up my boyfriend without even a courtesy call, fuckhead. Then you turned him over to some spook asshole who calls himself Captain Midnight and who's probably going to torture him. You think I'm going to walk away?"

"Lady, you're in violation of so many codes here they'll probably hang you."

"Let's forget the dick-waving for a moment. I want to know where Jack is, and I swear to god I'll burn this building down with you in it if you don't tell me."

"I don't know where he is."

She waited, staring at him angrily. Then he sank onto his low shelf and relaxed, surprising her. "I'll find out, I promise. Just tell me how you got in."

"You never heard of shapeshifting? It's a special Indian thing. I turned into a spider and came in under the door."

Thirteen

The Second Sex

"They swear they'll tell me tomorrow. It's not easy, Ramirez. Some of these guys would eat my nuts for breakfast."

Each day for over a week now he'd had an excuse, some more plausible than others. "O'Brien, you got one more day. I mean it. I WILL torch your building and nobody will ever know how I did it." She thought she might actually be able to find a way to carry out her threat.

She hung up on him because her mind was somewhere else, and it wasn't a good place. She had seen Maeve once, for two minutes, and the girl had looked frantic and raw. They'd shouted at each other and Maeve had run off. For a moment, Gloria had come close to putting the little Toyota Echo on the hot list, just to find her again. She knew that she needed to call Jack's ex and let her know her daughter was running wild in East Los.

She dug out Jack's tattered little pocket phonebook from the previous year, the cover cracked and reattached by Mylar tape. Every year he laboriously copied the numbers he wanted over into a new little book that was a standard Christmas stocking-stuffer.

He wanted nothing to do with anything electronic. LIFFEY, KATHY, and an address in Redondo. He'd squeezed in a work number, too, and a cell number sideways and June 16, which gave her a pang. Was he still sending her birthday cards?

She flipped forward to RAMIREZ and there it was, her birthday and her mother's name, too, a fact she had once revealed to him in a moment when alcohol had softened her resolve.

She went downstairs to the land line in the living room. The cordless phone kept going on the fritz, and she wanted no static and no batteries dying in the midst of this call.

"Hello."

"Kathy, it's Gloria."

Something guarded entered the woman's voice. "Hello, Gloria. It's good to hear from you."

"I'm sorry. This time it's not going to be very good. Nobody has died or been hurt, but there's trouble."

"Please. Just spit it out." She could perceive an edge of panic. She'd heard it often enough on the job.

"It's Jack. I don't know exactly what happened, but he's been arrested by some Homeland Security outfit and they're holding him somewhere, to question him. He's been gone almost ten days now. I'm doing my best to find out where he is. I think I'll know by tomorrow."

"Oh, god."

"I'm not done. With Jack gone, Maeve wouldn't listen to me at all. You know how strong-willed she is. I should have called you sooner, but I thought she'd be back at any time. She's run away."

"Run away!"

She wondered if she should tell Maeve's mother everything. "She's acting on strange impulses these days, trying to make herself over into a Latina. I think she wants to feel she belongs."

"She *does* belong."

"I know. But it's never simple. Anyway, the phone's not the best place . . . I think she might be with a guy, not such a nice one. She's in love with him, or so she believes. In some ways, it's normal enough."

"Who—"

Gloria broke in. "Just come over here, please, and we can help each other with it." She paused. "We'll figure it out."

Kathy's voice was controlled now. "Give me your address again."

She did. "It's best to take the 10 and just stay on it where it becomes a mess across the river and then get off at 4th Street. It'll say Boyle Heights." She gave the rest of the directions. "I'll be waiting. You're welcome to stay with me for a while if you want to bring some things with you." If you can handle East Los, she thought.

"Thanks. I'll be there."

Gloria sat back and breathed heavily.

He never did figure out what the siren had been, but it had signaled a real change in his treatment. Afterwards they'd hustled him down into a new steel cage built into the corner of an old cellar and left him to stew, with only an army cot and a seatless toilet for company. The man with the ski mask brought meals twice a day but refused to say a word. After a couple of days of this, Jack Liffey began to realize what a punishment solitary confinement could be. He'd have given just about anything for company, even a raving schizophrenic, just for the distraction from his own gloomy thoughts and an end to the incessant napping that left him permanently groggy. On the brick wall he'd begun scratching out the days with his belt buckle like someone out of *The Count of Monte Cristo*. Four uprights, a diagonal, and three more uprights now, counting as best he could from the day they'd nabbed him.

It was a strange place, obviously the basement of some old building. There were a few areas of glass brick in the ceiling on one side that might have been set in a sidewalk. It suggested New York to him, but that possibility seemed pretty unlikely. Now and again a shadow crossed over the glass bricks and was gone. Pedestrian? Guard? He heard vehicles rumble past from time to time, and once he'd heard a very loud motorcycle ratcheting by the building.

He wondered what Gloria and Maeve were thinking about him. He wondered especially if Gloria had realized he'd been snagged by an official outfit of some kind and not just run off to Vegas or splattered his pickup into a ravine off some mountain road. No, Gloria'd know that was out; the car was still home. There was a cop fraternity that, in his experience, had a very long reach and could usually find out quite a lot when one of them needed help. The problem was, he wasn't sure how well the gears turned over for women cops, especially when it came to taking on the old-boy political network. The hopeful part of his soul expected her to kick open the door upstairs and come down the wooden staircase at any time, with a couple of friendly L.A. SWAT cops trailing behind her.

He was beginning to notice signs of a change for the worse in his morale, his sense of himself. He felt more and more guilty, as if he'd done something to deserve all this, and he experienced a strange need to confess. It was as visceral a feeling as the memory of any sin he'd ever committed—but for the life of him he couldn't figure out what he'd done wrong.

. . .

The old woman settles back and closes her eyes.

KUM HAK-SOO

I returned to Korea finally in 1951, but the
war had swept over my village so many
times there was nothing to go home to. I
could not find a single soul of my family.
Then I stayed in Pusan in the south and I
moved around. I lived in miserable huts with
thatched roofs and even in the streets. I was
still young but I was worn out, and I wanted
to live the rest of my days in a country at
peace.

(she smiles gently)

A Korean businessman I met said if I would
be his slave, he would take me with him to
America. I knew the houses were made of
gold here and I only had to get here and
break off a piece and I would be able to live
comfortably forever. So I went with him, but
of course it was not that way.

Maeve had accumulated a lot of books for the afternoons when
she was expected to stay home—though what she was expected to
do at home she didn't know. She carried the last load up the steps
with a bit of a bowlegged waddle, she was so sore from all the
lovemaking. Not that she would complain about it. She'd never
thought she'd be so steamrollered by passion, and it was such an
amazing discovery that she was letting it run as long as it would.
All she had to do was hear Beto's voice and she'd be wet for
him—but all this desire was also starting to give her strong
twinges in the know-better part of her brain. He was mostly

sweet to her, but there were moments when hints of a different kind of treatment crept in, and she knew it probably couldn't last. Whenever she tried to talk to him about anything that mattered, he shut her off.

"Hey, *chavala*, that's man business. You get me another *cerveza*."

"*Orale*, don't I take good care of you?" he'd say. "Here, go buy something."

"You want to talk, tell me how you like *this*." And he'd run his hand under her skirt and up her thighs.

Then sometimes he'd say, "Baby Girl, your skin here is like velvet."

Or, "Baby Girl, you so good to me I want to keep you in a box and keep you near me forever."

One night he came home with a cut lip and let her nurse him. Then he fell asleep exhausted in her lap.

Another night, he must have taken some drug because his erection just wouldn't go down and she lost track of the number of her orgasms. "I open up my heart to you, Baby Girl," he said, but even she, in all the heat, understood he was mistaking his heart for another organ.

In quiet rebellion, she began to read *The Second Sex* by Simone de Beauvoir.

Kathy and Gloria sat opposite one another, status total alert. Loco had nuzzled Gloria's ankle a bit and then skedaddled. "My contact claims he'll tell me tomorrow where Jack is being held. But he's been saying that for several days running."

"Can you trust him?"

Gloria shrugged. "No. But I have some leverage on him. It doesn't look like Jack did anything to deserve this."

"That'll be a new one. He can't seem to not meddle where he doesn't belong."

"I suppose that's the job he's chosen."

They were sipping an herbal tea that was new to the house. Kathy had brought her own little basket of food necessities with her. Gloria really wanted a beer, but feared it would put her at some kind of disadvantage and didn't want to risk that. Kathy Liffey was older-looking than Gloria remembered, but probably that ruddy freckled skin picked up crows' feet faster than other skins. She was getting a wattle, too, under her chin and on her unmuscled upper arms.

"I never liked this job Jack let himself fall into," Kathy was saying. "He was a senior engineering writer, you know. For a good company. It paid well and got him home at six every night. We had a boat and we took vacations to Europe and we were going to put in a swimming pool. He was good at the work and it seemed to keep his ego intact, too. When he lost it, he went to pieces."

"I'm sorry. It must have been hard for you." Harder for him, you bitch, she thought. But not many people saw it like that. They just know how *they* feel.

"It did spoil something between us. After he started drinking and became a real mess, I wasn't sure I loved him any longer."

Gloria thought of her own breakup with Steelyard when she'd still been a rookie and he the seasoned old pro—and how painful it had been to make herself let go. He'd rescued her as a lost teenager and was the reason she'd become a cop. There was a time after the breakup when she hadn't even liked him very much, all the hurt he had inside from his failed marriages that he spewed around. But she'd never stopped loving him, even after aborting the child she had never told him about.

"We've got to find Maeve. Let's do *something*."

Gloria had already been over it with her. "Beto's mother claims he hasn't been home in over a week. If she's with Beto, he probably won't move out of Greenwood territory. Though things aren't really as rigid as that. People do move all the time, and when they're on foreign turf, they just keep their heads down."

"I *hate* all this gang stuff."

"I've driven the Greenwood area a dozen times," Gloria said patiently. "She could have a garage, of course, or just a tarp, but there's no white Echo with her plates. Maybe she swapped the car with someone. I don't know."

"Can't you use your police contacts?"

Gloria wondered how Kathy would react to knowing her daughter's photograph was up on the gang-girl wannabe board at the substation. It was better not to mention it.

"I considered putting her car on the hotlist, but that's filing a false report. I'm already in plenty of trouble, stepping on toes looking for Jack. Informally, I've asked a few patrol cops to keep their eyes open. She's not in a hospital. I know she's basically okay because she came back and we had that run-in."

"Tell me again."

"I said she was being a fool over a man, but she wasn't ready to listen. She split immediately. You're right, I didn't tackle her and tie her up, but she isn't my daughter. I think she must have come into the house a couple of other times when I was at work. Books are gone, but not many clothes. She's dressing different now. I wish I'd thought to tell her her dad was missing. It might have shocked her out of her groove."

"Groove?"

"Sure. Haven't you ever dug yourself into a groove out of sheer cussedness, and then wished for a way out of it?"

Kathy thought it over but didn't reply.

"You just need a kick in the pants, really. Gives you a chance to scream and complain but you get to be dragged home. Most of the half-assed fights I see outside bars, the guys are just begging inside for somebody to stop them."

Kathy sighed. "Do you think you could drive me around the territory? Just once, so I have an idea."

It was evening and they wouldn't see much, but it would give them something to do other than shadow box, so Gloria agreed. Discreetly she armed herself with the Glock and put on her jacket. Outside, Kathy stared at Jack's pickup parked at the edge of the driveway.

"You've checked the car thoroughly?"

"I've talked to the last several people Jack contacted, too. I'm less worried about him than Maeve. He's a big boy."

"Not always," Kathy said glumly. She pointed at her Buick on the street, offering to drive, but Gloria shook her head and they got into the RAV-4. She wasn't about to have this *gabachita* driving them around East Los at night, stopping suddenly in all the wrong places, looking like a social worker hunting down a truant or maybe just somebody who was anxious to give up her purse.

She started over by Hollenbeck Park, technically out of Greenwood's barrio, and let Kathy get a good look at the *vatos* who inhabited it at night, floating ghosts with white T-shirts, rings of shadowy forms marked by red cigarette embers, here and there a glint off a beer can.

"Are those gang members?" Kathy asked.

Gloria nearly laughed. "You could say that. That's probably White Fence."

"Pardon?"

"That's the name. It's one of the oldest sects in the country, going back to the '30s. We'll take an alley behind the church. Look for Maeve's car."

"I don't suppose you could ask somebody if there's a new girl in town."

Gloria thought about it. It was just dumb enough to catch somebody off guard. "We'll have to find some Greenwoods." She'd been keeping careful watch but they weren't hanging in the Montalvos' backyard at the moment.

There were no white Toyotas of any kind in the alley, but Gloria crossed 4th and kept going across to the alley again, springing the bouncy RAV-4 over ruts and humps. An old full-size Pontiac was parked close to the side of the alley, leaving just enough room to get by. There were four sinister heads in the Pontiac, watching them approach. "Don't look at them," Gloria said urgently, and Kathy obeyed, slumping back in her seat and staring forward as she inched past in the narrow space.

"I show you something real special." It was a purring voice, eerie with menace.

Gloria didn't change speed. She'd come near to flashing her badge but she didn't want to steam around the barrio, advertising. She headed then for Greenwood Park, while Kathy warily kept an eye on the world outside, murals, gang *plaka*, little groups of teens walking home.

They parked alongside some grass, not far from a group of taggers, twelve and thirteen at the oldest—cigarettes disappearing fast into the grass. "Let me do the talking," Gloria said.

Kathy followed her out of the car. "*Qué tal, amigos? Orale, no problemas.*" Two of them had got up and were about to book out. "*Nadie se mueve.*" Gloria showed her badge. "You're not in trouble."

"We din't do nothing."

"I know. It's all right. I just want to ask a question. Have any of you seen Beto the last few days?"

They all shook their heads.

One looked as if he was about to say something, so she concentrated on him, thin as a rail with jet-black hair that he couldn't keep slicked down. Incredibly cute, she thought. "What's your name?"

"Puppet."

"Well, Puppet, we're looking for Beto's new *chica*, Baby Girl." She thought of lying, saying they had something valuable that belonged to her, but then decided to hell with it. These kids deserved the truth as much as anyone else. "This is Baby Girl's mother, and she's very worried about her."

"We don' know. Hones'."

She talked to them for a while longer, even let Kathy plead with them, but they probably didn't know. Beto would keep a hideout somewhere, just some nondescript apartment or converted garage. Gloria took Kathy's sleeve and tugged her back toward the car.

"They don't know, but by tomorrow she'll have heard you were over here looking for her."

Kathy tore loose and grasped Gloria's arm hard. "What aren't you telling me? What's this Baby Girl stuff?"

"It's okay. We're making progress."

Kathy fumed for a moment, standing with her arms crossed and refusing to get in the car.

"Get in," Gloria said finally.

She drove them straight to the substation, and, as luck would have it, Dean Padilla was in, taking a report on a bag-snatch from an old woman who spoke no English. Gloria waved to him and made a sign that there was no urgency. She took a deep breath and led Kathy to the WANNABE board. There were eight Polaroids now, but Maeve was still there under the heading: WHO IS THIS? LET'S "INTERVENE," GUYS.

Gloria pointed to the shot of the new Maeve and heard Kathy Liffey gasp. She obviously hadn't been picturing her daughter with dyed black hair and a spaghetti-strap top, and those big *chola* hoops. The typed note beneath still said: "BABY GIRL." GREEN-WOOD PARK. MAYBE 18. ANGLO. APPARENTLY BETO'S GIRL. SHY. NO TATS.

When she glanced up, Kathy had both hands to her cheeks, still adjusting to what she was seeing.

"I'm sorry, Kathy. If I hadn't been preoccupied with Jack and other things, I would have called you sooner. He never got a look at her quite like this."

"How did it happen? She looks ridiculous."

"It's a style. Not one that the fashion magazines feature much, but some ordinary people manage to live with it."

"It's cheap and it says, fuck me."

"And leather Versace miniskirts don't?"

Kathy glared at her but didn't reply. "Will he know anything?" She nodded toward Padilla.

"Maybe."

Padilla was finishing up with the snatch victim and walking her sympathetically to the door. When he let her out, Gloria introduced them.

"So, you're Baby Girl's mom. I was pretty sure she was Anglo." He looked Kathy over, and for some reason she seemed to invite his flirtation. "You could be her sister."

Gloria didn't let her exasperation show. She'd heard enough about Padilla to think he ought to be on traffic detail somewhere. The penny hadn't even dropped that he should have recognized Baby Girl as the one who'd been shot last year.

"I'm worried to death," Kathy said. "Do you know where she might be?"

"Last I heard, Alberto Montalvo was living at home next door to Sergeant Ramirez here. But the bangers all got places to go.

He's almost an O.G.—that means a true old-timer. The longer you're around, the more back doors you got."

"Do you have a picture of him?"

"Sure. Have a seat." He got the Greenwoods gang book and opened it to the first page, pointing to Beto's picture, and Kathy glared at it.

"Here's some information."

She read his jacket, which Gloria already knew—a lot of arrests, a couple of convictions for weapons and drug possession, and one bust that had gotten him some hard time for cutting a rival in a fight.

"This part has his background."

"It's got his birth date." She obviously did the math in her head. "My god, he's thirty. Maeve's just seventeen."

"*Hey*, you don't look like you could have a seventeen-year-old daughter." He winked.

"Can you help me find her?" She did everything but bat her eyes at him.

Gloria realized suddenly that Jack's ex-wife was trying to flirt her way into getting help. After all, it was Padilla's jurisdiction, not Gloria's, so why not let her switch horses?

"Well, we could try," Padilla said.

Gloria decided it was time to make herself scarce. "If you two want to go out looking, I've got stuff to do. Good hunting. I hope you find her."

"I'll call," Kathy said to her, ambiguously, as if she might not make it back that evening.

Fourteen

The cosine of one is zero

He stared morosely at the scratched ticks on the wall. He was afraid that he'd forgotten a day. There were twelve marks, two sets of five and two over, but he was almost certain there should have been thirteen. Better not to exaggerate the ordeal, he thought, so he left it at twelve and lay back on the cot again. His dinner tray sat by the door. He had taken to eating every bit of it, as much for something to do as any craving for nourishment. The food was not bad, just tasteless, textureless, and somewhat unclear as to its character. Mystery meat and mystery gravy with some kind of green vegetable puree. Coffee that tasted more like tea. Some chilled yellowish mess that might have been custard. In the last five or six days, no one had spoken a word to Jack Liffey, and he wondered if his own voice apparatus still worked. He spoke aloud in the cell regularly, just to hear the sound, but then he would forget whether he had actually spoken aloud or not, and he'd have to do it again.

A half hour after each meal was delivered, footsteps clattered down the wooden staircase and a man in a ski mask—it may or may not have been the original man in the ski mask—appeared to collect the tray before there was time to break up the hard brown plastic and hurriedly fashion keys, knives, firearms, Ferraris. But this time, his guard gestured for Jack Liffey to get up and follow him.

What joy! Variety in his day! Even another interrogation was preferable to this enforced stasis.

"Where are we going?"

The man gave a single shake of the head and led him up the stairs, so confident he didn't even take the trouble to grasp Jack Liffey's arm.

"Do you have any kids? I can't help wondering how my daughter is doing. I've been away a couple of weeks, and she was into a little trouble when I last saw her. Is there any way I can send her a note, let her know I'm okay?"

Jack Liffey knew he was making a fool of himself, but it was such a delight to have an ear that he couldn't stop himself. The man was not going to respond. He unlocked the door at the top of the stairs with a big old-fashioned key and he led him along a gloomy corridor, choked with dust, past doors with frosted-glass transoms and niches for missing fire extinguishers. It gave the impression of some civic building that had been abandoned many years ago and then put back into use in a hurry. His guide opened an unlocked door into a large room, brightly lit by fluorescent fixtures. Once again there were no windows, but what captured Jack Liffey's attention was a deep steel tank of water in the middle of the room like a very big horse trough, and above it a pivoting inquisitional apparatus with straps for a man's arms and legs, an obscene piece of equipment whose only possible purpose was immediately apparent.

A pudgy man with a mustache waited placidly in a plastic raincoat, but Jack Liffey turned to his escort, who evidently had no intention of entering with him, only standing behind him to make sure he did not bolt.

"Don't do this. We're all responsible for more than the things that we do personally," Jack Liffey said. He had stiffened up staring at the big tank. "This is not acceptable. You can't let it happen."

The escort pushed him gently into the room. The door shut behind him and the Grand Inquisitor himself made a sinister beckoning gesture, absurd in his plastic raincoat.

She guessed that she'd finally graduated past some critical point in acceptability, because Beto let her come along that evening to Husky's house. It wasn't exactly a Greenwood party, more a hanging-out, but a lot of them were there, eating from a big cardboard tray of tamales and burritos and drinking from three cases of beer somebody had scored. A plastic salsa bottle was open and lying on its side amongst the tamales, slowly dripping onto the cardboard. *Norteño* music was chugging away from the bedroom. She'd heard enough of it now, she thought, to recognize the classic group *Los Tigres del Norte*. It was a small living room with muted-plaid wallpaper and a number of standard devotional items—a crucifix, saint's candle, a print of the bleeding heart of Jesus. A grisly image, Maeve thought, but not as disconcerting as the three-year-old in diapers on the floor who was playing with a toy submachine gun that every once in a while burped its rat-a-tat as it lit up a red plastic barrel. Several people were smoking from a shared pack of Shermans and a glass bong—the room was dense with haze.

She sat at the end of an old sofa with the other women, who seemed to accept her now. Ruby and Ivana had their minds on other stuff. Funerals, for one thing.

"We gotta go to Manny's funeral Friday," Beto said. "All together, in colors. He wasn't G, but he always show up strong on the street."

"*Ese,* who you think cap him?" It was Sparky, scratching under the brand-new Mighty Ducks cap somebody had given him as a joke.

"I don't know, man. It was a old school drive-by and whoever, they in the real shit for that. The *Eme* says everything got to be walk-up now, that's the rule. Got to end this spray shit that gets the little kids and moms. '*Chucos* who do that shit gonna be in bad with the *hombres.*"

They talked about other funerals they'd attended—for Chivo, Bugs, and a really big one for an O.G. named Oscar—and Maeve realized how normal a part of life funerals were for them. Their lives were surrounded by rituals relating to death—car washes to pay for the casket; little displays of flowers, photos, and notes at the death site; building homemade altars to the victim made up of pictures, items of clothing, foods—all the things the victim had liked in life. Maeve had only been to one funeral ever—a girl in junior high who'd drowned in high surf. Nobody she'd been close to.

As they talked, she hung back and listened with great care, unable to stop comparing them to the kids across town. She saw how essentially conservative and fatalistic Beto and his friends seemed, making them old and grim beyond their years. What they respected most was a kind of dogged determination to be what they considered honorable and to stay loyal to a sense of worldly and religious order. The guys mostly held back their feelings, remaining curiously stiff and formal, hanging out together and participating in macho rituals, like butting shoulders, that revealed next to nothing. And there was a suppressed anger inside a lot of them that she didn't understand.

A little sister brought Ruby's twin baby daughters out for feeding. Ruby told Maeve without any embarrassment that the father had split about two minutes after conceiving the twins, but her current boyfriend, Chilango, didn't mind. Maeve had just found out that Chilango was slang for somebody who came from Mexico City.

"Did you think about an abortion?" Maeve asked innocently

The girl looked at her like she was crazy. "We don't do that. We're Mexican."

The small girl brought two plastic bottles, and while she was bottle-nursing, Ruby leaned, and whispered to Maeve, "You making Beto happy?"

"I hope so."

Maeve watched Beto, and how still and quiet everybody got when he spoke. She wondered what it was like to be like that, a little Napoleon. She guessed it would be a terrible temptation to use that power over people for selfish purposes.

Just then Chilango, who sat by the door, waved his hand urgently. Once Beto's attention was caught, everybody's was caught. Then the only sound was the music from the back room until they all heard footsteps on the porch. It could have been any of several missing Greenwoods, so nobody seemed too worried. But the knock was so peremptory it was obvious that it wasn't a friend. Yet an enemy would just have barged in or shot through the windows. The Shermans, the bong, and the beer quickly went into the back of the house.

"Greenwoods. This is the police. Open up. *¡Abre la puerta!*"

Chilango looked to Beto. Beto nodded, so he got up and threw the bolt back, revealing Dean Padilla.

"*Nadie se mueve.*" His eyes went straight to Maeve. "It's you I'm looking for, kiddo."

It was like a double bolt of lightning. Not only was the policeman's gaze fixed directly on her, but behind him as he stepped into the room, stood her mother! Kathy's face was as grim as she'd ever seen it, and her arms were folded tight across her chest, as if she needed protection from this strange world.

"We ain't doing nothing wrong, Padilla," Beto said.

"How old you think this girl is, *cabrón?*"

Maeve saw her mother motioning urgently for her to come out on the porch, presumably so she didn't have to step into that hostile living room. But Maeve pretended not to see. She had no idea what to do, but what she wanted just then was to shrink down to a dot and disappear behind the sofa cushion. All at once she was self-conscious about her huge earrings and her crimson lipstick, to say nothing of the red bra that rose out of her skimpy top. She was caught between two worlds and could not move or act.

"Forty-two," Beto said, looking scornfully at Padilla.

"This girl is seventeen years of age, and if I choose to do you for a 261.5, you go down for hard time. You just gotta be three years older than her, Beto *mi amigo*—and I know you are—and we've got a felony." He stepped closer to Maeve and spoke softly. "Has he interfered with you?"

She couldn't help herself. "*Interfered?* Like in softball, when you're running the bases?"

He wasn't in the mood. "You know what I mean." He was almost whispering now, hoping her mother in the doorway wouldn't hear over the music.

"That's none of your business." She wanted to say that he was her man, her boyfriend, her *novio*, but was afraid of getting him in further trouble for rape. She tried not to look at her mother, but saw the look of shock on her face.

Padilla took Maeve's arm and wrenched her to her feet in one tug. "You're coming with us now. The rest of you, stay where you are."

"I don't want to leave," she said futilely.

"Oh, honey," her mother said. "*Please.*"

"You're going to have to lock me up," Maeve said defiantly. This was sheer bravura. "I'm coming back," she called before the cop slammed the door, and the three of them were face to face on the porch.

"Let's go home now," Kathy said.

"I am home, mom. These are my friends. Just understand that you're kidnapping me."

"You'll feel better when we get back to the house, honey."

The old woman seems to be trying with great dignity to keep from presenting herself as an object of pity.

KUM HAK-SOO

I landed in this country like Mr. MacArthur
in the Philippines—

(she smiles gently)

—stepping from a small boat on a beach near
Santa Barbara with about ten other Korean
women. The freighter just sailed off. My first
days in the United States were spent in the
bedroom of a tiny house with these women,
waiting for someone to come get us. Of
course the man who was to marry me never
showed up.

Then we were taken to a big brick building
Downtown, and we worked on sewing ma-

chines in one room and slept on palettes and
rags in another room. It was a lot like my
first comfort station in Manchuria, except I
sewed during the day instead of the other
thing. We earned seventy cents an hour, but
we couldn't leave the building and we had to
spend our money on food they supplied us.
They charged us when we spoiled work, too.

This first job in America was making big
fancy wedding dresses, and it was like being
surrounded by snow, so much white. I fantasized all day about the girls who would wear
these dresses, how rich they must feel.

(she looks away)

But I knew that marriage can be a form of
servitude, also. There was a kind of peace
that grew in me. We worked twelve hours a
day, sometimes more, and seven days a week.
It was hard, but it was a rhythm that I could
count on without beatings and without soldiers. Once we climbed on some boxes to a
high window and saw many buildings around
us and none of them were bombed or burned.
I would sing my old village songs for the
other women as we worked.

"O'Brien, it's me, Ramirez."

She was using her cell phone down in the parking lot of Harbor station so the call wouldn't go in or out through Dispatch, or
even one of the direct lines that she was sure were monitored in

some random fashion. Being a cop taught you Paranoia 101. Actually, as she waited for him to get back with the information he'd said he had to hunt down, she noticed that the cell call was probably going out via a fake plastic palm tree ringed with cell antennas that she could see up by the freeway. She'd seen big artificial sequoias, too. Just the sort of thing that Jack might have ranted about, but she thought they were actually pretty funny.

"Sergeant Ramirez."

"I haven't gone anywhere."

"Uh-huh. Now I'm just saying this is a 'maybe.' But ISOC took over an old county facility down by El Centro that they were going to rent out to INS or whatever the hell it's called now—ICE—as a holding jail for illegals they picked up on the inland routes. It seems the government never bought into the idea, so ISOC decided to put it to other use. Mostly training, I'm told, but they do some interrogations on contract to various agencies. So the agencies can deny doing it themselves." He gave her directions to the place, and she realized there was no "maybe" involved.

"Thanks." She was grateful, but she would not forgive him for his part in making Jack disappear.

Then, on a whim, she called Padilla to thank him, too. It was free, and you could never tell when a little politeness might buy you an extra edge in the department.

"That information you gave me finally paid off, Dean. I might have found out where Jack is. Thanks a lot. I'll return the favor some day."

"I wouldn't mind seeing you in your underwear."

"I thought you had that all worked out with Kathy Liffey."

He chuckled. "Yeah, I kinda thought so, too. If only I hadn't found the girl right away—I'm just too good. Mama wanted to take her straight home, no time for us to get to know each other better."

"Well, it's good to know she's safe. Thanks again."

"Just forget you ever talked to me about this antiterror stuff."

She snapped her phone closed. There was nothing she could do about El Centro until the weekend, and she wondered what she could do then. She couldn't just flash her badge and walk into some ultrasecure facility being run by god-knows-who. She wondered if any of her friends—or Jack's friends—could help. You'd have to go pretty high up the food chain to find someone who could get anywhere with people who thought of themselves as mercenaries, and could probably prove it to you before you blinked twice.

Jack Liffey stared blankly up from where he lay on the floor. In the fluorescent glow, he could see above him one of those textured frothy surfaces, like a 1960s apartment ceiling, but what did it matter, really? He felt torn open, and parts of him were leaking out, carrying away his self-respect. What was left behind was an intolerable racket of reproach as all those deep, hidden spaces where he'd stuffed away his failures were now stirred up and wailing to one another.

Breaking him down had been a simple matter, as it turned out. With his head pinned under water, he was soon a blubbering wreck. Drowning always had been one of his worst fears. Even a dip in a shallow pool would be panic-inducing the instant his head went under water. What was it in *1984*? he thought—Room 101, they had called it, where they confronted you with your most scarifying phobia. They'd found it. He was having trouble now suppressing the memory, the utter helpless panic that would return like the event itself.

The door was opened now to fill him with dread. Look, he thought, at the moment I'm a bit under the weather and I'm just not in fighting shape. He rolled his head to look, but it wasn't the pudgy Inquisitor, nor Ski Mask. A brunette in a business suit and high heels came in and looked down on him with an impassive sense of total assurance, as if she owned the whole setup.

"Don't you dare look up my skirt," she said impassively.

He had been doing his best not to.

She knelt beside his head, bent forward and blew softly in his ear, which shocked his shaky psyche and left him more confused than ever. "We have your friend," she whispered. "Now she will suffer for your stubbornness. They're reading her sentence to her now."

"Who's my friend? Please."

"Don't pretend to be naïve."

"*Please.* Who do you mean?" He was terrified they might have Maeve—or Gloria. She blew in his ear again and he kept his face rigidly upward rather than roll his head and be accused of trying to kiss her.

Perhaps they'd captured Soon-Lin, he thought. It was like some moral conundrum from an ancient riddle—you could choose as a torture victim your own daughter, your lover, or a young Korean girl that you'd never met.

Her laugh was intimate. "Wouldn't you like to confide in me? Can I call you Jack? Can I touch you?"

Her lips touched his ear lightly and caused a great shudder to pass over him. He felt his penis swelling and he experienced a deep sensation of shame.

"I love men when they're helpless."

"Go fuck yourself," he blurted. "I've done nothing to deserve any of this, and if you harm my family in any way, you'd better make sure I'm dead, because I'll hunt you down."

"My, my." He felt her rest her palm on his erect penis. "You have such hospitality."

What was she talking about? Had she meant to say *hostility*? He took some comfort: even in their absurdly unequal situation, she had shown weakness, imperfection.

"Wouldn't you love to tell me what you know?" she suggested.

"I know the cosine of one is zero," he said.

Fifteen

Catch and Release

She'd taken off the big hoop earrings, more from embarrassment than motherly insistence, and she lay on the bed in her room in Redondo now, revisiting a lot more unstudied emotion than she knew how to get her mind around. It was all so confusing being halfway between two worlds. There was nothing she could do about the black hair dye, and to take off the red bra right away would be too much like conceding defeat.

She wished her dad were available for a talk, but when she found out he'd been missing for some time, she felt even worse because she hadn't been thinking of him at all but only herself. Thank heavens Brad had moved his stuff out, it appeared for good, as his three-foot-tall model lighthouse was gone from the living room. And there was no evidence of her mom's new boy-friends.

It occurred to her that sex created an awful lot of mischief in life. She had certainly come to appreciate some of the ways the sex drive could be acted out, though Beto wasn't all that inventive or even considerate. He had only licked her once, and that briefly; she squeezed her eyes shut now, remembering it. She ran her palm thoughtfully over her belly.

Her period had been due a few days ago. It was probably too soon to start worrying about it, but she was normally pretty regular. She had every intention of going back to Beto, but being in her mom's familiar home again cast a new perspective on everything and made her life in East L.A. seem pretty far away—unreal in fact. Once summer was over, what about finishing out her last year at Redondo Union High School? What about college? She'd been acting and living as if this other life, for some strange reason, was off in some parallel realm and had no consequences for her more accustomed existence.

Her mother knocked once and opened the door before she could even reply. She came in holding a tray with two glasses.

Maeve was a little embarrassed. This was clearly her mom's attempt to buddy up, which wasn't really her strong suit. Maeve decided to do her best to make it easier for her. She sat up and took one of the glasses as her mother settled onto the little desk chair. She noticed how the wrinkles had puckered up around the corners of her mother's eyes—but she was still a handsome woman and Maeve figured she could probably find a man again, though she dreaded who it might be.

She tasted the drink. Her mom seemed to have mixed up fairly weak gin and tonics with big chunks of lime.

"Why don't you tell me about it?"

That was mild enough. "I'm just really crazy about him, Mom. Totally. I guess it really doesn't make sense, but he's like nothing I ever ran into in our world. I'm in a different place when I'm with him."

"Is it a better place?"

Maeve sipped some more, starting to like the drink's sweet bite. "I don't know. It's confusing."

Her mother smiled. "I have trouble seeing you with that dark glossy hair. I don't mean it's bad," she added quickly. "I just never saw anything like it in our family."

"I was getting tired of mousy brown, but I wish I had more body. It's so limp." She ran her fingers through a tress. It didn't look anything like Gloria's, or even Ruby's.

"Maybe our whole family searches out intensity," Kathy said.

"All of us?—or are you just taking a run at dad and me?"

"Honey, you never met my geologist."

"You had another guy when you were with Brad?" Maeve was dumbfounded.

Her mother bit her lower lip. "You know it wasn't working out with Brad, and this just overwhelmed me all at once."

This was going to take a little digesting, Maeve thought. "How did you meet him?"

"I was out for a walk. I was tired and sitting on a big rock in one of those last areas of the PV hills that isn't developed. Jeremy was striding along with a big leather backpack, looking for out-crops, he said. He had a British accent. We shared a bag of Oreos I had."

Maeve almost laughed. "Did Brad find out?"

"I only told him when he was packing up to go. Jeremy was long gone by then, off to Canada and then Australia. He was too young for me, but . . . wow."

Too much information, Maeve thought. This was her *mother.* "Will Jeremy be back?"

"With a man like that, it's always catch and release, hon. It was a summer romance, but never say *just* a summer romance—they can be the most wonderful things in the world."

They finished their drinks and then went downstairs for two

more and talked on and on about men and love and passion, and they used sexual words she thought she would never use with her mother or hear from her mother—and then they wept and held each other.

It confounded her emotions terribly, but she was still determined to go back to Beto. She wasn't interested in catch and release.

He awoke staring at the same ceiling, without the least idea of how much time had passed, or whether it was day or night in the windowless room with its big water tank running with rivulets of condensation. It was a great luxury to be left alone, he thought. But now the door opened and Ski Mask led in a swarthy middle-aged man in some kind of paramilitary getup. They were speaking Spanish and he couldn't get much of it.

We can do that.

Friends.

Usual business.

One phrase stuck out that was easy enough for him, even with the odd accent, even with parts of the words swallowed by the *para*.

"*Vemos cuidarlo para Usted.*" We will take care of him for you.

Ski Mask knelt and cradled Jack Liffey's neck, pressing a strip of silver duct tape around his forehead, right over the hair in back and then around again, so it would be hell to rip off. He used a felt pen to write something on the tape across Jack Liffey's forehead. Then he slapped him, almost affectionately, on his cheek.

"Rest up. Travel is broadening."

The men went out, audibly locking him in with a snap. After a long time of concentrated but unproductive thought, he rolled over and came up onto his knees, feeling weak. He pulled himself up the sweating metal of the water tank, until he could see the surface of the water. By boosting himself a little more, he could tilt his face forward and just make out his reflection in the water. The hand-lettered word read YAUGARAP.

KUM HAK-SOO is sitting next to another elderly Korean woman on a sofa, each with a cup of tea. The second woman glances with affection toward her friend from time to time. She seems to have some difficulty swallowing her tea.

KUM HAK-SOO

This is Peggy. That's her American name.
Cancer has taken her voicebox, and one lung.
Maybe it was all the cotton lint in those
places we worked. Maybe it was something
else.

Peggy makes a gesture, and Kum Hak-Soo interprets.

She wants me to tell you about Time Fash-
ions. We worked there for a long time. The
boss was a very kind Persian man named
Farshad. We stayed with him for nine years, I
think. We had holidays and he brought in a
doctor every few months to look at all of us.
He was almost the only one who never
changed our time cards to steal from us.

It's a sad world when a kind man like that
can't stay in business, but he was undersold
by the other little companies that were not so
kind.

(she looks at Peggy)

Sometimes I ask myself what sort of a world

it is when working for a simple honest man

is the high point of one's life.

YOUNG VOICE, off

Was that the high point of your life?

The woman looks straight back at the interviewer, who must

be just off camera, and answers slowly. Her friend watches

her.

KUM HAK-SOO

I don't know yet.

"Hey, they got me on traffic, and even taking a dozen kids to Chuck E. Cheese would be a nice break from that."

"You do something wrong?"

She and Paula Green had gone through the Academy together, had once been close friends, but Paula had been stuck up in Foothill Station in Pacoima for years, which might as well be on Mars, it was so far from the centers of power and promotion.

"Yeah, I think I probably said I preferred the term African-American one time too many for the watch commander we called Bubba the Hut." Green had light olive skin and straightened hair and could have been an LAPD poster girl for minority recruitment. "He said he preferred black, but I think *Neegra* would have made him happier."

They were sitting side by side in a *pupusería* emporium called Costa del Sol. Gloria was happily smearing the peppery cole slaw called *curtido* over a cheese *pupusa*, a sort of stuffed fat tortilla. Both of them were hearty eaters and this was a favorite snack.

Back in 1997 the LAPD'd dropped the obligatory weight maxi-mums, and you only had to be "appropriate for your height and build" now, but Paula was pushing a pretty liberal interpretation of that—appropriate for someone 7-foot-6 maybe.

"So, how's Pacoima?"

"It's away from a lot of the heaviest stuff down there in Ram-part or 77th. Traffic detail sucks, but when I get back to patrol I can do some real neighborhood policing. My Spanish is getting a lot better. Last week I actually got to snap out, '*Basta con tu des-fachatez!*'"

Her pronunciation was pretty good. A slangy version of Cut out the sass.

"But they still get me sometimes," Paula said. "What's '*nariz boleada*?' Polished nose? What the hell's that?"

"It's border slang. It means nothing. Literally. *Nada.* I have to work at it to keep up myself. Listen to the *cholo* rap and *El Cucoy* on the radio."

Paula Green tossed down some beer to clear the hot peppery food. "Whew."

Gloria finished her last bite, licked her fingers, and began to explain about her fears for Jack Liffey. "He's a good guy and I don't want anybody using rubber hoses on the soles of his feet or whatever those pricks are doing these days. I want to go down there and get him back. I can't manage it without backup. Do you think you can swap some time?"

Paula Green held up the flat of her hand. "It's done, girl. This sounds like my kind of job, sticking it to the big shots."

Gloria gave her a soft high-five.

"You're an absolute living, fucking, quote book of Comrade Lenin."

Jimmy Park offered the right middle finger, and then pounded the wrist several times against the palm of his left hand for emphasis, like something an Italian might do, though he was, of course, Korean.

"Every cook has to learn how to govern the state," he quoted.

"Yes, of course."

Jimmy Park and the goateed Richie Yu frowned a bit at one another as Peter Kim went on videotaping them all, backing across the room now to get a wider angle, his bright red hair like a flag over the camera.

Jin Dong-Sun, who was probably the only Korean under fifty in the United States to insist on having his name the Asian way round, muttered away to himself in the corner, doing his thing. And the old man, Al Siegel, sat back watching but not interfering.

They had taken four rooms of a decrepit motel along the Salton Sea, and now congregated in the biggest room to hold a plenum of the full active membership of the Front, which was, in fact, down to eleven, not counting the missing two.

Fishermen had given up on the dying inland sea decades ago, and they were the only guests in what had once been a fancy resort. The old window air conditioner didn't work but still the windows were kept shut because the hyperpolluted sea out the window was in the midst of one of its periodic fish die-offs. The manager had told them it was due to a bloom of algae from all the organics that the Coachella Valley's agricultural fields emptied into the sea. Because of this, the smell outside was a bit like . . . well, nothing was *like* 50 million belly-up bass and tilapia floating in amber-colored water, tempting the wary, squawking pelicans with a dose of botulism.

"It's really very simple," Soon-Lin Kim said. "They have two of our comrades, and they're torturing them. We can't allow that. It's state-sponsored kidnapping. And these guys aren't even the state."

One skinny young man shook his head. "All we're really capable of is armed propaganda," he said. "We've been doing pretty well at it, but if we go head-to-head with the ISOC . . ."

Richie Yu shrugged. He was their Minister of Defense, or as he preferred it, the Guy with the Guns. "A lot of these ISOC types are ex–Special Forces. They'll gut you guys like deer."

"You were a Green Beret," Soon-Lin said.

"Sure. Can you guys keep your intervals in a squad-in-column assault?"

"No fair, man. Explain it and maybe we can. We got more weapons than a small country."

Richie grinned. "I get a kick out of you. You want state power, but we couldn't runthis motel property."

Al Siegel sat forward at last, and they all paid attention. "We're keeping the movement alive, Richie, until there's a renewed impetus from workingpeople. It's not glamorous, but it has to be done."

"If you have no faith in that, you should get out," Soon-Lin put in with her characteristic bluntness.

"Don't tempt me," Richie snapped. "All right, I'll go over to the facility and I'll do some passive reconnaissance. Maybe not so passive if the *impetus* moves me."

"Take me along," Soon-Lin insisted.

"I'm better off alone."

She shook her head. "I want to see. We can't rely on you for everything."

He shrugged and turned to rest two fingers under Peter Kim's tiny camera and frowned at it, as it whirred at him. "I should smash this."

He moved the two fingers to under Peter's chin. "Or this." Peter moved away from the wooden chest he'd been perched on, his little video camera whirring away. Richie Yu lifted the lid on a tangle of shotguns, automatic rifles and wax-wrapped bricks of explosives, but all he took out were black 7x50 binoculars and a pair of night-vision goggles, then he locked the lid down again.

Jin Dong-sun's mutter seemed to be coming to a crescendo: " . . . Mind the in innate they are? No. Skies the from drop they do? From come ideas correct do where?" He broke into a grin. Once again he had proved to himself that he could recite backwards the entirety of Chairman Mao's key essay, *Where Do Correct Ideas Come From?*

She'd dropped Paula Green at a nail salon in the little one-street town of Niland so she could ask about the big fenced facility a few miles south, and then she had talked herself through the gate of that very facility alone, with a little badge-flashing and a suggestion she might want to come over and work for ISOC.

Waved on at the gate, she drove up the unpaved road to the main building with its unlikely portico of Corinthian columns oddly suggesting the White House. Up close she could see that the columns had started to decay in the desert sun, revealing that they were only plaster over lath and chickenwire.

It was hard to tell what the whole compound had been built for originally, probably back in the '30s. Mainly, there were concrete-block buildings, but dressed up here and there with entablatures and pediments like movie sets for a remake of *Intolerance*. It could have been a fertilizer plant owned by an eccentric old Italian or maybe a World's Fair pavilion fallen out of high orbit into the wrong place.

A young guy in fatigues met her before she got to the door. "Ramirez?" was all he said.

"Yup."

He turned and led her up the broad staircase toward some old wooden doors with a new sign that said AUTHORIZED ONLY ISOC. The reception area had arched niches for busts of emperors that had long been missing. One of them now held a big plastic novelty switchplate with an oversized red button labeled PANIC BUTTON. Oddly enough it looked like it was actually wired up. Their path led them along a bilious yellow-green hallway. The woodwork on the old-fashioned transomed doors was darkening with reticulated varnish but had once been pretty classy. A paper card on the door he chose said COS. She played with that a moment, wondering if it was Chief of Station or something else.

A broad-shouldered man came to his feet behind a desk and she recognized the type immediately—police captain, hard-eyed and unforgiving, overweight now but once in superb shape.

"Roger Fuqua," he said, holding out a hand.

There wasn't a single personal item in the office, making it feel like he had just parachuted in and taken over.

"Gloria Ramirez." The only seat was a stiff ladderback chair, and she took it. She knew the type through and through. He hated cleverness. Almost anything you said was an affront to his whole worldview. They had the right to a certain crude kind of put-down, but you didn't.

He got straight to the point. "What makes you think you'd like to work for ISOC?"

"I scored the highest anybody ever scored on the sergeant's exam, and my career is at a dead end because I'm a minority woman. I'll never go any higher with LAPD."

"We mostly have SWAT veterans and ex–Special Forces. Our business mostly lies in bodyguards and sometimes rescuing kidnapped executives."

"I'm sure you do quasi-police work, too. I'm a damn good

cop."

There was a crash somewhere in the building, like a metal filing cabinet going over, but he acted as if he hadn't heard it.

"You don't do interrogations?" she asked.

"What makes you think that?"

"I'm not a fool, Fuqua. I read the papers. Two of your guys were at Abu Ghraib, and you turn up all over the place. Wherever the Pentagon is stretched thin."

"Ever stolen a car?"

That startled her, and she wasn't sure how to answer, but she decided to go for it. "As a matter of fact, I have. I had a troubled youth, but that was a long time ago."

Something was going on in his mind, and she didn't think it had a lot to do with her.

"Ever shown off your tits?"

That one did bring her to an angry stop. Why did it always come down to this with the guys who worshipped power? Everything in the room went a little out of focus.

"Have you ever waved your weenie?" she replied.

"Answer me," he said. "Or show."

"I lost one to cancer. You want a peek at that one?"

"I'm looking to find out what kind of woman Jack Liffey's got searching for him, and how far she'll go to help him."

The world came to a complete standstill. *Shit*, she thought. Shit, shit, shit.

Sixteen

The Wrong Movie

Now that Brad was gone, Maeve didn't feel quite so bad about the Redondo house, which hunkered down inland just over the crest from the really desirable homes that possessed a glimpse of the ocean. She'd finally swapped the red bra for an ordinary white one, and now she was out in the back yard swinging lightly on the truck tire that hung off a limb of the ash tree. In her hand she had a mug of strong coffee.

Something in her mother's entreaties the night before had touched her deeply, and she tried to imagine sharing the house on equal terms with a much older, divorced woman who was into dating again. Her mother had said, "I want a man who does more than drop a little blue pill and go metronome with his gearshift." Maeve smiled and sipped.

This morning her mom was sleeping in. The gin-and-tonics she'd made for herself had definitely been stronger than the ones she'd impulsively given Maeve. Her mother needed a dog, Maeve thought. Who was taking care of Loco? she was reminded; he was all alone over at Gloria's. She'd called there very early, and a little later, but no one had answered. Maeve missed Beto, but she had a sad inkling of the impossibility of it all. However, it wasn't over yet. She knew that. She lusted for him too much.

"Whoop!"

If the big tire hadn't been so entrapping she might have leapt a foot in shock. An opossum waddled out from behind an azalea near the fence and stopped to give her the once-over, only a few feet away. She stabilized herself with a toe to the ground. She'd thought they were nocturnal animals, but this one was definitely up and about in the morning, with its ugly, naked tail stretched out straight behind. The creature looked her over, like a talent scout from some other universe, then turned heavily and headed away as if she hadn't quite measured up.

"I'll do better later in life," Maeve promised.

"What time is it?" Jack Liffey asked as a man finally led him back to the downstairs cell. He must have slept the whole night on his back on the floor beside the hideous water tank. His back and neck were rigid with ache.

"Why do you care?" his guide asked. It was someone new, a callow-looking guy with a square-jawed handsome face and what appeared to be a permanent edge of annoyance.

Why *did* he care about the time? Here he had no control whatsoever about what was happening when.

"Time is important to me," he suggested, just to be saying something to someone new. "Without time, everything would happen at once."

"Huh?"

Another genius, Jack Liffey thought. "My birthday would bump into the Second Coming."

"Don't blaspheme, petunia."

"I thought we were just about to the End Time," Jack Liffey said earnestly.

The man's eyes lit up. "I can get you an Armageddon Survival Kit, Tee-Em—the real one, by Joe Mailander."

"What's that?"

He slapped a Gore-Tex packet on his belt. "There's my flint-lite firestarter, and my tinder-fast wax-impregnated cotton wicks, there's twenty-two inches of duct tape and some heavy foil that folds into a stove, and a rescue whistle. There's the Lexan signal mirror and a genuine space blanket, and a survival compass. There's almost a hundred items that will be of great need in the time of tribulations."

"No miniature Bible?" Jack Liffey tried to remember what was in the survival kit in the B-52 in *Dr. Strangelove*. "No condoms or silk stockings?" He remembered Slim Pickens observing that a man could have himself a pretty good time in Vegas with that stuff.

Jack Liffey stepped into the corner cell without urging. Sooner or later someone in this madhouse would have to figure out that he wasn't a threat to anything they valued.

Paula Green was waiting on a bench outside their motel room with the door open and her feet up on a planter, nursing some coffee, when Gloria finally made it up. Despite the menace she had felt, Fuqua and company had simply grilled her most of the night and let her go when they'd satisfied themselves that she didn't actually know where Jack was. She was merely an interloper in an armed compound, and her suspicions didn't count for much as long as they held all the cards.

Paula held up her cup and pointed toward the courtesy pot on the dresser inside.

"It's lousy but it'll wake you up."

After Gloria got her coffee, Paula told her how she'd talked to the gossipy beauticians in town, the sheriff's deputy, the volunteer watching over the firehouse, and several kids that she cornered and intimidated. There was no question that what the locals called the Lost Temple, ten miles south of town, had recently been taken over by some secretive organization. But the scuttlebutt stopped right there. The newcomers didn't shop in town, or even pass through much, having their own landing strip on the back forty for light planes and even STOL cargo planes.

"Thanks for coming out here with me," Gloria said.

"You look beat."

"I only got a couple hours. I don't know who was interrogating who most of the night. They know I'm Jack's girlfriend, but I guess that's not too hard to find out. I think he's there. They know I think he's there. But I can't prove anything and we're no closer to getting Jack out."

"What do we do about it? We can't take on those characters, girl."

"They've got Jack. I'm sure of it," Gloria obsessed

"Listen, you go lie down. I understand, but you're thrashed. I'll wake you at noon and we'll think again. There's a few more people around I can talk to."

Gloria sighed. "I'd better. Right now I wouldn't even be good backup. I can't believe I got inside and I never even got a fix on where they're holding him."

It was the same buzz-saw siren he'd heard days earlier, that braying that had sent most of the interrogators hurtling out of the room, but he'd never found out what it was about. Now he heard it from his cage in the basement. The sound got on his nerves, made him want to hit something to stop it. He plugged his ears with his fingers and that helped quite a lot when the explosion went off, deep and powerful and not too far away, a shock wave transmitted down to the basement hitting like a punch in his chest.

Now, a rattle of gunfire chased along the hallway at the top of his staircase, and from somewhere else came the repeating thud of a much larger automaticweapon. There was a pause and then the sounds of a whole lot of firepower, as if a platoon had just arrived on the scene. Some of it seemed to come from pistols. Overhead there were running footsteps, and something heavy being dragged along a floor. He had no idea what was happening, but he was not unhappy about it. These people had done him no favors and Jack Liffey could contemplate a little payback himself. The milder pops of pistols sounded for a while and then the chatter of what he guessed were little spray guns, Uzis, or MAC-10s. There was a war going on above him, but he couldn't imagine it lasting much longer. Suddenly, the firing came very close to his dungeon, abruptly becoming personal as a whole magazine tore up the old door at the top of the basement staircase. The door was kicked open, and a man with a red-and-black bandanna over his face hurried down the steps toward him. He came to a stop facing Jack Liffey through the bars.

"Who are you?" He seemed Asian and rather young. He was obviously very jumpy, with an overflow of adrenaline, and his eyes had a bewildered look.

Jack Liffey took a chance. "I'm a prisoner of these assholes. I'm not here by choice."

The young man's teeth chattered, maybe just a nervous mannerism. He dug what looked like a big candy bar out of the cargo pocket of his fatigues, stripped off some olive cellophane and then tore it in half and pressed a ball of putty against the lock mechanism of the cage. Then he inserted what looked like an ampule of some drug into it.

"Get behind your mattress."

"There is no mattress. I'll do my best." Jack Liffey crouched in the corner of the cell, facing away and using the thin pad off the cot to cover the back of his head. A single gunshot startled him, followed almost instantly by a dull explosion like a Fourth of July cherry bomb. When he glanced around, the door stood a few inches open, the lock smoking away like burned toast.

"Put this on." He tossed Jack Liffey his thick flak vest.

Noble gesture, Jack Liffey thought. He slipped on the bulky vest and followed his liberator up the steps.

As they reached the top, there was a woman's shriek outside and the young man fell back into a crouch.

"Wait."

The young man gathered himself and burst out the doorway to fire off a full magazine.

"Can it!" somebody called. "Cease fire! Jesus Christ!"

The young man looked back in the door at Jack Liffey, as if he owed him an explanation. "They say that's called recon by fire."

"I think I get it. Are you folks liberating this place?"

"You could say that. These macho types get so pissed when they're caught with their pants down. They always want to go back and do it again, as if you could reset some big video game." He beckoned Jack Liffey out, wiping his forehead with the crook of his arm.

"Did they torture you, man? We've got friends here they did."

"A little."

"And do you still believe in the innate goodness of man?"

Jack Liffey was so startled by the question, he blinked. "Not particularly."

"I kind of do. Makes me wonder how torturers come about. Maybe something in their childhood, you know? I guess I get to ask them, don't I? What did they do to you?"

"Water tank." It was all Jack Liffey could get out.

"Come on."

In the hallway it smelled of gunpowder and plaster dust. There were a few bullet holes, but not much else to see. It would be good to get out of here, to wherever, which reminded him he had no idea at all where he was.

"Where are we?" Jack Liffey asked.

"I don't know if the place has a name. You're about thirty miles east of the Salton Sea."

"In California?" He was thunderstruck. After two flights—presumably now only decoys—he'd been certain he was at least in Central America, at some old military base where they could get away with anything. But he was only a two-hour drive from home.

The hallway spilled into a round loggia that appeared to be the formal entrance to the building. He remembered it vaguely, with niches around for missing busts. Several freshly gaping holes in the marble-painted plaster showed ragged lath and chickenwire beneath.

A half dozen young Asians in bandannas stood guard over the people he recognized as his interrogators and captors—even Ski Mask, who was much less sinister with the mask off, just some pouting hardbody type. The captives all knelt facing the wall with their arms secured behind them by the kind of nylon wire-ties that the cops liked to use at demonstration when they ran out of handcuffs. One of his interrogators from what he'd thought of as a previous location was there, too, and the woman minus her high heels. One older man was bleeding from his arm, but it didn't appear serious. The sight of his captors subdued and bound lifted Jack Liffey's spirits immeasurably.

Then he recognized the Water Man in the middle. "Can I kick the shit out of one of them?" Jack Liffey asked.

"Not right now," a young woman replied. "Give us a chance to secure the building."

Secure the building, he thought. It didn't sound like the little guerrilla band was planning to run off after their raid. He hoped they weren't drawing him into some doomed John Brown scenario where they'd dig in and call down the wrath of the entire U.S. government.

Then he noticed bright-red hair across the room that could only be Peter Kim, videotaping. The camera panned around and stopped on him for a moment, staring back. The anarchist bandanna couldn't hide his identity. Jack Liffey walked closer. "Dude, I thought you were strictly post-modern."

"Who said, 'There are lies and there are damn lies?'" Peter Kim asked him.

"Lies, damn lies, and *statistics*," he corrected.

"But who was it?" Peter Kim insisted.

"Twain, I think, but he attributed it to Disraeli. So you've been political all along."

He shrugged. "Got to watch over my kid sister."

And for the first time Jack Liffey realized that the one woman he'd noticed amongst the guerrillas, the one in fatigues who'd talking about securing the building, was probably Soon-Lin Kim. He almost laughed.

"You might have told your dad she was okay," Jack Liffey complained.

"She wanted to disappear."

Just then two more masked figures carried into the rotunda a cot forming a makeshift stretcher, with a beat-up-looking young Asian on it who was wearing nothing but his underwear. They set him down, and Soon-Lin knelt beside the stretcher and talked softly with its occupant as the bearers headed off to some new purpose.

One of the handcuffed men now began to curse loudly, and the tallest of the guerrillas took a step toward him and clipped him hard with the butt of his rifle so that his victim cried out once and toppled to his side on the concrete floor.

"Listen up," the tall guerrilla said. "This goes for everybody! We've disabled the alarms, so if you start to hear loud noises and parts of the building fall down around you, assume we are receiving incoming fire and take what cover you can! We've got a fifty on the roof, so there won't be any cars coming down the road for a while, but even this miserable county's got to have a phone to call for help."

"Why don't you take your friends and go?" one of the captives said, just as a second stretcher was delivered from somewhere, carrying a girl who was moaning softly.

"We want to find out who gave you gentlemen the idea that it was ever okay to torture American citizens."

"First thing," another of the Front members announced. "We got to get us a sound system and fill this place with rock 'n' roll."

The young woman stood up at the stretcher and looked around, seeming to notice Jack Liffey clearly for the first time. She walked straight across to him.

"What's your story? It had better be good."

"If that's Soon-Lin under the bandanna," he said softly, "your dad hired me to find you."

"Man, are you in the wrong movie."

"I've been aware of that for some time."

She gestured to her tall comrade to come over. "Tie this one up with the others."

"Hey!" Jack Liffey protested.

As if to emphasize his protest, the .50-caliber machine gun on the roof opened up with its dull thudding. Out the windows of the rotunda he caught a glimpse of a police car in the distance, backing hastily and jolting as it took hits.

Seventeen

La Doucette

She stood in the drugstore aisle for a long time as canned music played overhead, working up her nerve. Then she grabbed the little carton as if someone might swoop down and tell her to put it back. She plucked another carton off a peg at random to cover it up as she carried it tight to her belly, and then she felt herself flush as she noticed that what she'd chosen for cover was a gaudy purple packet of condoms, "with ribs and extra-supple French ticklers for *her* ecstasy." She tucked the box on a shelf behind some antacid bottles and headed for the checkout before she could trip over a display or run headlong into an old lady to draw every eye in the place to her.

She bracketed her intended purchase on the conveyor belt with candy bars and kept her eyes gazing off casually into the distance. But the clerk rang it all up without fuss, without joking or hitting on her, and she hurried out to her car. She drove back to Beto's and walked quietly past Señora Jutiapa's, the Indio lady who was supposedly a little loco. Her key still worked and the apartment still smelled a little of her burned *molé poblano.* Next to the sofa there was a new stack of half a dozen identical off-brand DVD players still in their boxes. She wondered if they were stolen, and, if so, why they weren't in the locked room. Maybe Beto just hadn't expected her back.

She went straight for the tiny bathroom and opened her purchase. She laid out the little wand and read the instructions twice, about human chorionic gonadotropin and how soon it showed in the urine, her hand trembling a little. She'd never been very good at peeing into a cup, and she was happy that she was only being asked to hit a Q-tip, which she did without trouble. There was a depression on the little blue wand to which she applied the Q-tip. Then she washed her hands extra carefully and walked away. She was supposed to wait five minutes.

This is going to be the longest five minutes of my life, she thought. At least my life, so far.

In the kitchen she saw that the dishes hadn't been done for a while, so she ran the hot water and stoppered the sink. While she waited, she looked out over the backyard. Beyond the fence a short woman was hanging out laundry from a plastic tub, shaking each item and pinning it up with pastel clothespins. A chubby baby sat placidly in a car seat in her shadow and an older boy ran tirelessly in circles.

What confusion she felt: the sight of the children gave her both a sense of dread and of melting human affection. She did not see how those emotions could coexist, but they did. She felt her eyes start to prickle with tears as she watched the running boy throw his arms about wildly, and she turned away to stop the hot water overflowing just in time. She dumped in the dishes and squirted some dish soap and was afraid to look at her watch.

She collected KFC containers from the counter, and a big pizza box, plus some hardening corn husk wrappers from tamales, and crushed them down into a supermarket bag in the open space under the sink where doors should have been. There were only screw holes where the hinges had been. She was still delaying.

She went into the bedroom and saw that her books were all there, and the two cardboard boxes of her underwear and T-shirts and stuff. A few skirts and blouses hung in the tiny doorless closet. She wasn't sure whether she felt at home or not, it had all happened so fast and then she'd gone to her mother's which was different than she'd expected. She'd also called Gloria to touch base, but there'd been no answer and she hadn't left a message. She'd stopped by then to feed a very hungry Loco and snuggle him awhile.

Five minutes, she thought. It had to be time. She felt a tickle in her belly, but she had had a colostomy so recently that it could have been anything—an adhesion, but more likely her active imagination.

"*Lo que necesito ahora mismo es una pica de la cuca,*" she said softly, practicing. What I need right now is a joint.

She paced slowly back toward the bathroom, waited a moment at the door, then pushed it open with a self-dramatizing shove.

"Okay, pharmacy gods, show me." She went in, not believing for an instant that it would be positive, and there they were: the two blue stripes on the tiny apparatus. Her backbone seemed to shrivel up to half its size. She felt a sharp pinch in her side, as if a full-term baby had bitten her from inside. More imagination, but it was in there all right, growing. And she was a woman, having skipped over all the stages that she had looked forward to. Who would go to Lamaze with her? Who would hold her hand in the hospital? She closed her eyes and pressed the big hoop earrings against her cheeks as if it was all their fault. She wanted to talk to her dad.

. . .

Paula Green screeched and hit the floor of the sheriff's car behind the seats. Gloria felt another impact, rocking the car like a pothole, as a hole the size of a grapefruit opened in the beige hood. Deputy Fausto Ndoyet was cranked around in his seat as he backed like a madman toward the wide-open gate in the hurricane fence, his spinning wheels sending gravel and dust all around them. She could see flashes from the distant roof of the weird classical building and more shots hitting the graveled road behind them and presumably other rounds burying themselves among the scrub to the sides. Having already delayed far too long, she sighed and ducked down under the dash.

"Ay, mierditas!" their escort from the tiny burg of Niland exclaimed.

Earlier Ndoyet had explained to them that Imperial County had a few outflung sheriff substations but none nearby. For a lot of its vast almost unpopulated area, the county relied on what were called "resident deputies"—men like him who had been issued worn-out patrol cars and some other equipment and now had all the authority they could handle to police a few hundred square miles from their own living rooms.

From where she crouched fetally, crammed impossibly under the dash, Gloria's eyes went up to the ragged oval hole in the roof—that first impact that had torn off the driver's headrest and gone on through the back seat only a foot from Paula. Ndoyet still bled a little from his cheek where he'd been grazed by something. Gloria was down behind as much metal as she could manage, but figured only the engine block itself would do much good. Whatever it was, it was a hell of a weapon.

"Dios mio!"

He didn't stop until the big Chevy was fifty yards outside the gate, then he piled out unceremoniously and ran in a crouch to shelter behind a big sandstone outcrop. The firing seemed to have stopped. In the car the women could hear each other breathing heavily.

"You okay?" Gloria asked.

"Jesus Christ! What did you do to piss them off?"

"Something's up. The gate should have been shut, and there should have been somebody at that guardhouse."

"Our friend over there was sure a lot of help." They'd driven to his house in Niland after Gloria woke from her exhausted sleep. They'd explained Gloria's ordeal and showed their badges and asked for his help. Deputy Fausto Ndoyet had had some experience of urban police work from half a dozen years of patrols in the county area near LAX, and he'd been curious himself about ISOC for a year. This gave him an excuse to go out and look around. Now, when they finally joined him, he was sitting with his back to the rock and drinking from a flask that smelled suspiciously like tequila.

"I think you better call your headquarters," Gloria said. "Something is wrong in there. The gate shouldn't have been unguarded."

He nodded, but took no action, as if expecting the two women just to go away and leave him alone.

"You know what they're firing?" Paula Green asked.

He nodded again. "*La doucette*," he said vaguely. "The sweet one."

"Huh?"

"Some of the Vietnamese who'd been around when the French were there still called it that. *Douze-sept* really. That's twelve-point-seven, the metric for a .50-caliber machine gun. One time I saw a .50 chop down a big tree a mile away. Took only half an L.A. minute. The slug's bigger than your thumb."

"That's all very nice, but I think you've got to get us some help," Gloria said.

He sighed and peered over the big rock before duck-walking reluctantly for his car.

"What do you think's going on?" Paula asked.

"I don't have a clue, but if Imperial County can't do anything about it, we know some people who can. *There*," noticing something all of a sudden. She was pointing at a makeshift visitors lot outside the wire fence where four nondescript old sedans, real junkers, were parked aslant as if abandoned in a hurry.

She and Gloria stood, and when there was no gunfire, they walked cautiously to the cars. They all had a similar run-down character, as if somebody in a hurry had bought up the cheapest row at a used-car lot.

They peered in the windows. "I've got a discarded Doritos bag," Paula said.

"I've got a military cap of some kind and an empty magazine from an automatic rifle."

"Okay." They stood there side by side.

Gloria rapped with her finger, pointing to a large screwdriver that had been left thrust into the ignition switch.

"Oklahoma car key," she said. She tried the door, and it was unlocked. After a search that didn't yield much, she yanked the big screwdriver out of the ignition and then used it to pry at the trunk.

Deputy Ndoyet finished his radio call and came over with a real pry bar to help.

"We only got a little SWAT unit down at El Centro but they'll be here in forty minutes or so." There was a metallic squawk of complaint from the latch, but it only took him one jump on the big pry bar to open the trunk. They all stood there like naughty schoolchildren staring down at half a dozen rocket-propelled grenades, as seen in news footage of insurgents all over the globe.

"Son-a-bitch," the deputy said.

Gloria took out the 9mm Glock she carried in the small of her back and put a noisy round into one front tire of each vehicle. "Be a good idea if everybody sticks around."

A hotel dining room has been transformed into a committee meeting room, with a bank of tables occupied by men and women in business suits, plus half a dozen cameras. An audience fills maybe fifty of the folding chairs.

The camera pans slowly to KUM HAK-SOO, sitting at the witness table.

> KUM HAK-SOO
> No, sir, I have no trouble at all remembering so long ago. Not one bit. The name of the company that came to my village was Daeshin. They had a big Japanese military truck with the name on the door. The Korean language had been banned, so the name was written in Japanese, in kanji and katakana. I was forced to learn Japanese in school so I had no trouble reading it. The words on the truck would translate as Daeshin Recruitment of Factory Personnel. Or Factory Workers. Of course, they were not recruiting factory workers, but that is what they told us.

> MALE VOICE, off
> Were the men who came in the truck Japanese or Korean?

KUM HAK-SOO

Korean. They spoke very bad Japanese. Pid-
gin Japanese, with bad grammar and a
strong Korean accent. I don't think they were
very smart men. My stepparents sold me to
those men for a handful of Japanese bank-
notes. I never found out how much they got.
(smiles bravely)
Not many people get to find out their value.

Ironically, Jack Liffey now found himself handcuffed and
kneeling next to the man he'd known only as Ski Mask. He recognized the set of his lips and the smoky blue of his eyes when
they glanced guardedly at one another. The hammering of the
machine gun from the roof seemed to be over for the moment.
Without the mask the man was an ordinary-looking Irish type,
freckly and ruddy-faced, well buffed up by exercise. The Irish
had been mercenaries for centuries, Jack Liffey thought.

The older guerrillas in the red and black handkerchiefs were
conferring across the loggia while a younger one stood guard
over the prisoners and another watched at the windows.

"What's wrong with you guys?" Jack Liffey said. "Your pal
over there held my head under water, but you know that. Just for
his kicks, as far as I could tell."

The man glanced over. "Sounds like Anacleto. He's not a bad
guy if you overlook his peculiarities."

"Shut up, you two!" one of the guerrillas behind them snapped.

He figured they probably weren't going to shoot so he went
right on talking.

"What's your name?" Jack Liffey asked. "You know mine."

"Michael."

"I said shut up! I'm on full automatic!" The young man was getting nervous and stomped closer to them.

"Just calm down," Michael said pointedly. "We're not interfering with your self-respect. You're the boss."

"Do you have any idea why you guys were questioning me?" Jack Liffey asked. "Honestly, I'm not anybody you'd be interested in. I just look for missing children."

Michael glanced at him. "We have clients. I assume they have reasons."

"They didn't tell you their reasons?"

"Nah. I just heard you were a TA."

"What's that?"

"Terrorist associate."

Jack Liffey couldn't help laughing a little. "Like *junior* terrorist?" Then a kind of anger flashed through him. "I'm someone who looks for missing children. That's it. Where does this hysteria stop?"

Michael shrugged.

"Who was the client that wanted to know about me?" Jack Liffey asked.

"Listen up!" Soon-Lin commanded as the conference of the general command broke up. "We had hoped to have our comrades identify the torturers among you, and then we could book out of here before anyone noticed. But we find our comrades are in no condition to travel. Would the torturers like to speak up now and spare their friends the ordeal?"

They all waited a few moments.

"I thought not. We appear to have been discovered by the police in any case. For the moment, all of you are our guests and our insurance."

Jack Liffey yelped as Soon-Lin grabbed his hair without warning and yanked his head back. "You mustn't count on our kindly natures. We are quite pitiless. I am as brutal as the weather. We've already had to shoot one of your sentries when he drew down on us, so one more killing means nothing." He saw her clearly, but upside down and it was disorienting. Her face kept disassembling and trying to go back together right.

"Let go," he said. "I don't work for ISOC."

"We know that. Shut up."

Jack Liffey could just see Peter Kim's red hair, upside-down too, as he hovered nearby to record. "Your sister's not as nice as you are," Jack Liffey said.

At this, she gave him a full yank that pulled him over onto his back, but he managed to cushion his fall with one shoulder. The unswept dust on the cement floor whiffed up and irritated his nose.

"You will all now lie on your backs. Your knees must be hurting." After the briefest pause: "That was not a suggestion."

The line of men began wriggling around to position themselves on their backs, a surprisingly difficult operation with your wrists manacled.

There was another short conference, after which several of the guerrillas hurried away.

Before Soon-Lin could make another announcement, there was a dull concussion outside that he could feel come up through the floor into his back, and a fireball boiled up in the courtyard, an astonishing billow of red flame visible through several of the windows. The blast appeared to be well away from the building. The one Front member he could see was not happy about this at all. He was facing the window, pointing angrily, when the window blew in and he screamed as he was thrown backward. Immediately, the heavy machine gun on the roof began to fire again, and the men on their backs did their best to wriggle into the sheltered wall spaces between the windows.

The young man who had been hit by flying glass shrieked behind them, a single noise like something escaping a haunted house in an amusement park.

"You two are like herding squirrels," the deputy said grumpily.

Gloria actually gave a half grin where the three of them cowered behind the rock outcrop, while .50-caliber slugs tore off fist-sized chunks of exfoliating stone. It had been her bright idea to try out the RPGs on the machine gun setup on the roof of the facility. The sighting mechanism had been fairly straightforward, the safety over the trigger primitive and obvious. Unfortunately, the weapon was wildly inaccurate at that range. There had been remarkably little recoil, then a second *whoosh* as something ignited late, and she had watched helplessly as her projectile arced down into the dirt courtyard, leaving a rather obvious blue-gray smoke trail straight back to her.

Ndoyet sat with his arms folded. "I could have told you. My old gunnery sergeant said if they had invented howitzers first, they would never have bothered inventing rockets."

"I don't like people shooting at me," Gloria said. "It upsets me."

Paula Green had followed her lead and fired the second RPG, the one that actually hit the building. She seemed to feel she had acted in haste and now looked a bit regretful. "You know, we don't really know what the situation is. We should wait for backup."

In a lull, as the big rock stopped tearing itself asunder, Gloria peeked around the outcrop at the building in the distance. The flame on the outer wall was already dying down, and her own burst in the yard was just a smolder off a shallow hole. "Just so they don't rush us in the meantime."

"El Centro's got a chopper," Ndoyet said. "That'll be here quick."

"But it's not armed, is it? I bet it's just got a great big search-light, like most police choppers."

"If it comes to that, Miramar's got F-18s and some Marine Harriers, though I think they got to get some special okay. But the SWAT guys got strong stuff, don't you worry."

The firefight seemed to be over for now, and she tried to imagine the place overrun with shot-out police cars and SWAT officers crouching behind their disintegrating vans. If they'd left RPGs in the car, they must have others inside.

"Maybe we ought to go back down the road apiece and warn the next wave what they're facing," Gloria suggested.

Kathy sat heavily on the end of Maeve's bed as soon as she realized that her daughter had absconded once again. The closet was open and more of her casual clothing was gone. She thought they'd made contact the night before, the best talk they'd had in years. For the first time in a long time, she really missed Jack.

But where was he now?—now that she and Maeve needed him, really needed him. Kathy couldn't bring herself to go back to that Mexican cop for help. She was still embarrassed at how she had come on to him, good old half-unbuttoned blouse and all—and a little astonished that it had worked so easily. The cop—what was his name? Doug? Duane? *Dean*—had driven them home and angled hard for an invitation, and she was a little worried that he might still show up some evening, half-lit for courage, demanding his due.

Suddenly, she remembered that Maeve, who seemed to like Gloria well enough, had told her that the woman was an Indian, not Mexican at all. She wondered if that was what turned Jack on about her. He'd always had a soft spot for the exotic. She remembered a time when she had wanted Jack quite a lot, and then, a time when she didn't anymore. But now she needed him and so did Maeve.

Help me, she thought in a small lonely voice, but she had no idea who she was addressing.

Eighteen

A Constant Annoyance

"This is déjà vu all over again," Jack Liffey suggested. But nobody facing him at the table seemed to get the lame joke. "I mean, I was interrogated here by the other guys—aren't they your enemies? If you're going to do the same, it's ridiculous."

No one mentioned the sheriff's cars that had arrived some time ago, or the bullhorn that was squawking unintelligibly from the front gate because none of the guerrillas would pick up the phone. They even finally yanked all the cords out. He had no idea what lay behind their doomed fatalism, but it was as if none of the police out there even existed.

The bandanas were off now, and he could see that the New World Liberation Front weren't all Asians, though most were. He thought one young man was East Indian. One, a hard-eyed, distracted-looking man in full fatigues, was probably Latino, and another, an older man, was definitely an Anglo. For the moment, leadership seemed to rest with a goateed man who sat in the middle.

Peter Kim was still drifting around with his video camera, as if picking up clips for the news at eleven.

"We believe you may know things that you do not realize you know," Soon-Lin said to Jack Liffey. "Are you willing to help us try to unearth these things?"

"Can I be frank?"

"It would break my heart if you weren't," Goatee said.

"I'm not sure I want to help terrorists who are about to be arrested or killed."

That annoyed them all and Goatee almost came out of his chair. "We're not terrorists, I assure you! We came here to rescue two of our comrades who were being tortured. ISOC are the terrorists. We're members of a people's army and, at the current stage of the movement, we go to great lengths to avoid violence."

Something in the way he spoke suggested a graduate student. "I'm a rescuer, too," Jack Liffey said. "It's what I do, but I don't feel I have to run around with an M-16."

"Armed self-defense," the man countered. "Had the blacks had automatic weapons in Mississippi, the civil rights movement would have been over in half an hour."

"Or it would have been a terrible blood bath. I admire civil disobedience."

Goatee waved his hand dismissively. "A tactic, not a theory. It wouldn't have worked against Nazis."

He almost liked him. His finicky philosophical bent, and even something about his earnestness, reminded Jack Liffey of one of his tech crew he'd argued endlessly with in the radar trailers in Thailand so long ago. All of them had hated the war, that went without saying, but they'd argued night after night over the nuances of their intellectual mutiny—was Vietnam an unavoidable product of American imperialism or just some bizarre aberration? Was it driven by economics or global designs or just wounded prestige? Some of them had painted peace signs on their monitors and helmets. Others read history books and brooded about confronting any war supporters they could find. One insistent private wrote letters to every single senator and congressman plus the Johnson cabinet.

But there was this one, most memorable of all, a short sullen Texan named Moore who had been drafted straight out of Peace Corps training at the University of Michigan—who they suspected of much more than notional resistance, in fact, of the Military Act that Dared Not Speak Its Name. He'd come from a broken home, an abusive Army lifer dad who'd beat his mother nearly every night. Arlen Moore had arrived as an intense and distant specimen who read exotic books of literary criticism every spare moment but who gradually had drifted further off the planet to where he exuded a kind of glazed-eyed lunacy that no one wanted to confront. They all suspected he was simply ignoring the blips he detected going down into the jungle, signing off his radio on plaintive American cries for help and letting the pilots die or be captured.

It had been a time in Jack Liffey's young life when ideas mattered a great deal—as they obviously did still for Goatee. It was a connection he could appreciate without having to share the man's views. He knew those late-night discussions in Thailand had probably stayed with him in some inner echo chamber to play their part in his nine year odyssey of tracking down missing children.

"Be quiet, Richie," Soon-Lin ordered. Now Jack Liffey knew another name. "You say my father hired you to find me. Is that true?"

He wondered how far to cooperate, but he had already told her this much. "Yes. I liked him."

"Who else knows that you're looking for me?"

"Your brother."

She gave a half smile, and glanced at him where he crouched with the little digital camera. "Obviously."

The Anglo leaned forward abruptly. "Did you visit International House, Mr. Liffey?"

"I saw Soon-Lin in a photograph of a demonstration there, Mr. . . ."

"Never mind my name. Did you visit the place?"

"Yes."

"And representatives of Daeshin saw you there?"

"I spoke to somebody running the place."

The Anglo and Soon-Lin exchanged a significant look. This is their mentor, Jack Liffey suddenly realized, like the grain of dust that a raindrop supposedly coalesces around.

"Folks," Jack Liffey said. "I hate to remind you, but this place will be swarming with cops anytime now. The quicker you go out the back door, the better chance you've got."

They seemed not to want to acknowledge the unnamed inertia that had kept them there far too long. Bullhorns had been booming unintelligibly for half an hour. A lone helicopter had circled cautiously for a while, obviously wary of their weaponry, and then left.

It reminded him of what he'd read of John Brown's raid on Harpers Ferry, the small army of abolitionists who had taken the firehouse and then just settled in, clueless, as the Virginia militia gathered around them. No one had ever figured out why Brown's men hadn't fled to the hills—but he thought he could see it, an almost universal longing among people who had made such a fierce commitment to their ideas. To stay put against all odds, to make a stand and hope the world would come to its senses and see the justice of what they were doing.

"Really, it's over," Jack Liffey said.

"Shut the fuck up," Richie said, but he looked concerned. He looked straight at the older man. "Al?"

Now Jack Liffey knew yet another name.

The Anglo shrugged. "There's a whole motor pool of Humvees out back. We'll leave through the desert after dark. There's a lot of nothing out that way."

"Luckily, your opponents don't have airplanes, helicopters, or night-vision devices," Jack Liffey said.

"Enough from you." Soon-Lin pointed at him angrily. He made a gesture of surrender. "Put him with the others," she snapped. "Objectively, he's been nothing more than a spy for Daeshin."

"That's not fair."

"Listen to me," she said. "You're responsible for your role in the world, whether it's what you intended or not. Your actions led Daeshin to us."

"How?"

"No one knew our names in the Front, not Daeshin, not the police. They knew Asians United, not the Front. Any hint you gave them about *me*, you set my name vibrating in their ears and they linked and linked again. That's how our comrades were snatched for questioning."

He felt a terrible chill, wondering if he really had doomed them by hunting them. Somehow he doubted it. It was just their convenient rationalization for having enemies who had all the advantages. "You folks chose to trap yourselves here."

"We never leave anyone for the buzzards," Richie the Goatee said.

Kum Hak-Soo sits beside her friend Peggy in the International House visiting room. Several other residents sit on the sofa, while on other chairs are a few younger people in ski masks. The camera is obviously hand-held.

> MASKED GIRL
>
> Ladies and gentlemen, are you aware of who is behind Westlake Luxury Hotel Partners?

> KUM HAK-SOO
>
> No. All we know is men came and gave us eviction notices.

Another woman shakes her head.

> OLD ASIAN MAN
>
> They said they had new places, new apartments, waiting for us. They mean single-room occupancies. It'll be missions and shabby old hotels with hotplates and cockroaches.

> MASKED FEMALE FIGURE
>
> There's something worse, for some of you. There's a local partner, a big L.A. developer, but the other partner, the real money in this deal, is a Korean zaibatsu. Or, more properly, a chaebol. Some of you know this conglomerate already—Daeshin Industries.

Kum Hak-Soo is impassive. She reaches for Peggy's hand.

> KUM HAK-SOO
> (almost without emotion)
> Then we will die in this building.

She sat out in Greenwood Park on an empty bench away from the little groups of women, trying not to feel conspicuous. It was afternoon, the time of the *señoras*, the *mamacitas*, with their babies in walkers and carriages or just in blankets in their arms. They leaned over to peek at one another's babies and offer compliments in low happy voices. It was the baby that gained you unquestioned entry among the *mamacitas*—everybody equal before the stork—even the big *rubio* white girl with all the tattoos or the obese young girl rocking her double stroller. Here and throughout the barrio, having a baby made a girl somebody. The men treated you better, got softer—she'd seen it.

Me, too, Maeve wanted to shout. I've got one inside, a little Latino-Irish fetus—though right now it's only a few hundred blastocysts. You all just wait. Maybe it'll be a boy and look like Anthony Quinn—she remembered that he was Mexican-Irish. It's Beto's. You know, from the Greenwoods. He's my man. The thoughts seemed to make her dizzy.

An older woman carried her small blue bundle across the pathway and knelt on her heels in front of Maeve, perfectly balanced and comfortable, to put her cool palm on Maeve's forehead. "Honey, you got the morning sick?"

She was astonished. "I just found out."

The woman smiled and leaned closer, exuding a reek of spices and something else that might have been baby vomit. "*Felicitaciones. Tienes una alma nueva en la cuerpo.*" You have a new soul in your body. She tipped her own bundle slightly until a small round brown face appeared in the cowl of blanket, devouring Maeve with its black eyes and moving its small perfect mouth as if trying to form a greeting.

All words left her, and she had to struggle for the simplest Spanish. "*Muy hermoso.*" She hoped it was male.

The woman's smile broadened. "*Tu novio, imágino que es un*

amante tremendo y que sabe como chichar como loco. Alcáncelo fuerte."

Maeve sat woozily, doing her best to work it through. My man, my intended—that's Beto—I should imagine that he's a tremendous lover . . . and he knows how to *something* like crazy. Hold on to him tight.

Suddenly she pressed a hand to her mouth to suppress an urge to throw up. She needed fresh air, but, slowly, as she watched the older woman's kindly face, the urge passed. Amazing how it changed your whole perspective on staying alive, that sensation of nausea. For a moment there she'd actually flashed on dying. The woman hadn't budged an inch, and her presence seemed to be encroaching on space that Maeve needed to breathe, to think, but words started to come back on their own.

"*Estoy embrujada,*" Maeve said sorrowfully. I'm bewitched. "*Pienso en nada más que hacer el amor con él. El padre de mi bebé.*" I think of nothing but making love with him. And she felt so alone and lost, so needy for Beto, that she began to weep uncontrollably.

Jack Liffey and his new friend Michael ended up together in his old basement cell, with a second thin mattress pad thrown in. Michael had gotten there first and appropriated the one cot.

"If you want the bed back, pal, you can fight me for it."

"That's not very neighborly." Jack Liffey bunched up his rubber pad and sat.

"Tough shit."

"How did you end up among the mercenaries?"

He shrugged. "We call ourselves contractors," he said, but with an edge of self-mockery.

"I'm serious."

"Jesus, man, how does anybody end up anything? You go from

job to job and then the music stops and that's where you are. I can't stand working under a roof. I did a tour in Afghanistan for a hundred grand for nine months, and I loved it. Every day, I had life and death in my hands."

"That must charge you up."

Michael sat up on the cot and lit a cigarette. The smoke smelled French to Jack Liffey. It had been a long time since he'd smelled a French cigarette, but odors really burrowed in deep. Gauloises or Gitanes.

There was a rattling noise overhead as if heavy equipment were being dragged along a hallway. They both listened for a while until it died away.

"I spend about nine months a year running on adrenaline in some flyblown troubletown, mostly protecting some fat stupid foreigner in a suit. Then I did R&R for a while."

"Does it give you satisfaction?" Jack Liffey asked.

Michael glared at him. "No. It's a fucking total annoyance."

"Maybe you need to change jobs."

"Maybe I need to become Mother fucking Theresa. What have you got, Jack?"

"Right now, I think we'd better come up with a plan for getting us out of here. This is all going to go to shit."

"You got the stones to try it on?"

"I don't see anybody else here."

They'd parked a couple of big fire department pumpers full of water against the fence. Somebody had figured even a .50-caliber round wouldn't penetrate that much water. Behind the fire trucks there were now canopies against the fierce afternoon sun, a SWAT truck from El Centro, several police cars, and even a mobile command center, just a big RV really. Gloria and Paula sat on folding chairs a little apart from most of the other law, like moms at a kids picnic. The SWAT guys in their flak jackets were too hyped up to sit and they conferred self-importantly at one side, their assault rifles and stubby machine pistols all at port arms. Reportedly San Diego City was trucking out its armored personnel carrier with the big ram welded on the front, its drug-house buster.

A Chevy Suburban full of suits had shown up a half hour back, and the darkest suit seemed to be in charge now, though he was in no evident hurry to do anything. Every few minutes, a deputy tried futilely to telephone all the numbers he had on a list and then called out, "No answer," and waited to start over. The bullhorn had grown too irritating for everyone concerned, and they had stopped barking through it. Gloria guessed it was about five hours to true darkness, when things would probably happen.

"All we need is a campfire and marshmallows," Paula said. "I was a Scout, you know? We used to guess what our lives would be like as grown-ups, when we were twelve and out camping."

Gloria smiled. "Me, too. I used to do that."

But for all her outwardly calm manner, Paula's eyes now betrayed anxiety, glancing around regularly at the hubbub.

"You worried about something?" Gloria asked.

Paula smiled. "They ever drag you into one of those big mobilizations for a presidential visit?"

Gloria shook her head. "I must be lucky."

"I was put to guard a building in Century City once, in a whole row of L.A. uniforms. The motorcade of big Lincolns rolled up Avenue of the Stars and screeched to a halt right about where I was, and far too many guys with mirror shades and buzzcuts jumped out with one hand on the little Uzis on slings under their coats. They did everything snappy, jumping out, looking around. *Alert*, you know, but not quite *rational*. If I'd'a shouted, I didn't

vote for that prick!—I woulda been shot about a hundred times."
She made a gesture that meant, Look around. "It's a little like
that now."

"They're pros."

"There's too many jurisdictions. I don't like it."

And, just then, a man with a silver flattop headed their way. He
signaled them to stay seated.

"Good afternoon, ladies. I'm with the Bureau. My name is
Special Agent Leonard Emerson. I'm told one of you has been
inside and knows the layout."

"That would be me," Gloria said. "Sergeant Gloria Ramirez,
LAPD." They shook hands. "I also think I have a close friend
being held in there."

"Are you certain?"

"No. I didn't see him."

"Could you come into the CP and try to sketch out the place
and tell us who and what you saw in there?"

She stood up, and Paula patted her butt gently. "You go, girl."

Nineteen

In the Playbook

It took her two trips to bring up all the shopping bags, and she wondered if it was the early stage of the pregnancy that was making her feel so winded at the climb. She realized that for a while now she'd be blaming just about everything on the coming baby—zits, weight gain, clumsiness, anxiety. . . . The special feast she was planning for Beto included a complicated recipe for *adobado*, a chile-marinated pork that she'd never seen listed on a menu but she *had* seen scrawled on the windows of tiny authentic-looking dives. And she had bought some big translucent cactus paddles to try to make *nopales*.

She tidied up first and put stuff away from the shopping bags and then used a spoon and cup to grind up some dry brown-red chiles so potent they set one eyelid alight when she touched it without thinking. She added cumin and oregano and garlic and salt and started the meat marinating. There wouldn't be enough time, really, but it ought to have some flavor.

Then she used a potato peeler on the *nopales* to get rid of the skin and the little nobs where the spines had been. She bit into a corner and decided it tasted like a cross between bell pepper and asparagus. The recipe said to steam them and serve with lemon juice as a side dish. Luckily, she had some tortillas, too. That seemed like enough variety. It was hard to make sure you got one item from each of the old "food groups" when you were cooking out in culinary left field. Maybe she should warm up some *frijoles*, too. You could never go wrong with *frijoles*.

As she worked, she noticed herself cupping her belly from time to time, as if cradling an infant underneath her skin. She'd have to see a doctor soon. She wanted to know if the scarring left by the missing section of her intestine would cause any difficulties. The path of the gunshot hadn't gone all that far from her uterus. She had a sudden chill, thinking how arbitrary life was, and how easily she could have been left barren—or dead. Then she thought of Beto and desperately wanted his arms around her, wanted to grasp his penis and feed him deep inside her. She'd barely had a chance to experience the joys of sex and here she was, water-over-the-dam, or something.

The tall glass-encased candle on the counter was something else she'd bought today. You saw them everywhere, with their colorful images of different saints printed on one side, and some account of their martyrdom on the other. She'd bought it at random for its pretty colors, but now she looked closer and noticed with surprise that the image looked like a Roman centurion: *St. Expedite.* A centurion, she thought—that ought to be really meaningful for East Los. She let the tip of her finger graze the embossed print on the glass and then squinted to read a bit of it: *Saint Expedite is the patron of those who hope for rapid solutions to problems, who wish to avoid or put an end to delays, and who want general financial success. His aid is also sought by those who wish to overcome procrastination as a personal bad habit, as well as by shopkeepers and sailors. His feast day is April 19.*

That was Beto, all right. She'd read that in Santería each of the

saints was a stand-in for one of the old pagan gods, a way the Indios and Africans and Afro-Cubans semihoodwinked their priests
in a substitution called syncretism. This must be a substitution
for the god of FedEx, she thought.

"Watch over my baby, FedEx," she said aloud. And she giggled.

She didn't have a steamer, so she put the *nopales* in an aluminum colander and balanced it over a big pot of water. It fit just
about right, making her proud of her ingenuity. She didn't have
a lid either, but a dinner plate would just do it. She was setting
the table when she heard a rumble in the drive that sounded a lot
like Beto's old 50s Lincoln, with the suicide doors in back, and
she perked up. She wondered how she'd tell him about the baby,
but she wasn't in any hurry. In truth, she was worried how he'd
take it.

There were no noises on the steps, and she decided she'd
heard wrong—there were lots of resounding mufflers on old
muscle cars over here in East Los—so she went into the bedroom and started to sort out the paperbacks she'd brought
home with her. It was hard to think of the beat-up apartment as
home, but she knew it would probably grow on her over time.
There was a Spanish dictionary, two Wallace Stegners, a Willa
Cather, and a Polish science-fiction novel that her friends had
insisted she try. These were just the beginning of the contents
of the carton she'd scooped hurriedly out of her bookcase in
Redondo . . . she was still looking at the books when she heard
footsteps along the walkway outside and the scratching of a key
that fought a bit with the door. Probably because it wasn't
locked.

She waited in the bedroom doorway, a book in her hand, as if
that were the natural way he would often find her, this intellectual girlfriend of his, and finally the door came open. It was Beto

all right, dark and handsome—but his right arm was draped possessively over Ruby's shoulder, and Ruby's blouse was half-unbuttoned, showing a lacy black bra, and her hair was already mussed. It was impossible to miss the bright purple lipstick smeared over Beto's face.

Maeve's heart plummeted to her toes and hit hard. She couldn't think of a single Spanish word and it made her feel stupid. Her skin prickled and her mouth went dry, and in the merest instant she realized that there was nothing that would be the same in her life again. This would tear it for her with Beto, no matter what came next—and he didn't even know about his child yet. Would she be able to tell him now?

"Baby Girl, what you doing here?"

"Coming home, I thought."

With a hint of embarrassment Ruby tugged away from him and set her arms on her hips. "Why don't you go back where you belong, little *chavala*?"

Maeve felt her eyes burning and tears starting to form. "I belong here, with Beto. You're a man-stealer."

"We'll see, bitch!" She advanced on Maeve, but Beto caught her arm. He spun Ruby half around and put his face a few inches from hers.

"*Cierre la boca* and go outside. Make no trouble, *ruca*."

Ruby took a good look at them—first one then the other—and then swaggered out the door and slammed it. Beto looked Maeve up and down, not unkindly, just checking her out like some girl in a bar.

"You a good kid, Baby Girl, but I can't be being with you no more. Didn't you see that *chingada oficial* Padilla, the way he wanted me *arestado*? He love to fuck over Mexicans, and he got a special thing for Greenwoods. He see you with me, I go to *la pinta* for statuary, for sure. Maybe you come see me next year when you old enough."

No words at all would come out of her. By next year, of course, she would be a mother. She fought the blockage stuck fast in her throat.

"I loved you, Beto," she said finally. She said it defiantly, and the past tense was like tearing something open inside her, something that let all her outraged feelings pour out.

She could see that he wouldn't say anything about love, not even a few words as a parting gift. "Baby Girl, you okay, but we can't be together. You go give it up for some nice gringo boy."

Abruptly there wasn't enough oxygen in the room. She dropped the book she was carrying and walked away from all the books and clothes in the bedroom, knowing she would never see any of them again, went through the kitchen and turned all the burners to high, and then walked past Beto and out the door. Horribly, Ruby was right there resting her back against the railing, not even buttoned up, smirking at her.

"I bet you gone and got caught," Ruby said with great satisfaction. "How is it being knocked, *esá*? Go on home to *blancolandia* and live your little half a life."

"Go stick your finger up Beto's ass," Maeve said as she walked past.

"Did you tell him I said that?" Ruby shrieked at Maeve's receding back.

Soon-Lin is carrying a largish microphone, with a placard that says 34 Korea News. She enters the door of a large modern building and holds it open so the camera can follow. It's a corporate lobby, with marble dominant. An African-American security guard sits impassively at a high walnut security desk.

SOON-LIN KIM

We are here to see Mr. Park Chun-Hee.

GUARD

Do you have an appointment?

SOON-LIN KIM

He will see us if you mention comfort
women. And the reparations commission.

GUARD

(watches them suspiciously)
I don't think so. Would you shut the camera
off, sir.

Soon-Lin ignores him and starts to walk past. The guard hits
some kind of panic switch that sets off an intermittent ringing tone nearby, at which point he picks up a card and reads:

GUARD

"I have activated a lockdown situation. The
elevators are disabled, the stairwells are
sealed, and more security personnel will arrive in a moment. You are being taped by
several security cameras. If you remain in
the building, you will be arrested for criminal
trespass and prosecuted to the full extent of
the law."

SOON-LIN KIM

That's crap . . . sir. It's not criminal trespass
if you do no damage.

GUARD

I don't know nothing about that, sister. All I
know is I got my job here.

She holds out a manila envelope toward the guard.

SOON-LIN KIM

Maybe you could see that Mr. Park Chun-Hee
gets that.

He won't touch it, so she sets it on the guard station.

GUARD

I done said all I got to say. You best go quick.

SOON-LIN KIM

This corporation has a lot to answer for. It
has done evil in the past and continues to do
evil today. You are oppressed, too—and you
should know it.

As a door down the hallway swings open, the clanging of the
security alarm redoubles, and half a dozen security guards
spill out into the lobby.

It was night now, and a SWAT squad, jogging, passed out of
sight. Maybe they were planning to assault the back of the compound, or maybe they just liked to jog around in the dark.

"Sergeant Ramirez, could you come back inside?" It was Special Agent Emerson.

She'd already been debriefed for about forty-five minutes,
until they thought they'd exhausted her store of information.

After this, she'd been pointedly dismissed. Clearly she was not meant to know what was going to happen next.

Inside the huge command RV there had been a lot of radio gear, racks of weapons, bunkers with more equipment, even something she guessed was an infrared monitor, a big screen that showed the buildings with a few reddish blobs moving behind the walls.

The layout sketches that she'd helped them draw were spread out on a big central table. Two other suits sat on stools, improbably playing rock-paper-scissors.

Emerson tapped his finger on the rear of the building on the drawing. She looked where he was pointing and just shook her head. "I don't know. Never saw the backside. Why don't you just take a big blowup with some satellite?"

"Right, why don't we just beam a squad inside from a spaceship?"

"You can do anything, can't you?"

"Actually, no. We're being quite cautious because we believe ISOC has some serious military weaponry in there, and the Front may know how to use it. I'd *like* an air strike, a couple of tanks, and immobilizing gas. But the Posse Comitatus Act of 1878 forbids the use of military equipment and federal troops against civilians."

"What happened at Waco, then? I distinctly remember tanks."

"Somebody seems to have made an exception, and a lot of people didn't like it very much, did they?"

"Worked real well, too," she said.

He shrugged. "I'm not after a war. We found the gate guard lying shot out in the chaparral, but he's going to make it. Nobody's been killed here, as far as I know. At Waco, the Branch Davidians killed four ATFs at the git-go and that meant nobody could back down. I want things to end peacefully, and I want to retire from the FBI in a few years with honor."

"Ah," she said.

"It's not such a bad motive, sergeant. Nobody wants a blood-bath. The NWLF won't answer the phone, but would you be willing to broadcast your voice inside to your friend? He's nei-ther ISOC nor Front. My boss in Yuma figures maybe your guy could mediate."

"I'm still not certain he's in there, but I'll try."

"Thank you, Sergeant Ramirez. Now could you wait outside again while I get the necessary permissions?"

Bureaucracy, she thought. You needed permission to try for a peaceful resolution, but you probably didn't need permission to fill a building full of people with flying lead. She wondered if it was the president himself giving the final permissions. After Waco and Ruby Ridge, they were probably going to be pretty skittish.

She went back outside and sat with Paula Green and Deputy Fausto Ndoyet under one of the canopies that were pointless now, except to deny them a good look at the stunningly star-filled sky. "They want me to shout through a megaphone at Jack, see if he can mediate. Sounds pretty desperate to me."

"It may be a cover for some SWAT move," Deputy Ndoyet said.

"I know that, but I've got no choice but to try."

They all sat glumly for a while.

"Hey, I've been meaning to ask," Gloria said. "What kind of name is Ndoyet?"

"It's both Maya *and* Zapotec. My family's from the village of San Juan near the ruins of Mitla. I was told we we're named after the god of death—so be very careful of me." He said it with such earnestness that she didn't know how to take it.

"Done."

"How do you two feel about all this?" Ndoyet now asked.

"What do you mean?"

"I don't like this standoff. Normally I'm the only officer for a hundred miles, and I've usually been able to fix things up. This smells to me like a lot of guys with their macho up. Maybe on both sides."

"That's police work," Gloria said.

"Not mine. I talk people down and send them home. It's mostly bar fights, around closing time. Even if they're hitting, they don't really want to hurt nobody."

In general, she agreed. Women officers were almost invariably better at de-escalating these bellowing standoffs—with both male parties working up little rages to do things they didn't really want to do. But there wasn't any other way she could intervene here.

She looked up to see Special Agent Leonard Emerson silhouetted by the faint light of the open trailer door.

"Sergeant Ramirez."

"Sir."

"We've written out what we want you to say on cue cards. You have to agree to read the cards word for word."

"Jack knows how I talk. It's not going to work like that."

"Never mind that. You just do it, and we'll take care of the rest."

She didn't trust him, but she had no other options. He led her to a folding table behind one of the fire department pumpers. She'd expected a handheld megaphone with POLICE lettered crudely on it, but what she got was a deskful of sophisticated electronics hooked up by a fat cord to what looked like a cable TV antenna on a tripod, stationed between the pumpers and pointed directly toward the compound.

"This is new," she said.

"State-of-the-art," Emerson said. "From inside there it'll sound like you're standing at the front door talking in a normal voice, without the usual booming and distortion." He looked around and spoke in a more private voice. "Sergeant, do you believe your love for this man is unconditional?"

"Pardon me?"

"How far are you willing to go for him?"

"Pretty far, all the way," she said, though she'd never said anything remotely like that to Jack directly.

"Here are the cards."

They were hand printed, double spaced, in all capitals on very white thick paper. The message began, DEAREST JACK, JACK LIFFEY, THIS IS GLORIA, YOUR GIRLFRIEND. There was no way on god's earth she was going to broadcast the word "girlfriend."

Michael began banging on the bars with an aluminum dinner plate, rattling it across several bars and then hammering relentlessly. Jack Liffey lay on the ground behind him, holding his gut and groaning miserably.

"Keep it up. You've almost got me convinced."

"I hope they can hear us."

"Me, too. Plan B is chewing through the bars with our teeth."

"Very funny."

"Keep moaning."

He could hear the upper door come open. "Knock off that racket!"

"This guy is violently sick. You food-poisoned him."

"Bullshit."

Jack Liffey tried to keep groaning, but he had to peek. The goateed Asian was clomping disgustedly down the steps. "Got no gun, got no keys," he announced, evincing a kind of world-weary disgust at people who would pull such ridiculous stunts. "If this is a trick, I'm useless to you."

"That's the plan, man," Michael said. "Lure you down here and throw up on you." Jack Liffey gave an especially over-wrought cry of pain and rolled onto his side, tucking his legs up like an appendicitis victim. Thespian lunacy, he thought. He'd never been very good at acting: it was too much like lying.

Their minder stood about ten feet back of the bars watching for a few moments. Richie, Jack Liffey remembered his name, and remembered he was probably the most formidable of them all—not counting the older Anglo.

"One of our guys has medic training," Michael said. "The guy with the blue sweatshirt. You'd best bring him down, unless one of you is a doctor."

"Alternatively I could just put your friend out of his misery."

"Listen, he's here but he's not one of us. He's practically an in-nocent bystander. That's the truth."

"Justice works in mysterious ways," Richie offered.

"We're not talking about justice here, just getting him some help."

"The guy in the blue sweatshirt?"

"Yeah. Name's Otto Twain."

Richie shook his head and started up the steps.

When the door slammed, Jack Liffey stopped moaning and looked at his cellmate. "Otto Twain?" he said.

"That's what he wanted to be called," Michael said. "The out-fit isn't finicky. I wasn't born Michael, either."

"You mean Otto's a serial rapist in some other state?"

"Presumably somebody knew who he was and decided he could be useful. Whatever. They're not picky. Why waste all that Special Forces training just because a guy robbed a bank?"

Now that he was not acting out, he noticed the dust smell along the floor and something else, a kind of rot. The room was warm and clammy.

"Should I kill them or just persuade them?" Michael asked, utterly matter-of-fact.

"These're just kids who got carried away, and an old guy who should know better." Jack Liffey sat up because he couldn't stand lying in decades of dust any longer. "I hope no one gets killed."

"Right now I hope they took us seriously enough to get Otto."

Jack Liffey lay down again and prepared to moan on cue.

Gloria handed the official script to Special Agent Emerson. She had marked the cards up heavily with her ballpoint. "Sir, here's what I will say—and what I *won't* say."

He frowned but took out a pair of glasses and began to go over the cards. As he read, she heard the sound of a helicopter coming in from the southeast. It landed, low and almost lightless, and let out two more agent types, who went straight into the command trailer. She wished she could trust all this bustle, but she did not have that much confidence in the feds.

"No, I want this in," Emerson insisted. It was a clumsy phrase toward the end about setting up a "stable means of communication," so she shrugged and gave it to him. Men always had to save face, somehow.

"How many negotiations have you run?" she asked.

"Enough," he said.

"I do it for a living," she said pointedly. "And this is my man we're risking. Let's do it right. You need to tell me if you're going to launch an assault while I'm talking to him."

"It's not in the playbook."

Damn all these sports metaphors, she thought, damn these guys, but she let it go. She knew she needed to keep her spirits up if she was going to do this.

. . .

Jack Liffey had never seen anyone move that fast in his life. Soon-Lin had been on the steps with a little spray gun pointed at them, while Richie led Otto to their cell door and unlocked it. Otto had a handlebar moustache and muscles like a trapeze artist and did not appear a very likely medic, but that didn't matter a bit. Michael had reached as if to greet him but, in an instant, he had been up off one knee with an arm around Richie's neck, holding the goateed Front member between himself and Soon-Lin's weapon. Richie struggled a little, but Michael had his left thumb in some kind of compliance grip that seemed capable of inflicting a lot of pain.

"Stop it!" Soon-Lin ordered. "I mean it!"

"If you fire a single round, young lady, I'll break this man's neck," Michael said coolly.

Jack Liffey scooted around on the ground to put the two men between himself and Soon-Lin's little MAC-10, just in case she did loose off a panicky burst.

"Jack and I are going out of here," Michael said. "Don't doubt it. Don't even think about it. You don't need us for anything, and I will make the price far too high to try to stop us. Back up now, two steps."

"Me, too," Otto said, but nobody paid him any attention. "I go, too."

"Let him go!" Soon-Lin demanded. Her voice held less conviction now.

"You mustn't hesitate or doubt or vacillate," Michael said. His tone was soothing. "I'm not asking you to do anything that will hurt you or your people. Jack and I are leaving, that's all. Don't feel you have to prove your strength. We respect you, but we have to go now. Just lower your weapon and take two steps up-ward. *Now.*"

She did, feeling behind herself with her foot so she didn't stumble. One. Two. Jack Liffey could see the logic of what Michael was doing. He had compelled her to obey a relatively harmless command, but, by doing so, she had given in to his will and the rest would go easier.

All at once, their careful little drama was interrupted as a god-like voice materialized in the room, coming from no evident source.

"Jack, Jack Liffey, this is Gloria. We all know you don't belong to either side of this fight and we would like to make you the mediator to re-solve the stand-off."

"What the fuck?"

They looked at one another, nobody seeming any less puzzled than anyone else—except Jack Liffey, who recognized the voice. Michael glanced at him.

"Yeah, that's Gloria, all right."

"Let's see if we can keep anyone from getting hurt. I assure you that no one out here is planning an attack, not as long as there is no gunfire from inside."

Three other Front members now appeared at the top of the steps, armed with assault rifles that were a lot more accurate than Soon-Lin's little spray gun. The one that Jack Liffey couldn't fig-ure out in this was Al—he was tough, but was he violent? He seemed more a thinker than a killer.

"Let's everybody stand down," Al ordered. He smiled coldly. "But if you insist on leaving, we can send your luggage on ahead."

Twenty

Nature Can Sure Complicate Warfare

Maeve sat glumly in the dark bleachers in the park, the vapor lights either off or shot out. None of the *klikas* seemed to be out that evening, and she had the place pretty much to herself, except for the overall night sigh of the city and a few couples or little grouplets strolling through with the kind of surly languor that suggested they would never be moved to urgency.

"*Buenas noches*," she said aloud, to the evening air. For the first time she realized the Spanish salutation was literally *good nights*. And *Buenos días* was good days. She wondered why, but she didn't wonder very hard. Idioms were always inexplicable.

She thought about what changed inside you when you gave up something you thought you'd wanted pretty bad. Did a lot of molecules rearrange themselves in your brain and now you were somebody else? My god, she thought, I've got this crazy G on my breast, my own scarlet letter—though it was in fact blue-black, ballpoint pen ink forming an amateurish blur. It was as bad as a tat saying "Property of the Hell's Angels." Once she'd seen a home-made tattoo across the forehead of a drug-skinny boy striding up Hollywood Boulevard: "Useless."

For the rest of her life she'd have to explain the G to boyfriends, unless she had it lasered off, and then she'd have to explain the scar. She was accumulating scars all over, as if trying to catch up with her dad, who had a metal plate in his head, titanium pins in his legs, a bullet scar on his shoulder and a weakened lung. But he was sixty. She already had an ostomy scar, plus the incision where they'd gone in to yank out a foot or so of intestine, and now, this thing.

Then she realized that she had been affected in a far more significant way: the consequence of her abject sexual surrender to Beto and her unwillingness to use any protection. Why? Even now, longing still, she remembered the desire for him inside her, tossing away all caution. How stupid could you get, Maeve? For just an instant she imagined Beto on top of Ruby, his hands pressing her bare fat thighs as she begged him to enter, but she couldn't stand the picture and shut it off. Okay, she thought, consider how I'm better off now. Be positive. The coldly calculating portion of her mind, the watcher, sorted through the easy answers—how she was maturing to the realities of risk, better aware of her own weaknesses, or even some dumb cliché like being sadder but wiser. The trouble was, nothing at all took up consoling presence in her thoughts, nothing but a great bitter resonance of loss.

Maybe tomorrow it would all make more sense, she thought. She got up, heading for her car and Gloria's house.

Jack Liffey could see the realization dawn on Michael that his leverage was pretty much gone. He still had his arm around Richie's neck, but two of the other guerillas had made it down the stairs and had their assault rifles on him at near point-blank range. He had amazing reflexes but not that amazing.

"You come with me, Liffey," Al said. There was an asthmatic wheeze between his words.

"Not till you let my friend go," Jack Liffey said.

Al smiled. "He seems to have the drop on *us*. Probably going to break our necks, one by one."

"Call them off him," Jack Liffey insisted.

Al made a small movement, a flick of his hand, and the rifles were lowered. Michael chose to honor the truce and released his captive with a little contemptuous shove. "We'll meet again," he said, as the others herded him back into the cage and headed Jack Liffey up the stairs.

The Big Voice started up again, condensing out of the air, soothing and disavowing violence, talking of communications and negotiations, offering everyone time to rethink over the standoff. There was no question that it was Gloria's voice, and the sense of her immanent presence was stunning. Jack Liffey felt he should be able to reach out and touch her though she was nowhere to be seen.

"How the hell are they doing that?" he wondered aloud.

"Maybe laser beams are turning the walls into woofers and tweeters—who knows? Do you recognize the voice?"

"It's possible." Let them doubt, he thought.

"You seem to have been tagged It. Mr. Neutral." Again, Al seemed to struggle for breath. It was an ordeal for him to make it up the staircase.

The camera wanders through an apartment that looks like it's been tossed by malicious burglars. Books and possessions are scattered across the floor. Stuffed furniture has been slashed so the cotton batting hangs out, and glass from picture frames has been shattered and left on the floor.

An older man, AL SIEGEL, wanders through the wreckage, eyes flicking about for something that might provide an answer.

                    MALE VOICE, off
        I found the place tossed like this and they
        were gone. Do you think it's all right?

                    AL SIEGEL
        No, it's not all right.

The camera picks up a muscular, goateed Asian, RICHIE YU,
carrying a pistol in his hand, who comes in behind the older
man and kicks at a pile of trash.

                    AL SIEGEL
        Let's just say some pros were involved.

                    RICHIE YU
        You think Tommy and Sunny are off hiding
        somewhere?

                    AL SIEGEL
        I talked to them last night. They were stay-
        ing in.

Richie picks up a piece of cardboard from the floor. He reads
it, makes a face and holds it up for AL SIEGEL. The camera
ZOOMS slowly on the message:

        TOO BAD
        TOO LATE
        TWO DOWN

RICHIE YU

We've got to find them. Get them back. Where
were they taken?

AL SIEGEL

We probably have to start thinking about that
secure facility.

RICHIE YU

I know you don't like the heavy stuff, but it's
time.

Maybe it was only the suggestion of the slight panting from the
man he was following, but Jack Liffey felt astonishingly weary,
for some reason. He wondered if he needed his heart checked
out. Probably not, he thought. He'd been through enough in the
last few days to slow anyone down.

"Don't think I approve of terrorism," Jack Liffey said. "I really
don't."

"Fair enough," Al said. "Neither do I. You know, Lenin was
against it on principle. He said, 'Hasn't the state committed
enough atrocities already? Why should we need more?'"

"And then he shot the kulaks," Jack Liffey said.

The old man rested for a moment. "Let's concern ourselves
with the present here. We need them to shut down that infernal
sound machine so we can talk over what we're going to do.
Specifically, what we're asking for."

"Your requisites might not fly, you realize?"

"Well, you stay neutral, Jack, and let us worry about that. My
name is Al Siegel, by the way."

As Soon-Lin stood scowling at them while her brother videotaped their slow procession along the corridor. Gloria's too-present voice was heard again, starting over from the beginning of her spiel, word-for-word, almost certainly reading. Listening for false notes, he felt it sounded enough like her natural speech pattern to be convincing.

"You've been around a long time, haven't you?" Jack Liffey asked. He'd decided Siegel was in his mid-seventies, though still hardy-looking despite the asthma, stocky and wiry like a manual laborer. Working out a time line in his head he guessed that Siegel had probably been in his thirties when the Communist Party had started breaking up like an ice floe in the late 1950s, and then he'd been in his fifties when the New Left in turn had fissioned away to nothing. About when Jack Liffey himself had flirted with the Vietnam Veterans Against the War. As he remembered, a lot of the political groups back then had had one or two "old guys" like Siegel, somebody trying to start over, to keep a lifetime of ideals going on pure willpower.

As if answering his thoughts, Al Siegel said, "Somebody has to keep trying."

He led Jack Liffey into an office with an absurd rococo desk and indicated a chair, where Jack Liffey sat with gratitude. His extreme exhaustion was puzzling, but it was night, and his emotions had been running wild on him. Plus, his confinement had meant weeks of inactivity and oversleeping, which was always debilitating.

Al Siegel picked up an inhaler from the desk and sprayed it into his mouth. Then he bent over to plug in a telephone cord. He lifted and dropped the receiver a few times to toy with the dial tone. "They'll figure it out."

Soon-Lin and Richie now came in. This was probably the NWLF's Central Committee, he thought. He wondered if they were all as tired as he was.

"Your father wants very much to see you safe," Jack Liffey said to Soon-Lin.

She raised her eyebrows and looked away, as if having a caring father were an embarrassment.

He turned his attention back to Al Siegel, who was reading over something on the desk in front of him.

"If I'm going to be your go-between, I think I ought to know your demands, or whatever," Jack Liffey suggested.

"I'm reading over our demands now, but they're a bit dated." He took another shot of the inhaler.

"Is it emphysema?" Jack Liffey asked.

"Chronic obstructive pulmonary disease," was the reply. "It's like nearly drowning all day long. But you know, Che had serious asthma even in the mountains and he never slowed down."

"He had a bit of a disconnect from reality, too. The Bolivia thing was really dumb."

"As Che said, revolutions are never made out of a desire for some ideal future—but a hatred of the past. Hatred of what has been done to your people. Che had seen Bolivia on his travels."

"Che didn't say that," Jack Liffey said evenly. "Walter Benjamin did."

Siegel's eyes widened to acknowledge his surprise, but he only stared at Jack Liffey.

A palpable noise against the dark window drew his attention. Even within the substantial building, Jack Liffey could sense the sudden gust of a really fierce wind outside, slapping its palms on the glass, and he wondered if a desert storm was brewing up, just to complicate everything. The southern deserts got a lot of the tropical storms that circled in off the Pacific over Baja but always bypassed L.A.

"So you read Benjamin."

Jack Liffey was abruptly sorry he had spoken. He wanted to

avoid this kind of philosophical piffle-paffle, but he had to keep talking to stay on top of things.

"You've been around long enough to know the forces out there are not going to let you waltz out of here to Cuba. Or drive away into oblivion on a bunch of Humvees, not in a million years. If they say they are, you better know they're only fibbing to get somebody in position for a better shot. You don't even have anybody interesting as hostages. Nobody cares about mercenaries. Certainly nobody cares about me."

"That's astute. But our demands go one better than that. We simply assume we're all dead. We have a political manifesto we want broadcast. And we're willing to trade our deaths—or our surrender—for that. Aren't you afraid to have your life go on and on and die old for no purpose?" he added with a half smile.

"I'm more afraid not to." Jack Liffey wondered what "old" really meant to this man. How much time did he think he had left? "Isn't it better to live to fight another day?"

"Ah, you *are* a negotiator. Those who choose to live we will let surrender. We'll even make it easy for them." He turned to look at Soon-Lin and Richie. "Does anybody here expect to live through this?"

They didn't make a sign.

"That's meaningless," Jack Liffey said. "Bravado. Nobody ever believes the bogeyman will actually get them until that red laser dot is resting on your chest."

"Did you ever believe in anything, Jack, deeply enough to fight for it?"

The wind gusted again, this time hurling grit against the window. It was like a signal from a secret lover, tossing sand up to the balcony.

"I'm not here to argue with you," Jack Liffey said. "That's not in my job description. Which means, first, you should get the phone working."

"It'll ring any minute now. But first we want to know a little about Jack Liffey—what he believes."

Jack Liffey noticed his carefully inclusive plural pronoun, speaking for them all. "I don't like talking about stuff like that. Sophomoric baloney."

"I insist." He took another hit off his inhaler.

Jack Liffey watched him a moment, the hard eyes and fixed jaw, though now there was something vulnerable about the lips or maybe the chin, and he'd already given away the weakness of the lungs.

"When I got back from Nam," Jack Liffey admitted, "I was pretty anti-everything. I'd seen a big blundering war machine that had turned a civil war into an ugly sideshow of the Cold War. I opposed it for a while. I marched to the federal building. But eventually all the true believers like you drove me out of the movement."

"Why is that?"

"You always insisted on the Big Solution, didn't you? That winds up getting people hurt."

Rain began to pelt the window with big drops, then dribble down the glass. It would certainly complicate the night, he thought, but maybe that wasn't such a bad idea.

Al Siegel smiled at him. "Can't you be more concrete?"

"For chrissake, groups like yours started talking about making a revolution in America, when they didn't have enough people to run a poker club in Gardena."

"You have a taste for the colorful exaggeration, Mr. Liffey. In 1970, in a Gallup poll, over a million American students defined themselves as revolutionaries." He shrugged. "But students are notoriously fickle, so you're not wholly unfair. Still, I can see that cynicism is your accustomed companion now. Once cynicism settles on you, you can flow with it or against it, but you can't break its hold. It's the one attitude we reject on principle, because we know it subverts all possibility of hope."

The raindrops were smaller now, pattering, running down the glass in rivulets. Al Siegel settled back for a moment and forced a long measured inhalation through his nose, resisting the recourse to his medication for some reason. "We aren't unrealistic, Jack. We know we can only achieve the most limited of goals given the relationship of forces in the world today. Isn't that true?" Again, he seemed to want to include the other two, though their deference was obvious.

Soon-Lin brightened and sat forward. "Individual action can always have an effect. If I didn't believe that, I'd be writing advertising copy in New York."

Al Siegel looked square at her. "Be charitable to yourself."

She shrugged. "Or writing about modern dance in *The New Yorker*."

"I think we're way past this," Jack Liffey said. "If I need to know any more about you guys, I'll ask. Right now, when the phone rings, you're going to want me to discuss some practical issues."

Al Siegel got down to business. "We want the principals—the president, the chairman, the CFO, everyone at the top—of the Korean conglomerate Daeshin brought before an international tribunal. For a half century of crimes against humanity." He leaned forward and handed Jack Liffey a manila folder that had at its top edges the metal fingers of a hanging file. The tab sticking up said "D–S." He opened the folder, which contained one sheet of lined paper. It was a list of monthly billings, with no indication of the recipient. They seemed to average about $25,000 a month, except for the last month when they were triple that.

"That's from the files in this office," Al Siegel said.

Light flared up against the dark window, like a movie effect, and he hoped it was really lightning. The distant rumble came as they all contemplated some form of the same worry.

"You sure this billing is for Daeshin?" Jack Liffey asked.

"One of the ISOC operatives confirmed it."

"After he lost his fingernails?"

"We don't do that. But you know they do. Note the increase in charges in the last month. They bill like lawyers, for their time. That *extra* is due to the vigorous questioning of our comrades, and maybe you."

Jack Liffey recalled the water tank. "So, you actually believe the FBI is going to extradite some corporate bigwigs from Korea in order to get you to surrender?"

"No," Al Siegel said, shaking his head sardonically. "We want publicity. We have at least a reasonable expectation of that. Remember that even the Unabomber got his manifesto published in the *Washington Post*."

"Have you got yours ready?"

"Better. We have everything we need on videotape, thanks to Soon-Lin and Peter. That makes it easy. That way it can be put on in the middle of the night on the albino midget wrestling channel—as long as they let people know. TiVo and videotape will perpetuate it."

"Assuming anyone is interested." It was a risk pushing him like that, Jack Liffey thought. But, in the end, nobody even noticed his statement because a lightning strike nearby announced itself with that high-pitched crackle-then-boom that means the gods have just spared you a direct hit. There was an answering rattle of machine gun fire—probably from a spooked comrade—and Richie hurried out of the room, probably to calm the troops.

Nature sure can complicate warfare, Jack Liffey thought, but saw no point whatever in saying it aloud.

Neither Jack nor Gloria had been there when she got back, and she had no idea why. There were no notes, but they probably hadn't expected her so there was no reason they should have left any. But they might have left them for each other. Her dad had been away for a while, Maeve knew, and he might even have headed back to his old condo in Culver City for any number of reasons—including some bad patch with Gloria. Gloria herself might be off on some business of her own. But Loco was there in the back yard, overjoyed to be let in and given some attention, plus some food.

Her own room was untouched, except for the things she herself had taken away to Beto's apartment and left there for good now. Books she'd probably never read now, or buy again with a twinge of shame.

It was late, and she lay down to nap a little but only tossed and turned. Maeve finally found a position that seemed comfortable, but slowly she became hot and sweaty, then started to get a cramp. Maybe it was humid out—something so rare in L.A. that when it happened, people tended to think they were coming down with a fever. Finally, she got up to read for a while. It was 1:30 AM. She took a copy of *Justine* to the living room and settled into the cozy chair where Gloria usually watched TV. She read until Durrell described some street music in Alexandria as sounding like "a sinus being ground to powder" and she giggled out loud. It was so perfect: that's just what Arab music was like.

Words began to blur on her, but still she wasn't sleepy, so she broke down and hit the button on the remote. She surfed till she found a news channel. There, suddenly, was a ragged-looking male reporter in a yellow rain slicker standing in front of a mass of police vehicles parked in a dirt field.

Like the book, the words emanating from the screen made her start to drift. Maeve jerked erect when she had one of those moments of daydream intruding on reality: she thought she heard a voice say "Sergeant Ramirez." She poked at the volume until she got it to where she could make out excited talk about a hostage standoff. They brought up a map that showed a dot somewhere northeast of El Centro, on the edge of a big blank section of southeastern California that must have been desert. The dot was labeled ISOC COMPOUND, which meant nothing at all to her.

Flipping down through other channels, she found that two of them had versions of the same thing—one from a helicopter and one in that sickly green that everyone remembered from the CNN night shots over Baghdad. It was all complicated by storm clouds and rain, and as she passed the green channel again, lightning punctuated the transmission with glare.

She defaulted to the disheveled newsman in the yellow slicker where she had begun. "The police are having difficulty reconnecting the telephone lines in the midst of an electrical storm, but it appears the terrorists have selected a negotiator." He frowned reading his notes. "Or . . . I don't know, Alan, they got some sort of word from inside." She thought the reporter seemed like an idiot, who deserved the drenching he was getting.

Then her jaw dropped wide open as a tiny photograph of her father came up in the corner of the screen.

The reporter stood silent and fretful as some clear voice back in his studio announced: "We're reliably informed that the negotiator selected is Los Angeles investigator Jack Liffey. You may remember that Liffey was involved in the Malibu firestorm nine months ago in which eight people died, some during a bizarre gunfight between narcotics traffickers and video makers." Yep, that was her dad.

She listened intently as the remote reporter was abruptly relegated to a little window up in the corner as an anchor sitting at a desk embarked on a description of the New World Liberation Front—which he portrayed as a cross between the Symbionese Liberation Army and the Manson Family.

She ran to her father's desk and got out the big floppy U.S. mapbook. She opened to the *California, Southern* page and worked out where this was all happening south of the Salton Sea. She figured she could get there in two hours or less if she really stepped on it, and she started thinking about what she should take with her.

Then she stopped short and told herself that the police would never let her get close. She'd see more by staying right there and watching the TV. And, unlike other times that she had dashed to her father's rescue, she had an unborn child to protect now.

She felt her belly and wondered if the fetus she was carrying was destined to become her universal excuse for bunking off on things she didn't want to do. Just then the little window on the edge of the TV flared up with light and came back full screen. She was about to dismiss it as more lightning when she heard what was distinctly gunfire.

Twenty-one

Some Relation to Bad Luck

The trouble with a *real* crisis, he thought, was that, psychologically speaking, there was probably only the one. It just came at you in new and different ways. But you were always reminded of all the other times you'd been there before, in much the same state of mind, whenever you'd accidentally steered your beat-up life off into some hellish ditch.

Apparently some high-tech searchlight had been trained on the office window from far away, and the light burst in, swimming a little with all the rain it had passed through, and then clobbered the far wall hard. He guessed there were other searchlights illuminating the rest of the compound, too, but nobody was trying to shoot them out, at least not yet.

"We've got fire discipline back," Richie said. "That bolt of lightning could have spooked just about anyone. It hit a free-standing antenna they've got about a hundred and sixty-five feet from the building."

A grumbling and gnashing rolled in occasionally to remind them they were still caught up in the storm.

Jack Liffey winced when Gloria's unearthly voice came back

on again, a little louder than before, if possible, probably to cut through the wind and thunder. She was obviously reading out the latest version of the message they'd already heard with an added plea for them to plug in their telephone again.

"Richie, would you go around and see if you get dial tone on any of the other jacks," Al Siegel said.

"Nobody's got a cell?" Jack Liffey asked.

Al Siegel shook his head. "I insisted. They can be tracked."

Halfheartedly, Richie slid himself off the bureau and left. It was going to be a long night, no matter what. Al Siegel tore a poster board off the wall, a black silhouette of an Arab in a desert turban in the crosshairs of a target. With a marking pen he wrote PHONE NOT WORKING in big letters on the back of the poster. Then he slapped it into the window, which brought blessed relief from about two-thirds of that huge dental drill of probing light.

"Listen, Jack, I need to know. How good a mediator are you?"

Jack Liffey considered the question. "How would I know? It's not something I get to practice a lot."

"Okay, try to put yourself in our place. We came here to rescue our comrades, not to hurt anybody. We're not going to try to shoot our way out. All we ask is a bit of non–prime time TV to get our message to people who need to hear it."

Jack Liffey frowned. Something didn't quite add up. "I'm sensing a disconnect here," he said. "Between this hostage situation that probably involves half the cops in Southern California and your one modest goal. Usually, people demand the release of a whole bunch of prisoners, new national elections, several billion dollars, and a plane to wherever. Then they negotiate down to just not getting shot up when they surrender."

Al Siegel nodded. "We thought we'd go straight to the bottom line."

Soon-Lin hopped off the sideboard, walked up to Jack Liffey, and slapped him hard across his left cheek.

"What was that for?" Jack Liffey said, rubbing his face.

"I don't like your attitude. They chose you to mediate, so mediate. That's all."

He nodded. But he was beginning to dislike her attitude, too. Or maybe just her. Hard to believe he'd been trying to rescue this young woman.

"It's imperative that attention be paid to what Daeshin has done. It's not trivial. Suffering is not." She was practically hissing at him, and yet she looked as if she wanted to cry. "We must achieve something for all our sacrifices."

"I've seen some of the interview," he said.

"Yes?"

"It's poignant. It's heartbreaking."

"Soon-Lin," Al Siegel said.

"This is *stupid*," Soon-Lin blurted. "This is all so *stupid!*"

He could see she was crying now.

"No," Jack Liffey said. "We'll get your video shown." Really, she just wanted somebody to pay attention, he thought. Maybe just her father. Like a lot of us.

They'd covered the sun canopy with a thick tarp over the folding table where she sat at the microphone, awaiting orders, and the tarp seemed to be catching most of the downpour and directing it off at a low point into a runnel that splashed steadily into a growing puddle, though a big gust brought the moisty feel of rain into her face from time to time. At the very horizon, yellowish glows blossomed briefly to be followed eventually by deep rumbles. Paula Green and Fausto Ndoyet sat on folding chairs at the edge of the big tarp, a respectful distance from Gloria and all the high-tech apparatus.

In the fortified building where the powerful searchlights were trained, one of the windows suddenly commanded all their attention. Special Agent Emerson and company studied it with a big pair of tripod-mounted binoculars, then conferred, after which, Emerson came over to her.

"Sergeant, key that a couple of times to make sure it's still working."

She touched the talkswitch twice and was greeted by an odd sense of presence each time, as if the air around her had hollowed out into a giant echoey canyon.

"Jesus, that's eerie," Paula said.

"Tell them we're sending a little crawler robot over there with a phone. It's a direct walkie-talkie, but it'll look like a cell phone."

"How do I address them?"

"Keep trying Jack. We're pretty sure he's in there now and I'd like to have him at the other end."

"You're not going to have snipers hit anyone while I'm doing this, are you?"

"I give you my word."

"Listen, I promise you," Gloria said, "if you do anything, anything at all that gets Jack killed, I'll shoot you dead."

He stared at her, then shook his head. "Everybody lives in some relation to bad luck, hon. You should have worked that out before you joined law enforcement."

Bad luck. It frightened her how easy it was for this guy to consign someone he didn't know to the hard luck end of statistical study. For his own sense of accomplishment, for some check mark on his record, for an orderly retirement.

"Just remember what I said," Gloria insisted. "You heard me."

"Talk to Jack."

She pressed talk. "*Jack*, this is Gloria. Listen, about the phone they're sending . . ."

She sat on the floor only a few feet from the television as if that would help her see better. Something was going on that had set all the newscasters abuzz. She was concerned about Gloria and her dad, but now something else began to assail her. It was like some kind of dread, or maybe like— She felt it rise abruptly from her belly. She fought it back, but was clearly losing and ran for the bathroom. Maeve knelt on the hard tiles and held her hair out of the way as she retched once and then vomited into the toilet. Very little came up, and what did was sour and burning. A string of spittle dangled off her lip and elongated slowly, bouncing a little. Her arms were quivery, but she felt a little better now and settled down on the cold tiles with her back to the wall. Then guilt told her she should be glued to the TV, and she crawled back to the living room.

Something had changed while she'd been in the bathroom. The camera was following a funny little tracked robot, like something out of *Star Wars*. It had a single metal arm thrust out in front of itself and was carrying something. It moved agonizingly slowly past bunchy weeds, and even then the faraway camera kept losing the robot to oscillations and adjustments and had to scan back to find it again.

She settled in with her back to Gloria's easy chair, wondering what was happening. Everything had changed too fast. She was on the edge of weeping, but wouldn't let herself. She wanted her father.

. . .

"They're keeping the press pretty far back," Jack Liffey observed. "I see one camera on a boom out there, but that might belong to the cops."

He and Al Siegel were waiting out front, more or less protected by two of the building's columns, as the promised robot jounced slowly across the chaparral well off the gravel road. The thunderstorm was receding toward the east, but there were still a few errant lightning strikes far away.

"If there's a big screwup," Al Siegel said, "nice to've met you."

"Sure."

The little robot was only about thirty yards away now, jerkily readjusting its course to aim for the steps that led up to the colonnade.

"Somebody's always getting hurt by somebody else's big solutions, aren't they?" Jack Liffey observed.

"Lie back and let the river take you downstream, Jack. It lets the powerful win every time."

"My job is to bring Soon-Lin home safe, and I intend to do it somehow."

Al Siegel nodded. "Best of luck to you. She's a tough customer."

The robot came to a stop at the first step, and they could hear a mechanical whine emanate from the thing. It tried to climb, but did not seem up to the task. "Don't go down there," Jack Liffey said. "They'd probably shoot you. This is my job."

He raised his arms and walked very slowly down to the robot.

"Jack, take the walkie-talkie," Gloria's disembodied voice advised from somewhere nearby him. At the same moment the little phone in the mechanical paw began to ring ominously.

Special Agent Leonard Emerson held the receiver to his ear, but there was no answer.

"Should I make another announcement?" Gloria asked him.

He shook his head. "We'll run with it now."

"His hand's on it!" an agent at the big binoculars shouted. Another agent was intent on the joysticks and knobs of a remote-control console sitting on the folding table. Gloria watched the tiny TV screen on the console and for the first time saw that it was definitely Jack reaching out to take the phone, the camera on the robot only a few feet from his face. It was really him, looking drawn and exhausted.

"He only has to lift it out now."

She was still suspicious of them because none of the over-equipped and overweaponed SWAT officers were in evidence. For all she knew they were tunneling toward the compound, or crawling in through some secret sewer duct. She took comfort in the legal restrictions against the use of military forces. But later she was to wish that she had listened more closely to the tone and the precise content of everything that Leonard Emerson had said to her.

The little telephone went on ringing in his hand as he carried it back up the steps and in through the crash bar doors toward the office, with Al Siegel following him calmly.

"If you need anybody else for a conference call, get them now," Jack Liffey said.

"We'll be fine. I trust you to report honestly."

"I will, but I wish it were a speakerphone."

"This will do."

Soon-Lin and Richie Yu were less sanguine though, standing against the sideboard, as Jack Liffey and Al Siegel came in the office door.

Jack Liffey looked closely at the little telephone and found the button labeled TALK.

"Hello, this is Jack Liffey. Who am I speaking to?"

"My name is Special Agent Emerson of the FBI. I'm the offi-cer in charge here."

"Hold on." Jack Liffey looked up. "His name is Special Agent Emerson from the FBI, and he says he's in charge." This repeti-tion was going to get tedious, he thought, like one of those earnest bilingual meetings.

Al Siegel made a gesture for him to continue.

"Special Agent Emerson, I want to tell you—and these are my own words—that these people have not hurt anyone in here to my knowledge. They came here to rescue two of their friends who they allege were being tortured. I myself was pretty badly treated here so I can well believe them."

He pulled the sheet of paper with their demands closer to him on the desktop: three-quarters of the list had been crossed out. "May I go on?"

"Please," the telephone voice said.

"He says, please go on," Jack Liffey announced. "They have given me their conditions for surrender and they seem quite reasonable."

He looked up and could see that they may not have been very happy with the phrase "conditions for surrender," but they weren't objecting to it. Soon-Lin seemed perturbed but let Richie rest his hand on her shoulder. The situation—talking to the FBI—seemed to remind Richie that he was unarmed, and he retrieved the M-16 that he'd lazily propped in the corner. Before Jack Liffey could read more, the man on the little phone began to speak in his ear.

"Jack Liffey, my job is to negotiate and see that no one gets hurt. But you should know that a guard here was wounded and we found him crawling in the desert. He's in critical care now at El Centro. They've also fired on several police officers, including your girlfriend, with a heavy machine gun, and it's only dumb luck that no one's been killed."

"Hold on." Jack Liffey repeated roughly what Special Agent Emerson had said. At the mention of the guard, Richie looked relieved.

Al Siegel told him about the rocket counterattack that they had suffered and the one Front member injured at the window.

"There's been trouble on this end, too," Jack Liffey reported. "They tell me one of their comrades got some pretty bad glass cuts from someone firing an RPG at the building."

Emerson cleared his throat. "That was a bit of a freelance action, I'm afraid. Long before I arrived. I wouldn't go pushing it, Liffey. It was your Sergeant Ramirez who found the RPGs in a car trunk out here, and she seems to have got herself pissed off at the .50-caliber fire and capped one of the rockets off at the building."

"Oh." Jack Liffey repeated the tale of the RPG to the room. "Well, I suppose offensive and defensive penalties cancel each other out."

"I have no comment on that."

"All right then. Here's what the people in here want." And he explained about Daeshin and broadcasting the comfort women documentary video. "They're not asking for *Sixty Minutes* or even prime time. They're not particular about when and where you show it, as long as it's announced in advance so people who care can record it."

"I can't authorize that on my own, but I can take it upstairs. We'll have to speak to some broadcasters."

Jack Liffey suddenly felt a tingling in his scalp and wondered if it was a portent of lightning. He looked at Al Siegel, with his lips caught between his teeth in anticipation, Soon-Lin who was nothing but hostility, and Richie who was professionally expressionless, rubbing a thumb absently along the blued metal receiver of the old M-16. The tenor of the night in the room had changed in some way, but he could not just say how. Was it simpler, the colors more basic, the air clarified? It was as if he had suddenly broken through to a place where language would no longer need modifiers and everything would be direct and straightforward, under control.

"Just to be clear, let me read—" Jack Liffey started, but the concussion of a nearby lightning strike cut him off. *No*—he thought—there hadn't been the crackle of proximity you got with lightning. *It was something else.* Then there were a half dozen more blasts and he felt each one distinctly in his chest like a punch from a great fist. He felt inexplicably paralyzed and sat watching Al Siegel sink down behind the desk warily holding a beat-up .45 pistol aimed at the door. Richie was on one knee, aiming at the door, too, with the M-16, and Soon-Lin was heading for her own rifle all the way across the room.

Jack Liffey moved finally, after the others. Grabbing Soon-Lin as she tried to sprint past him, he threw her to the floor and dropped on top of her as she wriggled and fought. However tough she might have thought herself, he was bigger and stronger—and that's the way they were when a blast blew the door off its hinges and two more flash-bang stun grenades went off only a few feet away, disorienting him and throwing everything out of sync. Big black insects behind Lexan shields erupted into the room. There was one burst of fire from where he thought Richie had been and then answering short bursts from several places. His attention went to the desk and he wondered if Al Siegel had hunkered down behind it, waiting to surrender.

"Stay down! Stay down! Stay down!" someone bellowed.

"Bastards!" Soon-Lin cursed into the floor.

He could hear vehicles arriving in front, a few more short

bursts of fire, and then somebody in the hall shouting, "Clear!"
And it was over as fast as that.

Gloria leapt out of the police car, leaving the door open, her
LAPD badge banging at her chest from a chain around her neck.
She brushed aside a SWAT officer who tried to prevent her from
sprinting up the steps.

"Get the fuck off me." Inside she yelled, "*Jack!* Jack!"

"Here!"

Another SWAT swung his ugly little assault rifle toward her,
startled, and she gave him the finger. "Shoot, and your career's
finished," she told him. She brushed past him, too, and found
the office where she thought Jack's call had emanated from, the
door blown right off the frame. Jack Liffey stood at an ornate
desk, looking sadly down at something on the floor behind it.
Two SWAT officers were handcuffing a hysterically weeping
Asian girl with plastic wire ties, trying to be as gentle as they
could with someone fighting like a wildcat. Off to the right a
goateed young man crouched forward in an unnatural posture of
prayer with his forehead against an M-16 in a spreading pool of
blood.

"Good work," she said sarcastically to the handful of SWATs in
the room. "Shoot 'em all and sort 'em out later."

"Anyone with a weapon had to be neutralized—that's the
rules," one of them said.

"We were negotiating a surrender," Gloria said. "None of this
was necessary."

"Orders were to go the instant we were close enough."

It turned out the SWAT team had simply crawled through the
chaparral in the dark fields at the back of the compound and the

Liberation Front sentries had been too inattentive to spot them.

"Experience tells us the longer you wait, the bigger the chance of a tragedy."

"This isn't a tragedy?" she said. "Ah, shit."

She dismissed him with a wave of one hand and went to Jack, where he was staring down at the body of an older Anglo with a tidy hole in his forehead and vacant open eyes, lying on his back.

"Jack! Oh, Jack!" she said. She hugged him hard and thought he seemed frozen in place.

"He wasn't a bad guy," Jack Liffey said. He sounded bewildered. "I'd just told your pal that their only demand was to show a video on some obscure cable channel, for chrissake."

"They didn't tell me, *honest*, Jack."

Soon-Lin shouted and then crooned and wailed.

"I guess I did my job," Jack Liffey said. "She can go home. Eventually." Even his voice sounded frozen, stunned.

"Well, you and I can go home *now*." Gloria tried to rally him.

"Um-hmm," Jack Liffey said.

On TV they were saying that none of the hostages had been hurt, but Maeve had seen and heard the brief firefight via the long-range cameras and knew better than to believe official announcements. Her mouth was dry, and she felt a great hollowness of utter disaster. "Oh, Dad."

Epilogue

Grace on Earth

A girl who barely spoke English was behind the counter in the doughnut shop. He tried asking for Kim Tae-Jin and then Tae-Jin Kim, but it must have been his accent because she didn't understand. "The boss," he said. Finally, she nodded. She made a number of golf-like swings and he got it. It seemed odd that a man with both his children newly imprisoned for terrorism would choose to go golfing, but maybe that was how he worked off his emotions. If the man was actually playing a round, Jack Liffey didn't have a clue where he would be, but he took a chance and went to the double-deck driving range off Olympic, and sure enough, he was alone on the top deck.

In a plastic chair Mr. Kim sat staring fiercely off into the distance. He seemed to be crying, the bucket of driving balls at his feet brim full, but he wiped his face quickly as Jack Liffey approached. There was an irregular *thwok-thwok* from below, and balls sailed into sight and on into the far metal netting where they gave a faint rattle and plop as they fell.

"Hello, Mr. Liffey," he said. He composed himself and then

shook hands. "Thank you, thank you. They tell me you saved my Soon-Lin's life."

"I'm sorry I couldn't prevent the other deaths."

"Peter, too—he was very fortunate."

"Yes, well. I'm only sorry I didn't get to Soon-Lin earlier. Maybe I could have headed off some of this mess."

Mr. Kim made a noise of protest. "You did the best you could. Your own life was in danger."

Now it was Jack Liffey who made a sound of protest. "Do you know what's going to happen to Soon-Lin and Peter?" he asked. He'd been too busy with his own family issue to follow the Kims.

"My lawyer says Soon-Lin will have to go to prison. This is not a good time in this country to be waving guns around. For Peter, it might be better. Everyone has testified he never touched a weapon. Of course, I will pay you your full finder's fee for your work."

Jack Liffey raised a palm. "I didn't come for that."

"But you earned it."

"Why don't you wait until the lawyers are all done with you and see if you have anything left?"

"No, I must pay you a debt of honor."

"I did drop by today for a reason."

"Oh, yes?"

"I assume the FBI have pretty much seized all of Soon-Lin's Daeshin materials that they could get their hands on. Probably all the stuff in the edit bay, the raw interviews that Soon-Lin was recording and certainly her finished documentary about the comfort women. They acted like it was ready to go. They just wanted it shown. It seemed a pretty modest request to me."

"Yes."

"You'll be speaking to Soon-Lin and Peter. Would you ask them if they have a hidden copy somewhere, a backup?"

"Why is this, Mr. Liffey?"

"I have friends here and there. At the very least, I'll make a lot of copies and spread them around—but I might be able to get it on the air. It's a story that deserves to be told."

"Why would that interest you?"

"Lord knows, your kids put their hearts into it and they paid for it. I've seen some of the documentary and was very moved by it."

Somehow it seemed a minor debt he owed to Al Siegel, but the minor ones were the ones you had to pay.

"Will this video change the course of history, Mr. Liffey?"

"Everything changes the course of history."

"I'm not sure stirring up these matters would be good for my children."

The answer seemed to have an extra dimension, and finally the penny dropped. "You do business with Daeshin, don't you?"

He waved a hand. "A little. Only a small subsidiary that imports my dresses. But I am nothing to them. Insignificant, unnoticed."

"Which is the way you'd like it to stay."

Mr. Kim regarded him steadily, but said nothing in reply. Jack Liffey had a flash of imagining how he'd feel if Maeve were facing a dozen years in a federal slammer. "I'm sorry I didn't find Soon-Lin earlier, sir," he repeated.

"Thank you, Mr. Liffey. I will get you a video."

"Oh?" He didn't want to show too much surprise.

"Everything in life is a risk. Daeshin can kiss my ass."

"When I was in the fourth grade, I told my teacher, Mrs. Cox—remember her?—that I wanted to discover new places and new animals and new birds and new insects. She said, 'Sit down, they've all been discovered.'" Maeve smiled. "I probably should have sat down."

She had a ginger ale in front of her, and so did her father. Gloria had a beer. Their reunion was long over, hadn't lasted more than a few minutes in fact, interrupted by Maeve's need to unburden herself, and her secret had been out for several minutes now. She had begun to weep uncontrollably while her father had tried to comfort her.

"Have you told your mom?"

"Lord, no. But we're doing better, a lot better. I will."

"Shhh. I'm not complaining. I just want to know your feelings." He was resisting asking the obvious question.

Gloria, sensibly, was keeping quiet.

Maeve grimaced. "You want my honest feelings right now? Okay, this is going to *kill* me—that's my feelings. I'm embarrassed and afraid and ashamed and humiliated and proud, too. How could I get myself into such a stupid place? It's like falling into two soap operas at the same time, and one's on a Spanish channel. And I have to confess my stupidity to all the people I love most."

He squeezed her hand again.

"God, I can't even say the word. I'm pregnant, pregnant, pregnant. I'm a girl who's way too young, and who got herself pregnant."

"Hon," Jack Liffey said softly, "without sweet girls who are way too young getting themselves pregnant by accident, there is no grace on earth."

She started sobbing again, and he decided not to move over to hug her, but to let her cry herself out. He met Gloria's eyes, and she smiled thinly at him. When Maeve had run down a bit, he felt he had to raise it.

"Do you know what you want to do about it?"

Music was coming from the house next door, not unhappy music but not too terribly chirpy, as if serenading the living and the dead together.

"I just don't know, Dad."